BEYOND REGRET

David Berardelli

BEYOND REGRET

GRAVESTONE PRESS

PART ONE - DARK MEMORIES

Chapter 1

Just as Laura raised her glass, Bill's jaw dropped when the young blonde strolled past their table.

My God!

Samantha?

His thoughts immediately went into full-blown chaos.

The music thumping from the juke had ebbed into a soft, nearly inaudible whisper that seemed to be coming from some faraway place. The laughter and chatter from the bar also diminished in volume. The clinking of glasses all around them faded into nothingness. Every sound he had heard during the last half hour had been replaced by silence. In this strange new atmosphere, all sounds and signs of life had simply vanished.

In just moments, the silence consuming him had grown into an unfathomable stillness.

Bill discovered that his existence had just been swallowed up by a darkness he had never experienced before. It had transformed itself into a heavy blanket of total black and seemed to be growing heavier as he wandered down a long, murky tunnel. At the end of the tunnel, a glint of light suggested movement. A slim figure appeared, watching him. This figure was much too far away for him to distinguish a face, but he was certain it was a woman—

Laura's voice shattered his frightening journey. "Bill?"

The darkness lightened, and a flurry of soft, faraway murmurings abruptly broke the heavy silence.

"Bill?" A nudge of his forearm. "You okay?"

The clinking of glasses made him start.

Snap to. Wake up.

Soft laughter…

Am I asleep?

What the hell just happened?

"Bill?"

Someone was shaking him.

The darkness lifted. Soft, hazy lights appeared in the distance, highlighting something across the room.

He shook himself. After taking a couple of deep breaths, he caught movement out of the corner of his eye. Someone was sitting near him. Someone close. Someone smelling of vanilla and *Obsession.*

It was Laura, and she looked frightened.

"What's wrong? You having a heart attack?"

Wake the hell up!

His inner voice had become insistent, instilling a sort of blind panic within him. He knew that he should pay attention and pull himself together.

He had to turn his back on that strange, uncomfortable darkness, once and for all. Otherwise, something terrible could happen.

He rubbed his eyes, shook himself again, and waited for his vision to clear. The music came back.

Then more laughter, followed by the clinking of glasses, which had grown louder. He took a deep breath, several deep breaths.

Laura was sitting very close, her face no more than three feet from his. Her large dark eyes were wide open; her lower lip trembled. She looked like someone who had just seen something frightening.

"Are you all right?" he asked.

She nearly gasped. "Are you serious?"

"You look, well, like you're—"

"You scared me half to death, and now you're asking *me* if *I'm* all right?"

"Well?" He shrugged. "Are you?"

"No. Not at all!"

"Good."

"Whaddya mean, good?"

"You don't *look* all right. Your skin's pale, and you're shaking."

She shook her head. "There's a good reason for that, you know."

"What's that?"

"I just found out that I'm having a drink after work with a crazy guy, the same guy I've been sharing my bed with for the last six months…"

He had no idea what she was talking about. The only thing that seemed to matter was what had happened just a few minutes ago. But just as his mind went back to it, he began wondering if what he had seen had really happened.

Or had he imagined it?

This was his second drink, after all. Granted, he'd been a seasoned drinker for the last ten years and knew from experience that he could down half a

7

dozen strong ones before the stuff started affecting him. But at least he had a good excuse this time. It had been a rough day at the office, and since he'd had two strong belts at the luncheon a mere four hours ago, his resistance wasn't exactly up to par.

Had he imagined what he thought had happened?

Was the girl who had caught his eye still in the room?

Or was it someone who looked like her?

Was it Samantha?

How could that be?

Was it even possible?

"Bill?"

Damn. He'd gone zombielike again.

"You're doing it again."

"Huh?"

"You're acting like a crazy person who lapses into some sort of weird mental state from one moment to the next, and I'm starting to think maybe I need to get you to a doctor to have him find out what's wrong. If I'm right, then I guess we'll have to make arrangements for you to…"

He barely heard the rest of her statement. Before he realized what he was doing, he'd gotten up from his seat and was squeezing through the small groups that had gathered in front of the bar.

More than a dozen women were talking to one another. Some were young while others were much older. Some sat at tables while others sat perched on barstools. Everyone appeared to be well-dressed. They were all professional people who worked in law and insurance offices on the upper floors of the building.

A small group just a few yards from the front entrance caught his attention. Three women and five guys, all well-dressed. He tried to remember what the girl who had caught his eye was wearing. All that registered was thick blond hair, large eyes, small, shapely breasts, and a slender figure.

It definitely looked like Sam from the side.

He reached the group of eight and, careful not to be obvious, approached the bar. He glanced to his right. Two of the women were probably in their thirties while the men all looked fortyish. The third girl was standing directly behind the tall, heavyset bald guy in the dark-blue double-breasted suit. Bill caught another glimpse of blond hair, but the moment her face was about to be revealed, the tall bald guy moved forward, hiding her from view.

Bill edged closer to the bar and made a play for the bowl of cashews. Just as he grabbed a handful, the girl's face moved closer, but someone else shifted between them, obscuring his view once again.

A moment later, the girl said something to the other women, and the three of them spun around and made their way for the restrooms at the far end of the room.

Once again, his consciousness automatically lapsed into the same unfathomable darkness.

Moments later, he began looking around. He had no idea that he'd even moved, but when reality finally returned, he discovered that he was staring dumbly at the door marked *LADIES' ROOM*.

He had obviously followed the women without realizing it.

What the hell am I doing?

More importantly, where do I go from here?

Do I just push open the door, walk inside, and pay them a visit?

Then what? What do I give them as an excuse for invading their privacy?

He shook his head. He was acting like a total moron.

"Whaddya doing now?"

Laura had apparently followed him over. She didn't look at all pleased. "Why are you standing here, staring at the ladies' room door?"

He just sighed and waited for his heart rate to settle down. He had nothing to tell her. Nothing he could say would make him sound less like an idiot.

"You're not…going *in* there, are you?"

"Of course not." Her question sounded ridiculous, but he couldn't blame her for wondering—especially since she'd obviously been watching his every move. Even so, the situation made him angry, and he couldn't help lashing out at her.

He really was an idiot. He was angry with himself for doing something totally ridiculous and yelling at Laura for asking him what he was doing.

Laura shook her head. "I'm gonna need a cab, you know. I don't intend to stay here and wait for you to sober up. If you wanna know the truth, I'm gonna get awfully tired standing here, waiting to see whoever comes out of that room. I'll be curious to see what *you'll* do when that happens, but I guarantee that I'll be *much* more tired than curious by that time."

"We can leave."

"You're sure?"

"I'm sure." He slipped away from the crowd and led the way to the front entrance.

She caught up to him. "What were you doing, by the way? And what's happened to you? You're acting very strange."

"I thought I saw someone I once knew." He opened the door for her.

"Some woman, obviously." She slipped by him.

"Yes."

"Someone you knew well?"

"*Very* well."

Laura was quiet as they went down the walk together.

They approached his BMW, which was parked near the curb.

"Was it serious?"

He nodded.

She was silent for several moments. "What happened?"

He took a deep breath as he fiddled with his keys. "Too many things."

"Like what?"

"Life is what happened."

She watched him as he reached around her and pulled open her door.

She turned around. "Bill?"

"What?"

He could tell from her expression that she wanted more of an explanation.

"Go ahead," he said.

"Can I ask more about her?"

"I wish you wouldn't."

"All I wanna know is—"

"She's dead." He turned and circled the car.

She watched him and waited until they were facing one another. "Then why did you act like that in there?"

"I don't know."

"How long has she been—"

"Don't know that, either."

"How do you even know she's dead, then?"

"I was told."

"Who told you?"

"Someone who found out about it."

"Someone reliable?"

He opened his door. "My mother wouldn't lie about something like that."

"Your mother?"

He nodded.

"But you still thought you saw her. And then you started acting weird."

"Something like that."

"Then you know that the girl you saw was probably just some doppelganger, right?"

"Maybe."

"What else could it be?"

He didn't reply as he got in.

"When did you know her?"

"A long time ago."

"How long?"

He sat perfectly still, gripping the keys in his hand. "Twenty years."

"Twenty *years*? You were a *kid*."

"I know."

"And you said it was serious?"

He nodded.

"How serious could this have possibly been?"

"I would have married her if her family hadn't gotten in the way."

***

The drive to their Winter Park condo was spent in a tense silence.

Worried and confused, Laura replayed their latest exchange over and over in her mind. With guys, she'd learned long ago that they seldom made much sense when a love from the past resurfaced. When this happened, they resorted to their former existence, often becoming incoherent and even silly. In a case like this, the situation had to run its course naturally. Conversation wouldn't solve this. Neither would threats or ultimatums.

She had never had this problem before with Bill. The guy was every girl's dream. He had looks, charm, intelligence, a terrific sense of humor, great business sense, and the delightfully rare gift for knowing what he was doing regarding his bedroom antics. He'd had more affairs and one-night stands than most guys in their forty-plus years but had never been married. And after being with him for the last six months, she'd grown confident that she could coax him to change his wild ways and settle down, perhaps for keeps.

She realized how it must have looked, her having what appeared to be a wild affair with her boss, who was seventeen years her senior. But she didn't care. She was happy and reasonably certain Bill was just as happy. Despite what many might say, she considered herself very lucky that her guy was just as active in the bedroom as any younger man she had previously been involved with.

In her view, she had won the Lottery.

Even so, she couldn't stop worrying about what had happened at the Paradise, and as they approached the last stretch of highway that led to their condo, she found that she was more determined than ever to find out what was going on. Only then could she concentrate on what she would have to do to get their relationship back to where it was.

She knew she had to. She had to because she didn't want it happening again.

There was no way she would let her man freak out over another woman.

She found it very strange that it didn't matter at all that this other woman was dead.

***

As Bill followed Laura down the hall leading to the kitchen, he couldn't stop thinking about what had happened at the bar.

He'd seen Samantha. It was that simple. The fact that Sam had been dead for years didn't seem to matter. A woman looking very much like her walked past his table and, along with five well-dressed men—approach the bar, engaged in bar chatter for a few minutes, then turned around and with two other women disappeared in the ladies' room.

He told himself that he shouldn't be agonizing over this. People resembled someone else everywhere these days. Thanks to cosmetic surgery, photoshopping, makeup and fashion trends, females with Sam's facial characteristics should be walking around in every city in every state in the country. Hairstyles made women look very similar. So did facial reconstruction. And cheek implants. And nose jobs.

He saw no logical reason why he should be obsessing over any of this.

But he was. It had happened, and he knew he couldn't stop it.

He knew he couldn't stop this nonsense until he found out for sure.

The only complication he could see was the slender brunette opening the cupboard and grabbing the bottle of *Absolut* Vodka from the shelf. And as he sat down at the kitchen table, he knew full well that she was not going to let this go.

This had nothing to do with Laura or her mental insecurities. Laura was a gorgeous, intelligent, outgoing young woman. However, Bill knew women, and when it came to a past love popping up in the middle of a relationship, he knew full well that they would all react in the same manner.

It took him less than thirty seconds for Laura to prove him right.

Just as she put the bottle on the counter and went to get glasses and cubes, she said, "So tell me about it."

He sighed tiredly, dropped his elbows on the table, and rubbed his temples. He knew how this would play out; he just didn't feel like getting into it right now. But he had no choice. Laura wasn't the type to let something like this go without an explanation.

Still, he decided to remain vague. He saw no advantage in telling her everything. Not at ten-thirty on a Friday evening, anyway.

"Tell you about what?"

"The girl you saw at the Paradise." Laura dropped two cubes into each glass and brought them over. She splashed two inches of vodka into each glass and sat facing him. Her expression wasn't reassuring. He'd seen it before. Laura had a short fuse. And once it was lit, it burned very hot, remaining so for quite a while. "The one you freaked over. Don't you remember? You followed her all the way to the ladies' room—"

"I already told you." He picked up his glass and downed the shot. The fire erupting in his throat relaxed him. He sat back in his chair and took a deep breath. Then he pushed the glass back at her and watched as she grabbed the bottle to pour him a refill.

"You didn't tell me everything."

"That's probably because I don't want to."

"Why not?"

"Why do you wanna know?"

"You don't think I should?"

"I'd just like to know why you're so interested. I told you the circumstances. The woman this girl resembles is dead. I've known about her death for years, but when I saw her come into the place, it kinda knocked me right out of my chair. Sounds

16

simple, doesn't it? It's really nothing more than a normal reaction."

"It does sound simple."

"Then why in heaven's name are you so interested?"

"Because of how it affected you. You freaked, and I mean totally. To me, it looked totally bizarre. Frightening, too. And it was anything *but* a normal reaction." She stared at him intensely. "You followed this woman to the bar, then to the restroom. The *restroom*. You—"

"I know what I did, thanks. I was there, too."

"Yes, Bill. You were there. But I honestly don't think you're totally aware of what you did. At least you didn't seem to be. Not at the time, anyway."

"Really?"

"I wouldn't lie."

He knew she was getting too close to the bone, but he had no idea how he could possibly distract her. "What exactly did I do?"

"While I was following you, I noticed that you weren't walking right. You were moving like some other person. It was like…like you were sleepwalking."

"Sleepwalking?"

"As I just said, you weren't walking as you usually walk."

"How is that?"

"Not like *that*…"

He shook his head. "You're not telling me anything."

"All I know is, it wasn't like you. Not at all."

"Who was it like?"

17

"Don't be funny. It just wasn't you."

"Too bad you didn't pull out your cell and preserve it for prosperity. We could all watch it on You Tube years from now, when we're too old to stay up and watch a full-length movie."

She groaned. "Don't make light of this, now."

"I told you. A girl I used to know walked right past our table—"

"Yes, Bill. A girl you used to know. A girl who happens to be dead."

"It was her double. It looked just like her—"

"You said doppelganger."

"No, *you* said doppelganger."

"It doesn't matter, does it? The fact is—"

"It does matter—don't you think?"

She sighed and stared at her half-empty glass. He could tell something else was on her mind. He also knew he was going to hear what it was very shortly.

"Tell me something." She finished her drink.

"All right…"

"You don't know when she died, do you?"

"Not exactly."

"Can you at least tell me that it wasn't recently?"

"As I recall, it's been years. Close to twenty, I imagine."

"Okay. Did you get a good glimpse of that girl?"

"You mean tonight?"

"At the bar."

He shrugged a shoulder. "I guess. Why?"

"Could you tell how old she was?"

"Not exactly. It was dark in there, you know…"

"I know. But since it wasn't dark enough to hide her features, you could tell about how old she looked…right?"

He hadn't thought of that before. His mind went back to his original glimpse of her. This was what got him thinking what he hadn't been thinking before. Was it because he had had too much to drink? Or had this girl's sudden appearance shocked him so much that logic had just vanished from his mind?

"You're not fading away again, are you?"

"I'm right here."

"All right, then. How old did this girl look?"

"Young."

"*How* young?"

He shrugged. He didn't want to venture down this road.

"C'mon, now. You can tell me. We know each other, right? I mean, we've been living together now for six months."

He nodded.

"How young, Bill?"

He sighed tiredly. "Twenties, most likely."

"Early twenties? Mid? Or—"

He felt his nerves beginning to twinge. "Does it matter?"

"Yes, Bill, it really matters."

He shifted uncomfortably in his chair.

"Early twenties? Mid? Or late?"

"Early."

"Like about my age?"

19

He picked up his glass and dropped another swallow of strong vodka down his throat. "Younger."

"Twenty, maybe? Or maybe even nineteen?"

"If she were nineteen, she wouldn't have been in the bar in the first place."

"We're just discussing our impressions. Nothing else."

He didn't appreciate her putting all this under an X-ray. "Don't make me go there, all right?"

"We're just talking, Bill."

"Just talking? You're sure?"

"I'm sure. Just you and me. No one else."

"Nineteen, then."

"Now…was that so hard?"

"Very."

"But now we know, don't we?"

"Know what?"

"We know that this girl you obsessed over back at the bar, this *child* you followed to the ladies' room, can't possibly be anything but someone else's daughter who resembles a woman you once had a fling with, back in the day."

"It was more than a *fling*." He felt his back muscles stiffen against the padded back of the chair.

Laura stopped talking and just stared at him.

"*Much* more…" He took another breath and forced himself to relax.

"How…*much* more, Bill?" Her voice had become a whisper again.

He shook his head. Laura didn't have to know the extent of all this. It was bad enough that Sam's image had come back from the dead after all these years.

"Bill?"

"You don't—"

"I need to *know*, Bill!"

His pulse raced. He couldn't back out of this now. She'd called him on it. Now he had to show his hand. He took a deep breath and felt his pulse racing. "I wanted...I wanted to...to marry that girl."

Laura didn't speak. Her dark eyes blazed.

He suddenly wanted to tell her the rest. He hadn't wanted to travel this road, but she'd called it, and now he knew that he had to tell her. It would hurt and anger her. Hell, she might even want to move out after he told her. But she wanted to know, and he knew he could no longer protect her because she obviously didn't want protection.

"If her family hadn't gotten in the way, we would have definitely married one another."

Silence.

Laura sat stiffly, not moving. Her eyes continued to blaze. Then, after about a minute, she seemed to let all the air out of her lungs. "Then it really *was* a little more than a fling after all."

"Yes."

She waited for him to say more. When he didn't, she asked, "Is that *all* there is? Or is there more?"

He didn't reply.

"Bill?"

He felt his pulse racing again.

"I need to know!"

He could barely look her in the eye. "Sam was the one true love of my life."

Chapter 2

The next morning, Laura got out of bed, put on her robe, and went to fix breakfast.

Bill remained in the bed, gazing numbly at the open doorway.

She was steamed, all right. Not a word since their talk in the kitchen. No communication in the bedroom as they undressed and got into bed. Not even a kiss good night. Her turning her back on him the moment her head hit the pillow strongly suggested that she was in no mood for fun games.

Nathan, you've really gone and done it this time.

He didn't need to search his memory to realize that what he had said the night before had been more than enough, and that he would have to weigh his words very carefully from now on if he didn't want more of a major flareup.

I should have known.

That certainly would have saved them both a ton of aggravation. He knew how sensitive Laura was, how insecure she could be at the most inopportune times.

"Sam was the one true love of my life..."

Had he actually told her that? Had something that cruel and unfeeling left his lips? Did he honestly think saying something like that would solve whatever problem they'd been having since his zombielike episode at the Paradise?

23

No wonder you've had so many failures with women.

He had had many. Too many, in fact. Three failed engagements, at least three dozen trashed relationships, and God only knew how many one-night stands had been crammed into his forty-plus years of life.

Fifty different women? Sixty? Or were there more?

It didn't matter, did it? The simple fact was that he had found a beautiful young woman nearly half his age who, until last night, worshipped the ground he walked on. She cooked up a storm in the kitchen and in the bedroom and satisfied his every wish.

But now he had to face the cold fact that this girl could join the rapidly increasing number of frustrated beauties who had left a man who had been running away from serious relationships for the last twenty years because of the demented delusion that the one and only perfect one had escaped him forever.

What the hell is wrong with me?

How can I toss them out after just weeks or a few months, for the simple reason that the relationship just doesn't feel quite right?

He was sick and knew it.

He just couldn't shake what had happened to him and didn't think he ever would. The only thing that seemed to matter was that Samantha had taken possession of his heart when he was just twenty years old. And as a result, he hadn't been the same since.

That was it in a nutshell.

She took my heart from that very first day and never gave it back.

And I've been trying to live without one ever since.

With these painful memories weighing heavily on his mind, he got up from the bed and plodded into the bathroom for his morning shower.

Ten minutes later, he stepped out of the shower, somewhat revitalized, but no less miserable or confused. After toweling himself off, he faced the mirror with eyes that looked at him with such contempt, he was certain they belonged to another person. And they seemed to be gazing directly into his soul.

What was going on now?

Now that he had brought back the past and analyzed it in a special new light, he realized that he would have to do something to repair what he had obviously damaged the night before, when he practically told Laura that she was not—nor could she ever be—the most important thing in his life.

Well, she wasn't, was she?

She wasn't for one very logical reason.

His memories of Sam had been foremost in his mind and would remain there forever.

But he knew he couldn't possibly keep them there—not as long as he wanted Laura in his life.

Fix this, you idiot... Fix it before it's too late!

He blotted his hair dry, fastened the towel around his waist, and opened the cabinet to grab his shaving gear. It occurred to him that no matter what had happened at the bar the night before, he could only change what would happen from now on if he lied to Laura and tried to convince her that she was in fact the only one he could ever love.

Would she *believe* that? Especially after their conversation in the kitchen the night before?

It didn't matter.

He had to convince her he was sincere.

After splashing his cheeks with cologne, he told himself that he *had* to sound sincere. He *had* to—if he wanted Laura to stay with him.

I can do this, he told himself, as he pulled on his jeans and went into the closet to select a comfortable tee shirt. *I'm the best investor in the damned company, for God's sake. I've been convincing people to trust me with their money for the last twelve years. I can convince anyone of anything.*

And as he went down the hall to join Laura in the kitchen, he smiled in confidence, convincing himself that whatever he told her was going to work.

It had to, because he wanted it to.

His confidence kept telling him it would indeed work, even though that other part of his brain—that part that always kept his innermost secrets hidden—had been working on a myriad of ways that would enable him to find out about that girl he'd seen the night before.

The one who looked like Sam.

So much, in fact, that he was afraid it might really be her after all.

***

26

Laura brought over a large dish of scrambled eggs, bacon strips, and several wedges of toast, and placed it on the dining room table.

Bill walked in and stopped in the doorway.

Laura appeared as sexy as ever in her light blue housecoat. It was the one he'd bought her just a few weeks ago, for her birthday. It came down to her knees, showing off her perfect tanned legs. When it was tied shut, it highlighted her cleavage, which exposed the small, heart-shaped mole on the inner part of her left breast. The fur-lined collar made the picture even sexier.

Although she had it loosely tied this morning, the effect was far from sexy. Even her hair, which hung free, failed in its attempt to arouse him. Her expression, plus the way she moved, suggested that she was not in her usual playful Saturday morning mood. He knew right then that he needed to do whatever was necessary to coax her into forgiving him for what he had said and done the night before.

Normally, this was not much of a challenge. Charm was something Bill had been blessed with since childhood. He had never had a problem knowing when or how to use it. But this morning, even though he desperately wanted to stroke this woman's fragile ego, he had something else in mind. Something he could not dismiss, even if he wanted to—which he did not.

"You're going somewhere this morning." She glanced in his direction on her way back to the stove and stopped cold.

"How could you tell?"

Her brows pressed together. "You're not wearing shorts, tennies, or one of your baggy tee shirts." She flipped her hair back over her shoulder and approached the stove. "It didn't take a brain surgeon."

He sat down at the table and poured coffee from the carafe. "I have to make a quick run to the office. I should only be an hour or so."

"You hate going in on Saturdays."

"I need to look over an account."

"Which one?" She brought over the butter and sat facing him. "I thought we had things pretty much squared away."

He sugared his coffee and stirred. "The Anderson-O'Neil. I need to—"

"You had me call them for a double check just before we closed up for this weekend." She stabbed a forkful of scrambled egg and fitted it carefully between her lips.

"I just need to verify something that's been bugging me about it since yesterday afternoon."

"What's been bugging you?"

He could feel the suspicion oozing from her. He knew he had to tread carefully. "I wish I knew. There's just something I need to see for myself."

"Was it something *I* did?"

"Of course not. I think it's something O'Neil told me when he handed me his latest list of holdings from his Bank America Account."

She nibbled on a piece of bacon. "It can't wait till Monday?"

"It'll drive me bananas. You know how I am with details like this."

She didn't reply.

He could tell she didn't believe what he was telling her. He knew right then that he should try softening the blow by checking out what was going on in her mind.

"Did you have something you needed to do this morning?"

She picked up her coffee cup. "I thought we'd do some flea marketing in town. I've been wanting to look for a new dresser for the bedroom. I never liked the one that's in there now."

"I know."

"I figured we should try and find something else."

"You didn't tell me about this before, did you?"

"I just thought of it when I was fixing breakfast."

So far, so good. Now he knew what he could do to keep this from getting out of hand.

"I'll only be an hour or so in Orlando. Then we can do whatever you like as soon as I get back. How's that sound?"

"Sure. I guess."

He could feel her disappointment. For some reason, it didn't seem to matter. "I promise I'll be back by noon. We can hit the tents, look for something, then have dinner at a restaurant of your choice. You've been wanting sauteed seafood and cracked crab…"

She thought that over. "Sounds good."

As she watched him, he had the feeling that she was trying to read his mind. He was very relieved that she couldn't.

If she could, she'd want to kill him.

***

After breakfast, Bill helped her with the dishes, then took her in his arms and kissed her.

"I'll be back by one, Laurie," he whispered, and kissed her again.

"You promise?"

"I promise."

Her eyes stayed on him. He could feel her heart racing. Under normal circumstances, he would have considered this a great time to take her into the bedroom. But after his huge blunder the night before, he could tell her symptoms were displaying uncertainty and fear instead of arousal.

"You still...care about me, don'tcha?" she asked in a whisper.

"What makes you think—"

She blinked, and those large, beautiful dark eyes clearly showed their suspicion.

"I know, I know. I'm very, very sorry about that. It'll never happen again."

"It made me feel...unnecessary. I felt invisible." She sighed and began to pull away.

He pulled her close and kissed her again. "You're *very* necessary," he said. "And *very* visible. *Never* forget that."

"But...what about—"

"I wasn't myself. I was tired. Don't forget that last conference call. And I obviously had too much booze."

Her eyes searched his. "You're telling me the truth?"

He kissed her again.

30

She sighed and rested her cheek against his chest. "If you keep doing that, I won't let you leave."

He smiled and stroked her hair. "Let's save that for tonight."

Her eyes sparkled. "It's a date."

He blew her a kiss as he left.

31

Chapter 3

Bill parked the BMW in his designated spot on the roof of the Centre Building on East Robinson.

For the next fifteen minutes, he sat behind the wheel, staring at the windshield and seeing nothing at all.

"I need to look over an account."

It sounded phony when he'd said it, but since he wasn't able to think of anything else, he decided to go with it anyway.

Now that he'd had more time to think about it, he knew he should have just forgotten all about the ridiculous scheme. The skepticism showing on Laura's beautiful face the moment he'd hit her with it made him feel like he'd just slammed a newborn kitten into the wall.

She knew he was lying.

Laura was a lot of things, but dumb wasn't anywhere on the list. Neither was naïve. Or clueless. If he'd wanted dumb, naïve, or clueless, the software profession would have provided him with dozens of qualified candidates that would have been up to the task.

Laura was mature for her young age, intelligent, sophisticated, and preceptive. She knew damned well what he was up to, she just didn't know what she could do about it.

However, she did manage to make him feel loathsome.

And he deserved every bit of it—her subtle pouting, her expressions of self-doubt and insecurity. Her soft, vulnerable, heart-rending voice.

"Was it...something I did?"

No, Laurie, it wasn't anything you did. It was me. Me and my total meltdown that started twenty-plus years ago and continued to eat away at me all this time but didn't really have the chance to show itself as magnificently as it did last night.

And now, to top it all off, instead of enjoying the weekend with a smoldering babe dripping with an insatiable sexual urge and a dynamite body, he was sitting in his car on the roof of the very building he eagerly escaped at each given opportunity, struggling with some sort of plan that would bring him into contact with a young woman who resembled the girl he had fallen completely in love with as a very young man.

Resembled? Was that accurate?

The word might be appropriate in this case. However, it didn't even begin to cover it. The girl he'd seen the night before was the spitting image of Samantha Lewes, the slender blonde who had literally opened his chest, ripped out his heart, and took it with her to her grave two decades ago.

Her spitting image.

Identical would even be more accurate in this case.

The girl he'd seen was indeed Samantha, although there was no logical way—outside of coming back from the grave—it could have been her.

But if it wasn't her, who *was* it?

He didn't know. That was why he was here, wasn't it? To find her again? To find out for sure? To look her in the face and let her see him as well? To focus on her reaction? To settle this madness once and for all?

Then what?

What would happen when or if he did find out?

He had no idea. He didn't even have a first step in this ridiculous venture. All he knew was that after what he had seen last night in the Paradise Bar & Grill, he had to find out if his eyesight had been accurate or if he was actually going crazy. He had no idea who the blonde was, where she lived or worked, or why she was there in the first place. All he did know was that she was among seven others who quite possibly worked in the same building.

What conclusion could he possibly make out of this?

I either find her or spend the rest of my life wondering if Sam is really dead while struggling on a daily basis to prevent myself from ending up in a padded room.

He glanced at his watch. 11:20. He remembered that some of the offices in the building were open on Saturday. Should he just get out of the car, step into the elevator, stop on every floor, and do a little good-natured stalking?

That would be stupid as well as pointless and time consuming. Laura was going to be seriously pissed if he didn't get back to the condo by one. In other words, attempting something like that would be dangerous.

He needed a drink.

The Paradise opened at twelve on Saturdays for its weekend buffet, but it was usually open for business by 11:30 for the tourist and weekend-working crowd. If Chuck was tending bar and handling the food, he might be able to help. Chuck was a smart, friendly guy, and got along well with the customers. He also had a decent memory for faces and might be able to help identify the blonde.

Bill got out of the BMW, walked over to the elevator, got in, and took it all the way down to the ground floor.

***

The bar was in the process of preparing for its afternoon buffet.

Two short, heavyset, middle-aged women in white aprons were wheeling an aluminum cart covered with buckets of food up to the long table positioned next to the end of the bar.

Bill went in and climbed the stool nearest the door. From his vantage point, he could see everyone coming in as well as anyone using the doorway behind the bar, which led back to the kitchen. The two ladies who had brought out the food were now arranging things at the buffet table.

Only a dozen or so customers sat at tables or at the bar. Two sloppily dressed, middle-aged men at the bar were having a heated discussion over their mugs of beer, while four couples and a trio of younger, casually dressed women sat at tables, chattering away quietly over their drinks.

A short, skinny redheaded woman around forty dressed in a loose-fitting white shirt, black slacks, and a red apron appeared from the kitchen doorway.

She saw him and came right over. He ordered a vodka gimlet and handed her a twenty as soon as she slid the glass over to him on a bar napkin.

He picked it up and tasted it. It was strong, so he decided to have just one. He didn't want to get shitfaced before chancing the six-mile trip back to the condo, which would be tricky with the heavy Saturday afternoon traffic. Being stopped by the OPD and forced to take the breathalyzer would be awkward and frustrating. He would obviously fail the test and be charged with a DUI. Laura would be waiting patiently for him to pick her up for their flea marketing and would be too angry to post his bail. He guessed that in this case, she would most likely tell him to fuck himself before packing up and walking out forever.

"How's the drink?" The redhead came over, polishing a glass with a soft white towel.

"Perfect. Chuck working this morning?"

"He's in back, helping with the buffet. He should be comin' out any time now." She went over to the sink and picked up another glass.

Chuck, carrying four small boxes of cloth napkins, appeared about five minutes later. He went over to the two women and placed the boxes on the table next to their trays. Then he turned and came right back.

"Workin' on a *Saturday*?" Chuck's sandy brows mashed together. "I thought you liked your weekends." He winked. "Especially since you hooked up with that pretty brunette lady."

"Love 'em to death. I just have one thing to do."

Chuck ducked under the counter. He pointed to Bill's half-empty glass. "Another round?"

"Not this time." Bill glanced at the room, then gestured him closer. "Got a minute?"

Chuck came right over.

"I was here last night and saw a young woman come in." He was careful to keep his voice down. "I was wondering if you might know who she is."

Chuck shrugged. "Quite a crowd last night. Fridays? What can I say?"

"This girl was with two other women and three guys. They all looked like they might be working upstairs. Insurance, maybe. Or one of the law firms. Could even be software."

"Ever seen 'em before?"

"Never."

"They were dressy?"

Bill nodded. "Professional. The guys had on pricey suits. Two of the women wore business suits."

"The one you're interested in... What'd she have on?"

"Black skirt, long-sleeve blouse. Spikes."

"Anything else?"

"One of the guys with her was huge. Six-three, maybe three hundred. Balding."

"In a good suit?"

"Looked like it fit, too."

Chuck thought it over. "Tall'n Big Store, obviously."

"Ring any bells?"

"Not right off. How 'bout the babes? Can ya describe 'em?"

37

"The two with her looked around forty, maybe close to fifty. Five-six, large breasted and, as I said, well-dressed. One was silvery blonde, but it looked like a wig. The other had light brown hair, piled up in back."

Chuck was shaking his head. "Describes a lot of 'em these days. Tell me more about the one you're interested in."

"She's around twenty, maybe twenty-two. Blond hair, and she wears it shoulder length. Big blue eyes, and she's small-boned and small-breasted, with a tiny waist—"

"Now, *that* rings a bell."

"You're sure?"

"About five-nine, but she was wearing spikes."

"Sounds about right. Go on…"

"That's about it. She's been in here two, maybe three times, but she really sticks out, if ya know what I mean…"

"I know exactly what you mean." He picked up his glass with a shaky hand and finished it in one gulp.

"I know it's none of my business," Chuck said softly, "but any specific reason you're checkin' 'er out?"

"It's personal." Bill's thoughts had gone chaotic. He knew he had just made some headway and was thinking of a subtle way of forging ahead without attracting attention. He'd known Chuck for a year or so. Chuck was young, maybe just two or three years this side of thirty, but he seemed to have a good head on his shoulders and wasn't the type to open his mouth at the wrong time. But Bill knew to be cautious. Chuck had seen Laura several times. Bill didn't want to do anything that might blow this up.

"Can you do me a huge favor?" Bill reached into his pocket and pulled out a thick wad of loose bills.

Chuck eyed the wad and shrugged. "As long as I don't get myself in serious trouble doing it. Whaddya need?"

"A little information and a lot of serious silence about whatever you get." Bill pulled a hundred from the roll and folded it neatly into a small green square. "Can I trust you?"

Chuck eyed the little green square. "I can keep my mouth shut, all right. As long as no one gets hurt."

"Next time this girl comes in?" Bill held the tiny bill close to Chuck's face.

Chuck's gaze didn't stray from the bill. "Yeah?"

"Try and find out who she works for."

Chuck frowned. "That's *it*?"

Bill reached into his pocket, pulled out his wallet, and took out one of his business cards. He put it with the bill and handed it over. "And call me when you know something."

"Does it matter when I call?"

"Not at all."

Chuck pocketed the bill and the card.

"Now…tell me exactly what you're gonna do."

"Next time she comes in, find out who she works for, then call you. Right?"

Bill smiled. "That was perfect."

Chapter 4

Bill got back to the condo at 12:40.

Laura had slipped on a maroon tank top and light blue shorts and had given her hair a light going-over with her wide-toothed brush and a quick dose of hairspray. She'd also dabbed her neck and earlobes lightly with *Obsession*, applied some lipstick and eyeliner, and looked fabulous.

"You're not even late." She looked surprised.

"You *expected* me to be? After my bone-headed blunder last night at the bar? How stupid do you think this boy is?"

"I don't want to talk about that again, okay?" She was smiling, but he could hear the hurt in her voice.

"You're the boss, lady."

She pressed against him and placed her hands on his shoulders. He wrapped his arms around her waist and they kissed, long and passionately.

When the kiss ended, she pressed harder against him and whispered, "It's still not even one o'clock."

He glanced at the clock on the wall behind her. It said 12:44.

"You're right. We've got sixteen minutes to kill."

She nodded. "I think I'm right about something else, too."

"What's that?"

"Something serious and very warm is going on between us right now."

"You noticed that, too?"

"I'd have to be dead *not* to notice…"

"Any suggestions?"

"Let's discuss it in the bedroom."

"You're a lady after my own heart."

"Among other things…"

***

The parking lot at the Fairgrounds was packed.

Locals and tourists strolled the large area, enjoying ice cream cones and sandwiches as well as the many fast food dishes they'd picked up from the long row of food trucks lined up outside the tents and stretching all the way to the enormous parking lot nearly fifty yards away.

The tents were set up in long rows, most of them under roof. Bill followed Laura up the grassy path and ducked into a tent where a sign, *HAND MADE FURNITURE*, had been painted sloppily in black on a large piece of white plywood nailed to a post stuck in the ground.

Rockers, end tables, hand-made cabinets, and sleigh bed framework sat in assorted groups separated by a narrow walk-through aisle. Desks for computers and other office accessories, as well as many types of shelves, sat on folding tables or on storage boxes.

Laura stopped walking and frowned at an immense entertainment center made from particleboard. "I just don't see what I really wanna see," she said flatly. "Do you?"

Just as he was about to ask her what she was looking for, he caught movement several yards ahead, on their right.

A young blond woman.

Her back was to them, making it impossible for him to see her face. However, he suspected that he was looking at the same girl he'd seen in the Paradise the night before. The cut and length of her hair looked frighteningly similar.

He was certain she was the same person. She was dressed in shorts, athletic shoes, and a short-sleeve tee shirt, and appeared to be the same height and body type as the girl he'd seen the night before.

She wasn't alone. The girl beside her was shorter and slightly heavier, with long, red hair, and was moving at the same pace.

His heart sputtered when he realized he was looking at the same girl. He also knew how much of a disaster it would be if he acted like a shithead once again and went after her. He'd already almost killed it with Laura and didn't want to tempt fate—

"Well?" Laura had moved closer. "*Do* you?"

Her voice startled him.

It took him only a moment to realize where he was but much longer to remember what he was doing here. Then he tried hard to recall why Laura was standing so close and what she was talking about.

I've got to stop screwing around!

Otherwise, Laura would know what was going on and tear into him. This time, there would be hell to pay. Laura had no *off* switch when she was pissed and didn't care where they were or who was standing within earshot when her fuse was lit.

"Bill? Did you hear me?"

Luckily, the crowd noise helped his situation by adding to the confusion. He'd have to bluff his way out of this, but he wasn't totally sure how he would go about doing it. The accusing look on Laura's face was intimidating.

"Sure did."

"All right. What did I just say?"

He felt his pulse quicken. Luckily, his brain hadn't yet abandoned ship. "This sort of stuff isn't really your style." He pointed to one of the cabinets. "I don't care for it, either."

His bluff must have worked.

"You could be right. I don't feel it at all."

"I really can't see any of this making a difference anywhere in the condo."

"Could be…" She thought it over. "I thought I caught a glimpse of mahogany in the next tent. Let's check that one out."

"Mahogany? You sure?"

"Why not?"

"Will it match?"

She shrugged. "It's worth a try."

"Let's check it out, then…"

She led the way.

Bill glanced toward his right and felt his pulse sputter again.

Up ahead, the blonde had stopped walking and was examining an entrance mirror with shelves. The redhead said something. The blonde nodded and moved closer to the mirror.

Bill waited to see a reflection of her face.

"Aren'tcha coming?"

He stiffened. Laura again. "Right behind you…"

Just as the blonde moved closer to the mirror, Bill followed Laura into the next tent.

I've got to find some way of checking out this girl…

His thoughts cascaded into utter chaos as he struggled to focus on Laura.

***

Half an hour later, Bill saw the blonde again.

She and the redhead had walked over to one of the food trucks and stood in line, studying the menu stuck to the front of the counter just above the owner's head.

"You're hungry, aren'tcha?"

"Huh?" He spun around. Laura was checking out the food truck on their left, which advertised burgers and hot dogs with several different styles of fries and onion rings. There were also various selections with shrimp and crab, plus a seafood basket.

Laura was nodding. "I feel like I'm in the mood for a shrimp kabob. How about you?"

"I'm not really—"

"Bill, it's nearly four o'clock." She was giving him her accusing stare again. "We haven't eaten since breakfast, and I'm *starving*. You can't tell me you're not hungry…"

It took every bit of concentration he could muster to keep from turning to gawk at the blonde. He knew what would happen if he lost the battle.

44

Out of the corner of his eye, he caught her and her friend walking away from the truck. Both had cold drinks in their hands and were drinking from straws. They disappeared in a small crowd, then reappeared and moved toward the line of porta potties standing on the far side of the open field.

If I could just sneak over there for a closer look... If I could just get a tiny glimpse...

But how could he possibly sneak over there while Laura was standing right beside him?

"Bill? What would you like?"

"Huh?"

"Food? Eating something?" She opened her mouth and pointed to it. "Since we missed lunch, and since we're right here, and since we've got all this food around us..." She shrugged. "Understand what I'm trying to say?"

It dawned on him that if he asked Laura to order, her back would be to him. This would enable him to check out the blonde. It would be even better if he told her he needed to use the bathroom...

"How about we stay in the safe zone and get your usual seafood basket?"

"That would be great." He pulled two twenties from his pocket and handed them to her. "I'll be right back. I need to use the can."

"Okay, I'll get the food."

"You're a life saver." He turned and hurried away, heading down the field.

Several small groups were milling around in the general area. Some munched on their food while others hurried into a porta john.

45

The blonde and her friend were dropping their plastic cups into an open trashcan on their way to the porta johns.

Bill hastened his pace, closing in on the gap just as the blonde reached out to pull open the door of a porta john. He was about to call out to her when someone behind him yelled, "Bill!"

He stopped and instantly felt his blood turn cold.

Footsteps approaching him grew louder, sharper. He knew who it was without turning to see.

"*Bill.*"

Sighing in defeat, he turned.

It was Laura. Her eyes blazed.

"Take me home."

He had no idea what to say but knew he should say *some*thing. An apology? That sounded right, since nothing else came to mind.

He opened his mouth.

"Now!"

"Laura—"

"*Now*, dammit!"

"But if you'll just—"

"I don't want to stand here and *argue* anymore! I've had *enough*!"

"I'm sorry—"

"*More* than enough!"

She turned away sharply and began walking away quickly.

Just as he took his first step to follow her back to the car, he heard a door click behind him.

He turned.

The blonde was coming out of the porta john.

She glanced at him, smiled briefly, then joined her friend as they began walking back to the tents.

His heart sank.

It wasn't the same girl he'd seen the night before.

Chapter 5

Laura sat stiffly in the passenger seat as Bill drove the BMW in the heavy Saturday afternoon traffic.

His mind was in turmoil and he knew he had to do something to make things right—not only with Laura, but also with himself. This sort of behavior wasn't like him at all. He was forty-one years old, for God's sake, but he was acting like an eighteen-year-old suffering through his first crush.

He couldn't continue acting like this. This was just *so* not him. It was juvenile and ridiculous. He was ashamed of himself and wasn't above admitting it. His parents would be ashamed of him as well.

Samantha was dead. He knew it, accepted it, and had been living with it. Many people he had known in his past were dead; he had learned to live with that as well. Death was part of life. He'd understood this since he was a kid.

Why was he acting like this? Why was he suddenly so obsessed with a woman who resembled a girl he'd loved years ago?

"Tell me what I'm supposed to do, Bill."

She'd said it quietly. And she sounded very calm. She'd probably been focusing on her composure for the last couple of miles and had finally triumphed over her hysteria. He applauded her for that. He also envied her for her self-control and cursed himself once again for causing all this.

"I just can't keep ignoring this—whatever *this* is."

She hadn't moved. She sat rigidly, staring straight ahead, her arms crossed over her chest. He could see only her profile but could tell she was struggling to hold everything together. A tear had been sliding slowly down her left cheek.

He wanted to kick himself for causing her so much stress.

"You shouldn't have to," he told her. "You shouldn't have to put up with *any* of this."

She turned and glared. "Then why are you *doing* this to me?"

"I shouldn't be, and I know it."

"Then why *are* you?"

"I wish I could tell you."

"Tell me *some*thing. Please. I really don't know what's going on. I *want* to, but…but…" She turned back to stare at the windshield.

"I don't know what's going on, either."

"Are you trying to tell me you don't know how you've been acting since last night?"

"Oh, I know how I've been acting, all right…"

"Okay…"

"I just don't know *why* I've been acting this way."

She sighed and shook her head.

He went right back to cursing himself for how he'd acted at the Fairgrounds.

"Tell me about her, Bill."

"Huh?"

49

"This girl. The one who is supposed to be dead but seems to be very much alive right now. Tell me about her."

"Laura...I really don't think—"

"Tell me, Bill."

"But—"

"I need to know—all right?"

"Are you sure you want to—"

"I need to know why a girl you knew a long time ago is suddenly tearing us both apart. A girl you told me is dead and has been for years. I really need to know, and I think I deserve to. Don't you?"

"Yes. You do."

"Then tell me."

"I don't know if—"

"Bill, do you care about me? I mean, do you honestly *care* about me?"

"You know I do."

She lowered her face. "I know you don't love me. Not yet, anyway. We're already talked about that and we both decided that it was all right, we could still spend our time together because we really care for each other and enjoy each other's company." She turned to him. Her eyes glistened. "But do you care enough about me that you'd want to do whatever it took to get me to stay with you?"

He didn't know what to say.

"Because if you don't, I'll just pack up my things as soon as we get back."

"Laura—"

"I'll pack, put everything in the SUV, and be out of your hair in an hour. Then you'll be free to—"

"I don't want you to move out."

"But can you be free if—"

"I don't *want* to be free."

She eyed him in silence before she spoke again. "You know how that sounds, don't you?"

"I know exactly how it sounds. I'll put it this way. If being free means being free of you, I don't want that. Is that better?"

"Much."

"Okay, then."

"So…tell me about her."

He had no idea what he should or shouldn't say. He knew that if he hadn't seen that girl at the bar last night, none of this would have even happened.

"Tell me, Bill."

He just sighed.

"I'll pack up and leave. I mean it. You know I'll do it."

"I know you will."

"I just can't put up with stuff like this."

"I really can't blame you."

"Then tell me."

"I…don't know where to start."

"Start at the beginning. Isn't that where we need to be?"

***

Bill had been pulling all-nighters for his studies at UCF and stopped at the Waffle House outside Orlando when he sensed someone watching him the moment he sat down at a table.

He rubbed his eyes. It had been difficult staying awake during the drive from the school. He knew full well that he wouldn't be able to make that last eighteen-mile stretch, where his parents lived just north of St. Cloud, unless he stopped for some strong black coffee to revitalize him.

Then he heard a soft, low-pitched feminine voice.

"Need some coffee? Looks like you could use the whole pot."

He stopped rubbing his eyes. He then waited anxiously for his vision to clear so he could see who belonged to that sexy voice.

He soon discovered that he was looking at one of the prettiest women he had ever seen.

"Should I bring the pot over?" She was smiling. Her large cornflower blue eyes sparkled in the harsh lighting of the eatery. "Or just hook you up to an I V and let you take the coffeemaker with you?"

He laughed. "I look that bad?"

"Worse."

"Ouch."

"Sorry. Didn't realize you'd be thin-skinned."

"Why wouldn't you think that?"

She shrugged. "You're, well, a *guy*…"

"Another ouch. Girl, I hope you've got a large batch of band-aids stuffed in that apron."

"Are you trying to say I'm kind of abrasive?"

"No, no, no, no, no… You're way *past* abrasive. The abrasive thing went along with your I V remark. I'd definitely classify you as highly combustible."

She laughed. "Wow! Thanks! Glad I could be of help."

"Help?"

"You're no longer yawning or rubbing your eyes."

"Oh. Well, thanks. And yeah, I would love some coffee. That is, on one condition."

"What's that?"

"You smile after you pour it."

"Why not before?"

"You mean I get the option?"

She suddenly looked serious. "We like to cater to our customers. It helps business—or so they tell me."

"Then I prefer both."

"You mean before *and* after?"

"Yep."

"Sorry. No can do."

"But you just said—"

"I said you get the option. I didn't say I have to honor it."

"But you also said you cater to your customers."

"We do."

"I'm a customer, right?"

"I don't know. Are you?"

"Why else would I be here?"

"You raise a good point."

"Then I'd definitely want a before *and* after smile, please…"

"Actually, I've been smiling since I approached your table."

"I've noticed. Are you always this happy?"

"When my customers are as cute as you are."

He could feel the room getting warmer. "Really? You just said I look much worse than bad."

"You seem to be looking better and better."

"How can that be possible?"

She batted her lashes. "You're obviously succumbing to my irresistible charm."

"Irresistible, eh?"

"What would *you* call it?"

"Alluring. Tempting. Appealing."

"Isn't that the same thing?"

"Just checking to see if you remember your synonyms."

"How'd I do?"

"Just great."

"Thank you. I'll be right back."

"Don't forget the coffee."

"I'll do my best."

Just three weeks later, they moved in together.

***

Bill parked the BMW in front of the condo.

He was tired and wanted to lie down and relax. His body was telling him that he'd been up for days even though it hadn't even been anywhere near that long. When he tried pushing the car door open, he discovered that it had mysteriously become much heavier and more cumbersome. Not wanting Laura to sense anything strange, he forced it open, forced himself out, and slammed it shut. After taking a few deep breaths, he circled the car and pulled the door open for Laura, who was removing her seat harness and picking up her bag from the floor.

But as he waited for her to get out of the car, he dreaded what would happen once they were inside. Since he'd already started telling her his story, he couldn't back out of it now. He detested himself for creating this impossible situation.

If only he hadn't gone all freaky when he first saw who he thought was Sam at the bar…

If he'd just reached for his glass while she was walking past his table…

If only Laura had rubbed the back of his neck at the right moment, as she had done only a minute before…

Too many if's, but the only thing that mattered was that none of them had happened. And as a result, his life had taken a bizarre turn he would never have expected.

"What happened, Bill?" Laura got out of the BMW and stared at him. "Everything sounded great. You two got along extremely well from the moment you met one another. You were obviously a matched set. What happened to mess it all up?"

He just sighed and pushed the door shut.

"Tell me."

"It really brings back a lot of—"

"I know what it's gonna bring back. I've been there too, you know. We all have skeletons. We all have closets. It's called baggage."

He wanted to tell her that skeletons didn't usually jump out at you at the most inopportune times. He didn't say anything because he knew that anything he did say would not go over very well.

"Just tell me. It had to have been complicated and all sorts of—"

"It wasn't complicated at all, and it was all sorts of nothing."

"But *some*thing happened. You two were in love and then you weren't. Something like that takes a lot of seriously nasty work to mess up."

"It didn't, believe me."

"Then it must not have been love."

"Oh, it was love, all right."

"What happened to end it?"

He cursed himself once again for putting her into the middle of this.

"Bill? I won't quit until you tell me…"

"You really want to know?"

"Very much."

"What happened to screw it up could be summed up in one word."

"Okay…"

"To make it simple, that one word would be *Daddy*."

***

"Hers or yours?"

Laura opened the fridge and took out two small bacon-wrapped chicken roasts they'd bought the other day. She pulled out a large metal bowl filled with salad makings and placed it on the counter.

"I'll let you guess." Bill grabbed a bottle of *Absolut* and a small bottle of sweet vermouth out of the cabinet and placed them on the counter. He grabbed a bowl of cubes from the freezer and began fixing the Martinis.

"Why'd he screw it up?"

"The answer's very simple. He hated my guts."

Laura stopped what she was doing and just stared at him.

He could tell what she was thinking. This wasn't making any sense to her, obviously, no doubt because she considered him one of the nicest guys she had ever met. And, judging by what she'd told him about the men she'd known in her past, he could see her point. Two of them had been abusers. Others had been players who didn't care much about how they'd hurt her or any other female. Her ex-husband had been the worst, draining both her checking and savings accounts the moment he'd walked out. Placing a close second was the moron who'd borrowed her refurbished Camaro and promptly totaled it in a DUI-involved accident on the East-West Expressway just two weeks after they'd started a relationship.

Compared to such low-class males, he realized he could not possibly fail to impress her.

However, Sam's father would have disagreed, and did so at every given opportunity.

"How can anyone hate you?" Confusion covered her fine features. "You don't even have any enemies at work—and that says something."

"He never liked me."

"Why not?"

"It might've been a chemistry thing. We just never got along. For one thing, he was a retired Marine Colonel, and a stickler for manners, morals—that sort of thing. I was kind of a rebel back then. Long hair, unshaven, lackadaisical attitude, rebellious. If I'd been born thirty years earlier, I would have been called a hippie. He didn't approve of me and thought Sam deserved better. I couldn't even carry on a conversation with the guy. He was the type who didn't hide his feelings and had strong ones—on every conceivable subject."

"It was a real shame he never got to know you. If he did, he would've felt differently. He might have even approved of Samantha's choice."

"Actually, I kinda killed that possibility in a single sunny afternoon."

"What happened?"

"He saw us involved in something he should never have seen." The darkness of the memories came right back the moment he'd said it. He could feel the same cold terror that had consumed him the day Sam's father had had it out with him.

"What did he see?"

"Guess." He'd finished mixing the Martinis and promptly poured one and drank it right down.

Her eyes grew. "You mean—"

"You got it." He refilled his glass and gazed out the window. "Bra draped over the back of the seat, panties on the dash, my shirt open, my pants down—you get the Kodak moment, don't you?"

"You two were ... having *sex*? In a *car*? And he ... *saw* you ... *doing* it?"

"Yep in all four cases."

"My *God*..."

"There's another yep." He downed the second Martini, poured another, then took the two glasses to the dining room table.

"I can see why he disliked you. Both of you were, what? Eighteen? Nineteen?"

"Sam was still living with them when we met. I was in the process of graduating from UCF, so I was still living at home, too. But I was also working part-time at the bank, and not too long after we met, I found a duplex that wasn't too far from the Waffle House, where she'd been working. She moved in with me just a couple of weeks after we met."

Laura sat there in stunned silence.

"Sam was his little princess. We both felt as if we'd mortally wounded him."

"In the eyes of a father, she would always be that."

Bill said nothing. He was hoping the discussion would end right then. There was nothing good that would come of this. After more than twenty years, bringing it back, in his view, would do nothing but harm to the present just as it had been to the past.

He just hoped none of this talk would ruin his relationship with Laura.

"What did Samantha think of her father?"

So much for hoping the story would end...

"She worshipped him. They were always super close."

"That princess thing runs deep. She'd always want to please him and would never want to do anything that might change their relationship one iota."

"Well, thanks to me, that ship sailed."

"I imagine it put a terrible strain on the family."

He gazed at his glass and struggled to keep from reaching for it. He didn't want to get shitfaced before dinner. The way things were going, he couldn't see any way of avoiding it. He had no appetite. The only thing he wanted right now was to go back twenty-four hours in time and forget all this.

"Bill? Did you hear me?"

He nodded.

"Well? Didn't it put a strain in—"

"You could say that."

"Did anything else happen?"

"Whaddya mean?"

"Did the situation ever change?"

"Actually, things changed much quicker than anyone could have imagined."

She paused before asking her next question. "What happened then?"

He went back to staring out the window. "Her father was killed in a three-car pileup on the Florida Interstate."

"My God! How horrible!"

"What made it even worse was that it happened just one day after he and I had a terrible row."

Chapter 6

Samantha wasn't the same after her father had seen them having sex in Bill's car.

She spoke less, rarely smiled, never laughed, went through long periods of silence, and slept with her back to him for weeks. They rarely had sex, hardly shared meals, and spent very little time together.

The magic that had brought them together had simply vanished.

And with it, the love they had once shared.

Six weeks after the unfortunate event with Sam's father, Bill came back to the duplex after working at the bank. It was a bright Saturday afternoon. He had just received a promotion and wanted to take Sam out to celebrate.

Sam hadn't been to work in several days. She'd been a bit under the weather and hadn't wanted to do anything.

Bill could see that she was suffering from severe depression. The changes in her had been eating him up inside; he'd been agonizing over it for weeks, struggling to find some sort of solution. He was determined to pull her out of it and didn't care what he had to do to accomplish it.

The moment he saw her sacked out on the living room couch in her bathrobe, he realized just how difficult his plan would be. But he told himself he could do it. Something had to be done, and he was determined to see this through.

"Get dressed," he told her the moment he came through the door. "We're going out."

No response.

He approached the couch. Her hair was a mess; she'd obviously not washed it in several days. The dark circles under her eyes told him that she hadn't slept much at all lately.

However, her appearance wasn't what concerned him as much as the fact that she hadn't even acknowledged his presence. Her gaze hadn't moved from the widescreen, which was showing the Weather Channel, with the volume muted.

He sighed tiredly and forced himself to deal with the problem.

"I was promoted at the bank today."

Again, no response.

He rubbed his temples and told himself he could do this. *You charm the ladies and the customers at the bank*, he reminded himself. *Dealing with people has never been a problem for you.*

"I said I was—"

"Heard ya."

"I think we should celebrate."

She picked up her mug and sipped from it. He guessed it was tea. Sam never liked coffee very much, and she'd never been the type to drink alcohol except on rare occasions.

"I figure we can go out to one of those fancy places at—"

"Don't feel like it."

"You still sick?"

A loose shrug.

62

He went over to the chair and sat. "Sam, I would really like to take you out and—"

"I don't want to go anywhere."

"Why not?"

Another shrug.

"What kind of answer is that?"

"The only one I have."

"You just can't stay here indefinitely, lounging around on the couch like this."

"How do you suppose I lounge around, then?"

"That's not what I meant."

She had another sip of tea.

"What are you gonna do when you go back to work? You've got to eventually get up from that couch and prepare yourself to re-enter the world."

"I don't know if I'm going back to that place."

"Whaddya mean?"

"Just what I said."

He was beginning to think her problem was much bigger than he'd suspected. "You didn't quit, did you?"

"Not yet."

"You mean you're actually considering it?"

"Maybe…"

"Sam, what's happening to you?"

"Whaddya think?"

"If this is about your father—"

"Leave him out of this." Her voice turned cold.

"Sam, I've apologized to you for that already. Many times."

No reply.

"Isn't it enough that I feel horribly bad about all this?"

"Not really."

"Why not?"

Her eyes blazed. "You're not serious."

"Yes. I really am."

Her eyes blazed. "My father has practically *disowned* me! He *hates* me! He doesn't even want to *see* me anymore!"

"You're exaggerating—"

"The *hell* I am! I tried calling them more than a dozen times since …since he saw us…that time. Mom's pissed at me, too, but at least she'll talk to me. She's distant, but she'll talk. She usually listens, then gives me one- or two-word answers. My father won't even get on the phone!"

He shook his head. "Just because he saw us—"

"Yes, Bill. Because he saw us. He saw his precious little girl kneeling naked in the back seat of a car, going down on a guy he'd only seen half a dozen times before! I was barely *nineteen years old*! Can you even begin to understand what that must have done to him?"

"Since I don't have any kids of my own, I guess not."

"I was his *little girl*, Bill! His *little princess*! I used to sit on his knee when I was a baby! Even though I'm all grown up now, he *still* thought I was his baby…" She sighed brokenly, then stared at the floor. "*No* father wants to see his daughter kneeling naked in front of a man, giving him—"

"All right, all right. I get it."

"Do you?"

"Yes. I get it. I really do. What I *don't* get is that you've folded."

64

"What?"

"You've folded. Entirely. You've given up. Closed the book on your life, on our life. Our love, our future. Because of what your father saw us doing, you've totally given up. I still love you, Sam. I love you more than you know, but we just can't live like this anymore."

She sighed brokenly. "I know…"

"We have to do something about this."

"I know that, too."

He struggled to guess what was going through her mind. He hoped she was thinking of a solution, too, but he couldn't be sure. Judging by her expression, she looked like she was hurting over the breakup with her father and that nothing else really mattered to her.

But he couldn't let that be the end of their relationship. He had to somehow forget about that—at least for now—and find some way to correct this. "What can I do?"

No reply.

"Sam?"

A shrug. "I wish I knew."

He got up from the chair and crossed the room.

"Where are you going?"

He stopped walking and spun around. "Do you care?"

She just stared at him.

"I figured as much."

He went over to the door and pulled it open.

"Are you…are you coming back?"

"Judging by your attitude, I wouldn't think you'd want me to."

She sighed tiredly. "*Are* you…coming back?"

"Eventually."

"What does *that* mean?"

"It means I'm coming back. But only after I try doing something about this."

***

"Where'd you go?" Laura asked as she had a sip of red wine.

"I went to see her father."

Laura's eyes grew. "You're not serious…"

"Serious as a heart attack."

She shook her head. "You went to see that man even after what happened? I mean, even though you knew how he felt about you?"

"I went to see him *because* of all that. All I cared about was that I was losing the love of my life because her father turned away from her, and I wanted to do whatever I could that might somehow clear the air. I knew I was being naïve about the whole thing, but I was determined to do whatever it took to get Sam back."

"But…wasn't that kind of dangerous? I mean—"

"It didn't matter—at least, it didn't at the time. I cared about Sam, and it was killing me to see her wasting away like that. I'd seen friends of mine waste away just like she was doing, but in their case it was drugs doing the job, so fixing their situation was a totally different kind of futility. This thing with Sam was nothing like that. It was workable, and all I had to do to change the situation was to have a heart-to-heart talk with the Colonel and hope he'd somehow find it in his heart to forgive us. This way, if things went south, I couldn't blame myself anymore, and Sam might appreciate what I tried to do and even forgive me. And if it did work, everything could just go right back to being how it was when we first met one another."

"Then you did talk to him?"

"I guess you could say I tried."

"What happened?"

"The crazy bastard tried to kill me."

Chapter 7

"What the hell do *you* want?"

Gordon Lewes stood six-two and weighed at least two hundred and forty pounds, much of it hard muscle even though he was on the wrong side of fifty. He wore a black U.S. Marines baseball cap that covered his salt and pepper buzz cut. His eyes were fierce blue slits. His thick black brows looked like two fat caterpillars squirming uncomfortably on his large square forehead. His reddish complexion suggested high blood pressure, and when he saw Bill approaching the garage, he straightened above the open hood of the classic '65 Mustang he'd been working on and glared at his unwelcome visitor.

A large crescent wrench extended from the man's large-knuckled, oil-smeared left hand. After a long, tense silence, he cleared the front of the car and took two slow, deliberate, and somewhat awkward strides in Bill's direction. His hard, lined face glowed a bright tomato-red, warning Bill of the man's dark state of mind.

"I'd like to…to talk to you, sir." Bill remembered that the man had been a Lieutenant Colonel in the Marines. He was careful to maintain an attitude of respect even though the man had been retired for the last two years.

No response. The glaring continued.

Nervous and uncomfortable, Bill stood his ground. His future with Sam was at stake, and he was determined to do whatever was necessary to get

68

things back to how they once were. If he had to humble himself with some serious apologizing, then so be it. Sam was worth the trouble as well as the aggravation. "Sam doesn't know I'm here—"

"Get the hell off my property," the man barked, moving closer. "You're not welcome here. And don't you *dare* mention my daughter's name again."

"Sir, I've come here to—"

"I told you to leave. I'm not gonna tell you again!"

"Why won't you just listen to what I have to say?"

The man took a large step toward Bill. Bill stiffened when he saw the wrench shift from one hand to the other.

"I'm not interested in *anything* you gotta say, you bastard!" The man's voice had become a low-pitched growl.

"But—"

"You deaf? Or just plain stupid? I told you—"

"You don't have to be insulting. All I did was—"

"This is my *home*, you stupid son of a bitch. I can be anything I wanna be! If I wanna be insulting, I'm gonna be goddamn insulting! Now get your worthless ass the hell outa my sight!"

"Sir, your daughter has been going through hell—"

"I told you never to mention her again!"

The arm holding the wrench suddenly came straight up and back, then shot right back down. Bill sidestepped, careful to stay out of range. The large head of the heavy tool missed him by more than a foot, screaming down and slamming into a heavy wooden work bench, splintering its surface and creating a thick U-shaped gouge at least two inches deep.

Bill didn't have time to react. Before he realized what had just happened, the wrench came back up with lightning speed. The man was getting ready to bring it down again, but suddenly lost his footing and nearly dropped to his knees.

His mind in panic mode, Bill raced back down the drive and jumped into his car. He got it going and peeled out quickly, nearly sideswiping the station wagon parked along the curve.

He didn't start breathing normally again until he was halfway to the Expressway.

***

"I guess acting like a reasonable human being wasn't exactly his thing, was it?" Laura asked, frowning.

"Believe me, the only thing that man wanted was to pound me into a bloody pulp, then dump whatever was left in his trashcan."

"That really was totally uncalled for, wasn't it?"

He sighed. "I'd had much better days."

"He was obviously a very nasty man."

"Actually, he seemed like a fairly nice guy when I first met him."

"What do you think happened?"

"You're talking about the part where he lost his balance?"

She nodded.

70

"I remember reading about it after the accident was covered in the local news. Apparently Sam's father had a brain tumor no one knew about."

"That could have been why he went off on you."

"It would explain how he moved when he came after me. I expected him to trip and fall on his face."

"If it had been me, I might've thought he'd been drinking."

"So did I...at first. I didn't smell alcohol, so I guess I ruled that out. But I knew *some*thing was off. And when he brought down the wrench, he brought it down way too wide. It looked like he was about to go sidearm on me. At the time, I guess I thought he was just too angry to have things under control. That's why I figured his aim was way off."

"Lucky for you."

"Even so, I felt the force of it when it sailed past my head."

Laura picked up her wine glass. "What about the accident that killed him? Was it his fault?"

"There were conflicting stories. Two eyewitnesses said his car crossed the solid line, into oncoming traffic. A couple of other accounts said he was only changing lanes, and a pickup from the oncoming lane swerved into him."

"Was the pickup driver charged?"

"He also died."

"My God... It must have been a bad one."

"It was."

Laura took another sip of wine. "Samantha didn't blame *you* for his death, did she?"

71

Bill didn't reply. He got up, went over to the counter, and poured more wine from the bottle. Then he leaned against the counter and stared at the backyard, which had become nearly invisible amidst the approaching darkness.

He wasn't thinking of the night or the backyard. His mind had gone back to the day he stood behind Samantha under the bright afternoon sun, watching her as she gently dropped a handful of sandy dirt onto her father's casket.

She was wearing a black dress with a black veil and hat. He hadn't seen her face since she'd come out of the bedroom just an hour or so earlier. Seeing the grief covering her face would have bothered him in other circumstances, but not in this case. She hadn't spoken to him at all since the family had gotten word of her father's death and gave her the horrible news.

He watched her and realized just how little she had become. How fragile. How different from the first day he'd seen her. She had in fact returned to her childhood, turning back into the precious little angel her father had always thought she was.

He couldn't stop going back to the first time he'd laid eyes on her. Standing there in her waitress uniform, smiling at him, her large, beautiful blue eyes sparkling in the bright room. Sharing insults with him. Laughing. Looking him over. Flirting. Making him feel great about himself and life in general.

It was all gone—the smiles, the mock insults, the flirting. The feeling that life could be terrific if you shared it with someone special. In just a few months, the love they'd once shared had withered away and turned into something else. Something dark and cold. Something foul. Something he hated with every fiber of his being. Something that made him shiver each time he thought of it.

She was silent on the way home. He tried a couple of times to get her to talk, but all she did was sit stiffly beside him, her hands in her lap, her eyes and cheeks wet with tears she refused to wipe away.

"I wish you'd talk to me," he told her as he drove. "I wish...I wish you'd stop hating me."

She didn't reply. This was, in his view, much worse than her telling him she really did hate him.

She went straight to their bedroom to change but did not come out until later that night. He didn't go in for obvious reasons. He knew that if he did, it would be a large mistake. However, curiosity eventually got the better of him, and he pressed his ear to the door a couple of times after an hour or so only to hear her whimpering softly.

When she did come out, she went right to the kitchen cabinet and got out a bottle of Jim Beam. She poured half a glass, dropped a cube into it, went over to the kitchen table, and spent the next half hour sitting there in total silence, staring at the night pressing against the window.

When he'd had enough, he went into the kitchen and forced himself to gaze at her. "I really wish you wouldn't hate me. I tried to apologize to him, but—"

"I don't hate you." She'd said it while staring out the window. She hadn't turned his way once and gave the impression that she was talking to someone standing in front of the window. She'd said it softly, but without emotion. Her voice sounded wooden, cold. She might have been telling him that it looked like it would rain.

"Then why do I feel like you do?"

No response.

"Why do I feel like you don't even see me anymore? It's almost like you don't even accept the fact that I'm here."

Again, silence.

"Why don't I feel that you—"

"I don't hate you," she repeated finally, again without emotion.

He continued watching her, wanting to ask her the next question but not wanting to because he was afraid of what she might say. Then, after the inner turmoil became too much, he heard himself say it anyway. "How *do* you feel about me?"

Silence.

"Sam, I really need to know. This is killing me, and—"

"Actually, right now, I don't think I feel anything."

That was it. The final blow.

He knew right then that further conversation would be pointless. His head had turned hot, his limbs cold as he turned around and faced the doorway. Then, forcing himself to ignore the rapid sinking of his heart, he left the house.

***

"Where'd you go?" Laura asked.

"To the closest bar I could find."

"Then what?"

74

He frowned. "That's where things get a little fuzzy."

"You passed out?"

He'd walked into the bar, found an empty table at the far end of the room, and sat down. A tall, broad-shouldered woman with large, blinking eyes and a face he could not remember came over and asked him what he wanted. She left and came back later with a glass filled with clear liquid and two cubes. He drank it down and asked her for another. And another.

Then everything dimmed.

"All I remember," he told Laura, "is waking up in a motel room. I think it was somewhere on the Trail."

"Alone?"

"I'm not even sure about that. When I woke up, there didn't seem to be anyone else in the room, so I guess you could say I was alone."

"Is this when everything stays fuzzy? Or did it get worse after you left the motel?"

It took only a moment before the image of the shower, the hangover, and the awkward stagger out to the car came right back. He sat in the car, wondering what he should do. He knew he'd messed up and that it wouldn't be long before he had to face Sam again. He had no idea what he'd say to her or what she'd say to him. They'd become strangers in the blink of an eye, and he couldn't remember exactly when that had actually happened.

But that wasn't the point. Her father was dead, and Sam—as well as the rest of her family—blamed Bill. They may not have thought that he'd been directly responsible for the Colonel's death, but they all agreed that he'd contributed to the man's stressful mental condition, which undoubtedly led to his death on I-4.

But the fact remained. He had to face her again, and he saw no logical way of avoiding it. After all, they had lived in the same place for several months. All his stuff remained there. He knew by their last conversation that their relationship had run its course, so he needed to get back to the place and move out as quickly as possible.

Before going back, he decided to stop at a diner and have a little breakfast and some strong black coffee. He wasn't the least bit hungry but knew that he should eat something before facing Sam for the very last time.

He stopped at one of the fast food places on the Trail and had eggs, toast, and a pot of black coffee. Then, after more than an hour of just sitting there, gradually draining the pot while thinking of his options, he left the eatery, got back in his car, and drove back to their duplex.

He sat in his car at the curb in front of the building, struggling with himself about what he should do or say, when it dawned on him that Sam's car was nowhere to be seen.

"Any idea where she was?" Laura asked, picking up the last of the dinner dishes.

"Nope. Didn't care, either. I was just relieved that she wasn't there. I wasn't in the mood to face her again, and with my hangover still alive and kicking, I knew I wouldn't have the stamina necessary to survive another argument."

"Then you went inside and packed."

"That's exactly what I did."

"Did she come back while you were packing?"

"Nope."

"Damn. I was hoping for a little more drama."

"Sorry. There's still more to come, but most of the really good stuff had already run its course."

He decided to stay overnight. Since she hadn't returned, he figured she'd be staying with her family. If so, this would give him the opportunity to grab a good night's sleep.

Later that night, at just a few minutes before midnight, he was proven wrong.

Just as he had fallen into a reasonably deep sleep, he was awakened by what sounded like someone coming in through the back door.

Since he didn't own a gun, he grabbed the first thing he could find. His Henry Aaron stamped baseball bat, given to him by his parents on his sixteenth birthday, stood propped up in the corner near the door. He squirmed into his jeans, grabbed the bat, went over to the door, gently eased it open an inch or so, and listened.

And heard Sam's voice.

Groaning, he tossed the bat onto the bed, pulled open the door, and went out into the living room.

Sam and her older sister Eileen, both dressed in jeans and loose-fitting tee shirts, were in the kitchen, fixing coffee. They both gasped when they heard him, and when they spun around to face him, they were glaring.

"What the hell are *you* doing here?" Eileen asked.

He didn't look at Eileen. He and Eileen had never gotten along. Eileen was one of those females who insisted that every guy she had ever met was lusting after her. And since he hadn't made a move on her or even shown the slightest interest, she hated him.

His gaze had settled onto Sam. He could feel intense anger, hatred, hurt, and disgust oozing from every pore. He realized right then that her violent emotions didn't hurt nearly as much as they had earlier. He hated to admit it, but he couldn't help sharing most of them. It hurt him very deeply that a girl he had very recently loved so much would turn on him so quickly, and because of something he had had no control over.

"I live here," he replied to Eileen's scornful question while continuing to stare at Sam.

"I take it you're moving out." Sam's voice was barely above a whisper. She'd said it flatly, without emotion.

"I'm gonna grab a few hours of sleep first." He hadn't made it a question.

"Really."

He wanted to unload some anger on her but knew it wouldn't help the situation. He thought it best to just let her do what she wanted and stay out of her way. Anything he would have said to her would have been twisted around by Eileen and reported to everyone in the family, so he decided not to give either of them ammunition they didn't need. He just said, "Don't forget to close the door on your way out." Then he turned around, went back into the bedroom, closed the door, and lay on the bed, staring at the dark ceiling and cursing life for making so many things so complicated.

About half an hour later, he heard the front door slam shut. He sighed deeply and closed his eyes. Then, despite the horrible feelings flowing through him, he drifted off into a deep sleep.

Chapter 8

"Then that was the last time you saw her?" Laura asked as she rinsed off the last of the dinner dishes.

"Unfortunately, no."

Laura watched him as she dried her hands with a dishtowel. "You didn't go back to her parents' place?"

"I didn't go anywhere."

"Then—"

"She came back to the duplex."

"And then I guess you two continued where you left off?"

"Not right off, exactly."

She sat down at the table facing him. "I guess I should just shut up and let you tell me what happened, then."

"I was out in back, in front of the garage, working on her rocking horse."

"Rocking horse?"

"Sam's father gave her a rocking horse for her second birthday."

"Okay…"

The horse was made of wood by a craftsman her father had known from his days as a Marine. The man was meticulous and knew his trade, and the horse was a one of a kind. Samantha cherished it and had it with her all her life.

However, during the years, one of its legs had loosened, compromising the integrity of the frame, and when Samantha told her father that she wanted his friend to fix it, he told her that the man had died just a few months earlier. Samantha didn't take the news very well, so she carefully wrapped up the horse in a blanket and kept it stored in hopes of finding someone who could fix the leg.

When she moved into the duplex with Bill, she told him the story and he said he could probably fix it. Bill's father had done carpentry work and had taught Bill some of what he knew when Bill was a boy. Since Bill had always been interested in making things, he retained everything his father had taught him. He guessed that all he had to do was use a few drops of glue, then give the leg a few light taps with the hammer to gently nudge it back into its niche. Then he'd carefully fasten and brace the frame, then put it aside to let it set properly.

Bill was moving out that morning when he spotted the horse on one of the shelves in the garage. The moment he saw it, he remembered his commitment to Samantha. Despite everything that had happened, he decided to do the right thing and complete the necessary repair work. He was in the process of setting it up when she pulled up the drive.

She got out of her car and stood quite still, watching him. Then she suddenly burst into a sprint and came at him. "What do you think you're doing?" She sounded panic stricken.

"I promised you I'd fix it, so now I'm fixing it."

"I don't *want* you to fix it."

He got up from his kneeling position and took a few steps in her direction. "I made you a promise—"

"I don't want you messing with it."

"But—"

"Just leave it in the garage. I've already asked someone else to work on it."

What she'd just said hit him hard. "You're...*staying* here?"

"I've decided to, yes. You're still moving out, aren'tcha?" She looked worried.

"If it weren't for this horse, I'd already be long gone."

"Then leave."

"Just like that?"

"Just like that."

"Sam, it won't take more than ten minutes to reposition this leg—"

"I told you to put it back. Just wrap it up."

"But I can fix it."

"I already told you I don't *want* you to."

"You actually think I'd *do* something to it?"

"It doesn't matter. I don't want to owe you for fixing it."

"I'd never charge you for anything and you know it."

A pause. Her eyes glared. "I'm not talking about *that* kind of charge."

Then it dawned on him. She wanted absolutely nothing from him and certainly didn't want to think fondly of him for doing something nice for her.

He couldn't remember anyone hating him this much.

"I'll just leave, then, and—"

"And take your hammer with you."

He brought it up and stared coldly at it. "Thanks. If you hadn't said anything, I probably would have just forgotten all about it."

She sighed and crossed her arms. "Just leave, all right?"

"I'm leaving."

"You sure don't look like it. From here, it looks like you're just standing there."

He found it difficult to stare at the same beautiful blue eyes that had captivated him so much not very long ago at all. Back then, they were filled with love. And caring. And desire.

But right now, all he saw was hate, disgust, and hurt. Lots and lots of hurt. It made his heart ache.

"Well? You're still standing there."

"I'm leaving, dammit. Just give me a minute and—"

"Please leave. I've got things to do. Don't forget your precious hammer. And make sure you put my horse back where you found it." She spun around and started walking back to the house.

That was when he decided he'd had enough. He gazed at the back of her head and struggled to force the forbidden thoughts away. Then he swung his arm and tossed the hammer. It sailed upward toward the two-story building, slamming down onto the Spanish tile roof and sliding halfway down, until it caught on a brace.

She cringed at the sound of the crash and spun back around. "What was *that* for?"

"I don't want that damned precious hammer anymore."

"What are you talking about?"

"Bad memories, as they say. Next time I pick it up, this wonderful conversation will jump right back at me."

Her eyes blazed and she trembled. "You're *such* an ass!"

"And you're just finding that out now? You lived with me for how many months, now?"

"However long it was, it was *too* long!"

"I'm glad we *finally* agree on *some*thing!" He went over to the two small boxes of odds and ends he'd just packed, picked them up, and carried them back to his car.

***

"That was *so* sad…" Laura reached out and touched Bill's cheek.

He drained his drink. "I thought it was, too, especially when I thought of what we might've had." He forced himself not to dwell on what had happened. "It started out so *great*…" He felt the cold darkness coming right back.

"But it eventually brought you to me," Laura said in a soft voice.

He didn't want to tell her that the love he'd once shared with Sam had been much greater than he'd ever had with anyone else, and had no doubt been the main reason why every other relationship he had had simply failed. Laura obviously knew how important Sam had been to him. He didn't want to remind her of that—especially now that she knew what had happened.

84

Laura had been very good to him. He didn't want her to think Sam would have been better. He also didn't want Laura to know how close he'd come to murdering Sam with the hammer he'd been holding in his hand during that last confrontation.

Sam had said horrible things to him. Things that had really hurt him.

What she'd said made him feel guilty, and since he'd already chastised himself for quite possibly being a major factor in her father's death, he didn't need help from anyone else.

Since she'd already insulted him, he found that his grip on the handle of the hammer had drastically changed. He was no longer holding it tightly but was now hanging onto it in a death grip. His hand began throbbing, and soon he discovered that he needed to let it go. And when she told him to put the horse back, he found that he was watching the back of her head and wondering what it would look like if he just walked up to her and pounded her with the hammer.

The sudden urge frightened him, telling him something about himself he didn't know.

"What are you thinking?" Laura asked nervously.

He didn't want to share his thoughts with her, so he just shrugged.

"I know you're agonizing about all this," she said. "Well, I'm telling you that I'm right here. I always will be, and I'm listening."

He reached for her hand and squeezed it.

***

The next morning, after Bill came out of the shower, toweled off, and put on shorts and a tee shirt, his cell buzzed quietly.

Sensing the call was important, he picked up the cell from his nightstand and turned on the display.

It was a message from Chuck from the Paradise Bar & Grill.

It said:

"Saw blonde. Name Miranda.
Works @ Peterson & Croft, 3d floor."

His pulse raced the moment he read the message.

Miranda. The blonde's name was Miranda. The young blonde strongly resembling Sam was working just three floors down from him, at Peterson & Croft.

The smell of fresh coffee and fried bacon drifting into the bedroom told him Laura was fixing breakfast.

He spun on his heel, rushed back into the bathroom, and closed the door. He pressed *Callback* and waited.

After two rings, he heard Chuck's voice.

"Mr. Nathan?"

"I just got your message." He kept his voice low.

"Yeah. I saw her late last night—"

"Why didn't you call?"

"Well, it was at two a.m. I didn't think you'd appreciate a call right then."

"You're right. So...she was there last night, then?"

"For about an hour."

"With the same people?"

"She was with two guys, and they were both young. I'd say around twenty-five or so."

"How were they dressed?"

"The guys? Or all of them?"

"I'd just like to know if they looked professional."

"They were all dressed for a night on the town. She had on this really hot sleeveless top, with little silver chains keeping the damn thing from pullin' open and showin' off her ta ta's. She also wore a pair of super tight Capri's and four-inch spikes. That babe looked hot!"

"And you say she works at Peterson and Croft?"

"I took a casual stroll and walked right past their table. One of the guys with her asked where she worked, and she told 'em she did errands and correspondence for a law firm on the third floor. Peterson's the only law firm on the third floor, so..."

"Good job. By the way, did you notice a wedding ring or band?"

"On her?"

"Chuck, why the hell would I care if two guys I don't even know are married?"

"Ya got me there. Well, I saw a pinkie on her right hand, and some sort of gem on the second finger of her left. Aquarius, I think it was. That's about all I got."

"That's a lot. Thanks, Chuck."

"Thank *you*. A Benjamin for two minutes of legwork is one healthy chunk of change—"

"And some brain work."

"Maybe, but—"

A knock on the door.

"Bill? You okay?"

"Gotta go." He pocketed the cell, flushed the toilet, then pulled open the door. "Hey, babe! Breakfast ready?"

She stood there in her denim shorts and red tank top, looking confused. "Why the closed door? You never close the door."

He shrugged. "Guess the a/c was a little much for me this morning."

"It's on seventy-two, just like every other morning."

"Can't help it. I got a chill. A shower tends to do that to you."

She frowned. "I sure hope you're not coming down with anything. You don't have a fever, do you?" She gently pressed the back of her hand to his forehead.

"I'm okay, Mom. The shower really hit the spot." He kissed her on the forehead. "Breakfast ready?"

"C'mon. The eggs are about to get cold."

"Great. I'm famished." He wrapped his arm around her waist and led her out of the room.

***

Later, Bill decided to do a little sniffing around the Peterson & Croft firm.

Knowing he'd be facing potential problems, he figured it would be necessary to come up with an alibi Laura would most likely believe. Because of his strange behavior the other night, her guard was already up, and she would most likely question whatever he told her. In this case, it was essential to make sure that whatever he came up with would keep her suspicions in check.

Once again, he questioned his motives for doing this. As with the other times, he came up empty. All he could gather was the fact that someone who was the spitting image of Samantha was walking around, and he knew he wouldn't be able to enjoy any sort of peace of mind until he found out more about her.

At around one-thirty, not long after they'd eaten lunch and cleaned up the kitchen, he went into the living room, where Laura had put on one of her TV shows on Hulu. He stood in the doorway, watching her as she put the remote on the table in front of the couch and settled into a comfortable position. She looked fabulous in her shorts and tank top. He'd noticed how great she looked during lunch, but he was so distracted by Chuck's message that he couldn't keep his mind focused on anything else.

So now, as he carefully thought up his alibi, he cursed himself once again for going through this charade, which, he was certain, would lead to total disaster.

"I've got to take in the BMW."

She turned in her chair. "It's Sunday."

"Stan and the guys usually work a short day just to catch up. They open at one and close the doors at four."

She shrugged a shoulder. "What's it doing?"

"That's just it. I don't know."

"Then how do you know something's wrong?"

"It was making a strange little whispering sound just before I killed the engine last night, when we got home."

She thought that over. "I didn't hear any strange sound…"

"But I did. This tells me that it could possibly be on my side."

"It's probably nothing."

"I need to know for sure."

She nodded. "Call me if it's something to worry about. I'll get in my car and pick you up."

Relieved, he went over, bent down, and kissed her on the lips. She reached up and wrapped her arm around his neck. "Don't be long," she whispered. "I mean that."

"Hold that thought." He kissed her again, then straightened. He gently stroked her hair and called himself an idiot yet again for doing this. "I'll do a repeat performance as soon as I get back."

"Then don't be too long, all right?"

"Gotcha."

Chapter 9

The parking lot of Stan's Auto Service on East Colonial was almost deserted. Only Stan's classic '68 Shelby and a late-model Cadillac SUV were parked in front of the two-story brick building.

Bill parked the BMW next to the SUV and went inside, where Lou, the part-owner, sat in the corner behind the counter, going over some figures on his laptop. He glanced at Bill over his reading glasses and gave him a quick wave. "Here to see Stan, Mr. Nathan?"

"Is he in?"

Lou pointed to the glass window, which showed the work area. Stan was walking away from a classic silver Aston Martin DB6, which had been put up on the rack. He spotted Bill through the glass and waved.

"This should only take a few minutes," he told Lou.

Lou nodded and went back to his laptop.

Stan Rizzo, a crackerjack mechanic, was the senior owner of the place and had been working on Bill's cars for the last ten years. Stan was tall, burly, and fully bearded. He was about fifty and walked with a slight limp caused by a fistful of shrapnel he'd picked up in Iraq. He came right over and stuck his head through the open doorway. "Long time no see, Mr. Bill."

"You're right. It's been, what? Close to five thousand miles?"

"Your babe need some special attention? You know we're not really open today, right? Just catchin' up on a few things."

"I just came over to talk to you. Got a minute?"

"Sure. Wanna talk here?" He glanced at Lou. "Or do we need to—"

"It'll only take a minute."

Stan looked down at his hands, which were covered in grease. "Looks like I oughta wash these boys again. Follow me."

Bill followed the big guy into the restroom down the hall.

The room was empty. There were only two stalls and two urinals. Stan went over to the sink. He focused on Bill's reflection in the mirror. "What's up?"

"I told my girl I was coming here to check out a strange whistling noise coming from the engine."

Stan thought that over and shrugged. "Is there one?"

"No."

"All righty…"

"She probably won't call, but if she does…"

"Gotcha."

"You're sure?"

He grabbed some paper towels from the dispenser on the wall. "You were here and just left."

"What'll you say if she asks what was wrong?"

Stan wiped his hands and dropped the towels into the trashcan. "A loose hose coupling always seems to work. No need for details, either."

"I owe ya."

"Just take care of that baby. You're almost due for an oil change, ya know."

"I'll be in touch."

***

The Paradise Bar & Grill was handling its Sunday lunch buffet activity as Bill went inside.

He took a seat at the bar, ordered a vodka and tonic, and took in the activity.

Tourists and middle-aged locals flocked the buffet. No one resembling the blonde was anywhere within eyeshot.

The tall, skinny barman brought over his drink. Bill slipped the guy a bill and took his drink over to a table in front of the window. The early afternoon Central Florida sun had already shoved its brutal intensity against the heavily tinted window, but the room remained comfortably dark and cool. Bill took a sip of his drink, pulled his cell from his shirt pocket, and logged into one of the available search engines, targeting Peterson & Croft.

What he found was standard stuff:

Peterson & Croft, Disability Attorneys
608 East Robinson Street
Centre Building, Suite 315
Established 2012, by Randall F. Peterson, Attorney-at-Law
Office Hours: 8:30-5 Mon-Thurs
8:30-4 Fri
Legal Team
Randall F. Peterson, CEO
Sandra J. Elwood-Croft, President
Larry Sandoval, Notary Public

R.J. Fennell, Claims Adjustor
Thomas Radcliffe, Attorney
Brittany Foxworth, Attorney
Miranda Resnick, Office Assistant

His pulse racing again, he found his gaze settled on that last name.

Miranda Resnick.

He put her name into another search and came up with four Miranda Resnick's, but none of them seemed to be the correct age. Another search found several others, all living in different states.

He tried Yellow Pages and two other sites but came up with the same information. He figured the Miranda Resnick he was looking for had just recently joined the work force. After all, she appeared much too young to have acquired much of a job history. If she was a college grad, her position with Peterson & Croft could easily be her first or second job.

His next logical step was to visit Peterson & Croft personally. He'd need some legitimate story to explain his visit, of course, but he'd been a broker for several years, dealt with people all the time, and knew how to stretch things.

Since the company would be closed, he decided to finish his drink and look around for a little while before heading back to the condo. It wouldn't be long before Laura would call, and he didn't want to get Stan involved in this. Laura was still suspicious and might want more details from Stan than they'd planned. If something didn't sound right, she'd know something was going on, and Bill wouldn't know anything unless Stan called him before he got back to the condo.

He finished his drink, got up, then walked out of the comfortable, air-conditioned bar. He didn't have the chance to take more than three steps when he saw the young blonde standing on the other side of the street, in front of a boutique.

She was staring at him.

***

Once again, he felt his heart hammering.

The girl was less than a hundred feet away, staring directly in his direction.

Without thinking, he began crossing the street. A horn blared, and he turned just in time to see a large black SUV heading his way.

Idiot! Get the hell out of the way!

He sidestepped an instant before the SUV reached him. It swerved out of the way and was almost sideswiped by a passing cab. Both vehicles honked angrily, and he felt like an idiot while he hastily found sanctuary between two parked cars.

For the next few minutes, he leaned against one of the vehicles, shaking while waiting for his sputtering heart to return to normal. His thoughts raced, and he cursed himself for nearly getting killed.

He'd stepped out into traffic. He couldn't believe how stupid he had just been.

You're a grown man. You're intelligent, educated, and independent. Why in heaven's name would you even think of doing the stupid, brainless stunt you just—

95

He stopped the sudden avalanche of angry thoughts. And spun around.

The blonde was gone.

***

Bill spent the next hour looking for her.

He checked the boutique first, asking about her the instant he pushed open the glass door. He was told by two of the women working there that no one fitting his description had recently left the shop.

Although he knew that checking each building in the block would be impossible as well as ridiculous and time consuming, he crossed the street, keeping alert for anyone looking even remotely like her. The wandering crowds revealed several young blondes, but he couldn't get close enough to any of them without attracting suspicion.

He soon realized that his only option was to stand at a street corner and carefully watch everyone passing, but he knew he couldn't do that for very long without getting arrested.

There were too many crazies in the world nowadays. Strange behavior had somehow become the norm over the last couple of decades. Not wanting to bring attention to himself, he decided that his best option was to convince himself that the girl he'd just seen was an illusion—and *not* the girl he'd seen at the Paradise.

Frustrated and angry, he went down the block where the BMW was parked.

His cell buzzed.

It was Laura.

"You okay? And where are you? Still at the shop?"

The shop. It took him several moments to remember what she was talking about. Then it dawned on him. The garage. Stan. The bogus story of the strange whispering noise in the BMW. The rest of the story tagged right along behind it. The lunch buffet at the Paradise. Looking for the blonde. Miranda Resnick. Peterson & Croft. Not seeing her, then spotting her across the street. Then acting like a complete idiot and crossing the street to confront her—*without* looking both ways to check out the traffic. And nearly ending up in the morgue.

"Bill?"

"Yeah. I'm here. I just left the garage. I'm getting into the car now."

"How'd everything go? Is it fixed now?"

"Yep, everything's back to good working order."

"Why'd it take so long?"

"Whaddya mean? I've only been an hour or so…"

He heard her groan. "It's way past four, Bill. You've been gone nearly three hours!"

He nearly gasped. His watch said 4:22. *Damn…* He had no idea.

What the hell is happening to me?

He immediately tried recalling his steps. First, he stopped off to see Stan. Then the Paradise. Then…

He'd left the Paradise. Saw the girl. Started crossing the street and nearly killed himself. Then he'd apparently lost all sense of time looking for her.

Idiot.

97

"Bill? You still there?"

"I'm sorry, babe. I guess the time got away from me."

A pause. "Are you coming straight home?"

"Huh? Yep. Definitely. I'll be there in just a few."

"Okay, then. I won't meet you anywhere for supper, then?"

"Want me to bring something home?"

"We've got more than enough stuff here. Don't you remember? We just went shopping the other day…"

"Yeah, you're right. I guess I forgot."

"C'mon home, babe. I'll have a drink ready for you."

Damn, Nathan. You've got a gorgeous prize waiting for you back at the condo, but you're here in town, looking for an illusion that nearly got you killed.

"You're too good to me, you know."

"I know."

"You could have been a little more humble about that, by the way."

"I don't *feel* humble."

"How *do* you feel?"

"Lonely."

"I'll be back there in twenty minutes."

"However long it takes, I'll be here waiting for you, okay?"

"Yes, ma'am."

He pocketed the cell and struggled to concentrate on driving back to the condo. *I can't let this get a grip on me*, he kept telling himself as he focused on the highway straight ahead, and not the small crowds walking along the sidewalk.

Even so, he couldn't help going into instant alert each time he caught a glimpse of shoulder-length blond hair flouncing onto the backs of young women walking briskly down the street.

***

True to her word, Laura had his Martini ready the moment he walked through the front door.

He took her in his arms and kissed her passionately. As he held her, he felt like an idiot for what he'd done earlier. He'd lied to her once again so he could drive to town to get a glimpse of another woman. He'd nearly gotten himself killed in the process, then lied to her when she called to ask where he was.

He told himself his near-death experience should be a definite wakeup call. He needed to snap back to reality and forget about the blonde, once and for all. Sam was dead. Even if she wasn't, there was nothing that could be gained by another encounter. Their relationship had run its course. The two of them had gone their separate ways and nothing at all could be done to turn that around. And even if it were possible, why would he *want* to?

Laura moaned when the kiss ended, then picked up the glass from the counter and handed him the drink. "If you do that again, I can't promise dinner will be on time."

"Are you trying to tell me that if I give you another kiss, dinner will be late?"

"You got it, baby."

"A *little* late? Or a *lot*?"

She was watching his mouth when she said, "That depends."

"On what?"

"On how good your next kiss might be."

"We'd better hold off, then. I'm feeling pretty damned excited right now."

"Then I guess we'll both have to wait. That roast cost you a small fortune."

After dinner, they relaxed together on the couch and sipped their Martinis. He tried very hard to remind himself how lucky he was… However, each time his thoughts seemed like they'd settled into a safe, comfortable sphere, Sam's image came right back, upsetting the works.

After about an hour, Laura finished her drink and began rubbing his chest, as she often did when she wanted to have sex. "Are you watching this?" she asked softly.

He knew what she was referring to but decided to be playful anyway. Laura had been incredibly understanding—especially during the last few days. He could not have expected anyone else to have reacted in a more sympathetic fashion. He wanted to kick himself for letting something like this happen in the first place.

She deserves better. And she's gonna get it.

"Watching what?" he asked in response to her question.

She smiled, then shifted on the cushion and began kissing his neck.

It took them less than a minute to make it to the bedroom.

100

Chapter 10

Monday morning came, and the work week began as usual.

At around 11:00, after dealing with a conference call and two difficult exchanges with high-profile clients, Bill decided to leave the office for a few minutes and buy a scone for Laura. She loved scones and hadn't had one in a while. He wanted to do some thoughtful things for her in gratitude for her putting up with his strange behavior during the last few days.

Since her work area was set up directly outside his office, he waited until she'd gone to the restroom before leaving and getting on the elevator.

As he rode the car down to the lobby, he thought of other ways he could express his gratitude. A terrific candlelight dinner would certainly do the trick. He decided to arrange for something special for Friday evening.

The main thing he needed to do, of course, was to forget about the blonde. There was no way he and Laura could move forward with their own lives unless this obstacle was removed. He knew how difficult it was going to be, but since he could not think of any other option, he had to seriously consider it. It wasn't doing him any good, for one thing. But what made it even worse was that it was taking a toll on his relationship with Laura.

And even if he did manage to meet this mysterious blonde, what would it accomplish? The girl was obviously not Sam, so what could he even say to her? What would she do if he told her that she strongly resembled a young woman from his past? Why would she even care? She didn't know him—why would she concern herself with a stranger's troubled past?

He had to consider the possibility that she might think he was some sort of nut job. Even if she didn't, what would happen then? Would she think he was trying to hit on her?

The way he saw it, nothing positive could come of this. That chapter of his life had ended more than two decades ago. Why reopen it?

He was crossing the large, heavily tinted lobby area when one of the other elevator doors rolled open. Just as he was about to reach the heavy glass door that led to the street, he heard the sharp clicks of high heels on the tile behind him and turned.

And froze.

The blonde had come out of the elevator and was walking briskly in his direction.

As she drew closer, he realized in horror that he'd been right all along.

It was Sam. She was alive, and even though he knew that this was not possible, his own eyes were telling him otherwise.

He began trembling. The back of his neck grew uncomfortably cold and his limbs quickly turned numb.

Even though his inner voice kept telling him this was not happening, Sam kept coming.

His thoughts raced. A moment later, they began spinning.

His face grew warm, then hot.

Sam's image blurred.

The room suddenly dimmed.

A heavy wave of lightheadedness made everything shift, then turn sideways.

He had the sensation of falling.

Blackness settled in.

***

Bill opened his eyes.

He was lying on the couch in one of the conference rooms at the brokerage. Laura was sitting beside him, watching him closely.

His forehead felt cold. He reached up. A damp washcloth was covering his flesh.

The moment he moved, Laura's eyes grew. "Are you okay?"

"I *think* so…" He took a deep breath and tried to sit up. He quickly found that he couldn't. "I guess not…so much…"

"Don't get up." She put her hand on his chest. "Just stay there. Relax. Lie still."

"What happened?"

"We don't know."

"How'd I get *here*? I remember getting in the elevator, then—"

"The receptionist came in about half an hour ago, said Steve called from the lobby and said you'd fainted near the front entrance. So we hurried down here and there you were, lying on your side, mumbling."

"Who…found me?"

"Someone from Peterson & Croft, apparently. Luckily, whoever found you was in the process of

103

calling for an ambulance when Steve came in from lunch, revived you, then helped you into the elevator and brought you up here."

"What about the ambulance?"

"Steve told them it was all right, he'd get you back upstairs and make sure you'd lie down."

"He say who it was?"

"Who what was?"

"The person who found me."

"He said some young woman."

His heart sputtered. "From Peterson & Croft?"

Laura groaned. "What's going on, Bill?"

"Whaddya mean?"

"You fainted."

He shrugged and adjusted the washcloth. He was trying to remember what happened. Then it came to him.

The blonde had just come out of the elevator and was headed straight toward him. The blonde. Sam. Alive again and walking over to him.

"This isn't like you." Laura looked confused.

"I guess I was just hungry. I haven't eaten since—"

"You're a very healthy forty-one, Bill." Laura's long-lashed, brown eyes were enormous. "You've been extremely active all your life and have the body of a man ten years younger. Perfect blood pressure and a healthy heart. People in your condition just don't faint." She looked him right in the eye. "Talk to me, baby."

He just sighed. He wanted to melt into the couch cushions.

"A sigh won't help. Tell me what's going on. Why'd you faint?"

Tell her, his inner voice ordered.

I can't, he replied to the voice.

You don't have much of a choice. There's no other way.

Telling her isn't gonna help anyone.

You got yourself into it, so don't whine.

"Bill?"

"I saw her again."

Laura didn't reply. She sat very still, her eyes locked onto his. Her expression was a mixture of fear and anger.

I really got myself into this. Despite my good intentions, I'm fucked, and I deserve whatever she decides to do.

But now that he realized how much trouble he was in, he decided to use whatever get-out-of-jail-free card he could find. This time, he tried the most dependable—which would be the truth.

"I was on my way to the bakery down the street to get you those scones you like so much…"

"And?"

"I got off the elevator and crossed the lobby. The other elevator door opened, and she got off. I saw her coming toward me. Then I guess I fainted."

"And that was it?"

"The whole story."

She glared but said nothing.

"The truth, Laurie. That's what happened. I turned, saw what looked like a dead woman coming at me, and then everything went sideways."

Laura still didn't reply.

"You don't believe me."

"I do." She got up. "I really do."

"Honestly?"

"Yes."

"Then why do you look like you want to kill me?"

She didn't respond right off. She continued her glare, then sighed tiredly and said, "Because right now, I'm really tempted to." Then she turned and marched out of the room.

***

"I'm leaving, Bill."

Laura blurted it out just a few minutes after she and Bill got into the BMW after work that evening.

Bill had expected her to reach some sort of decision since his fainting event. It was obvious that she'd been preoccupied ever since.

As the day wore on, she spoke to him only for business purposes, concentrating on her job and even avoiding looking in his direction unless she needed to communicate with him. To make matters worse, she begged off going out to lunch with him, preferring to eat alone at her desk.

He knew she was concerned about him and didn't doubt for a moment that she was enraged over the business involving the mysterious blonde. He just didn't realize that her anger had been so severe that she would want to end their relationship so quickly.

"Laurie, I really and truly value our relationship—"

"So do I." She stared at the windshield. "Which is why I have to leave."

106

"I...don't think I understand."

"Hopefully, this won't be permanent."

Relieved, he relaxed in his seat.

"You've got to fix whatever this strange thing is before we can continue with the next level of our relationship. I just don't think you can do it while we're living together. Does that make any sense at all?"

She was right. There was no way he could find a way out of this without further damaging what they had together, and he wanted to curse at himself for not thinking of it himself.

"You're right. It makes perfect sense. I've got to fix this, but I can't do it without hurting us further in the process."

"And you've got to do it alone. I'm tired of being in the crosshairs."

"That's one way of looking at it."

"What other way *is* there?"

"There isn't."

He turned left onto Semoran Boulevard and they continued north in silence.

After about a mile, Laura said in a soft voice, "I really love you, Bill. I don't want to lose you. I hope you can believe me."

"I love you, too."

She turned in her seat. She was silent for a few moments before she spoke again. "Do you? Do you really?"

"You're the best thing that's ever happened to me."

"What about that girl? The blonde. Samantha. You thought she was the one, too."

107

He shook his head and cursed himself again, this time for letting that spill out.

"You told me you did. Was that a lie?"

"I was awfully young when I met her. I was a stupid kid."

"You loved her and you know it."

"It was a different kind of love."

"What kind was it?"

"You're young, so you should know. The young, reckless, uninhibited kind. Total, unbridled, wild, all-for-nothing sex and thinking it was love. Lots and lots of kissing, teasing, groping, pawing, gasping, wrestling, crawling around in back seats of cars... That kind of thing."

Laura shook her head.

"What's wrong?"

"It's a shame that kind of stuff is wasted on the young."

"You're twenty-four."

"And...?"

"You're young."

"So?"

"I'm not."

"To repeat myself...so?"

"It's different with us, isn't it?"

She suddenly looked sad. "I know. We don't exactly have that kind of thing going on with us, do we?"

Laura was right. He hadn't thought of that, and it made him feel even worse. She was a beautiful, healthy young woman, and after so many years of failures, he felt like he'd come to the end of the road. And it wasn't fair. Not to a quality babe like Laura.

"I'm sorry, Laurie. I haven't…well, I haven't exactly given you my best."

"I understand."

"That's just it. You shouldn't be so damned understanding."

"I can't help it. A girl doesn't usually find that really special guy, and if she's lucky enough, she does whatever's necessary to keep him."

"That goes both ways, you know…"

"Does it?"

"Yes. And I plan to prove it to you."

She turned away to stare at the windshield. He could tell she was thinking this over.

"How?" she finally asked.

"First of all, I plan to fix this thing with the blonde."

"Then?"

"I intend to fix whatever needs fixing with us."

"What needs fixing?"

He smiled. "I guess what I'm trying to say is that I'm gonna go back to being young, stupid, and reckless—as I once was when I was twenty."

"Can you honestly *do* that?"

"Why can't I?"

"You're…well, you're over forty, Bill."

"What did you say not too long after I woke up on the couch back at the office?"

"I said a lot of—"

"Using your own words, you said I have the body of a man ten years younger. Remember?"

"Bill, I don't expect you to risk a heart attack just so you can prove you can—"

"Don't sell me short, now. I just might surprise you."

"What we have is perfect, Bill...."

"But—"

"Perfect."

"Don't you wish I were younger than—"

"Never."

"Not even occasionally?"

"No."

"You never once wondered what it would be like if—"

"*No.*"

The way she'd said it made him realize that she meant every word she'd said. It also made him feel even guiltier than before.

"I'm gonna fix this, babe. Remember that."

She just smiled.

"I really am."

No response.

"Believe me. I will."

"I believe you."

110

Chapter 11

Laura moved out that same Saturday afternoon.

While packing, she'd assured Bill that she was serious about her move being temporary. As proof, she'd packed only two suitcases, her luggage bag and overnight bag, leaving the rest of her things in the condo.

He was silent as he carried her luggage out to her Nissan and placed them in the trunk.

Although he was relieved for her decision to give him space, he cursed himself for causing all this and promised himself that he would resolve it as quickly as possible. He was totally committed to Laura and didn't want her to leave. But he knew it was necessary—at least for now.

He watched her as she pulled her key chain out of her bag and selected the ignition key. He stared at her hair and the outfit she was wearing—shorts, V-necked sleeveless tee shirt, and athletic shoes—and wanted to kick himself once again for causing this rift between them. He wanted to take her in his arms and kiss her, then bring her back inside and have sex with her for the rest of the day.

But he knew that would have to wait. He had to find out what was happening to him. He had no idea where this journey would take him. He only knew that he didn't want anything to change between them. He just didn't know what was going to happen once he managed to figure things out.

"I really don't want to do this, you know." Laura was looking down at her keys as she spoke. Her hair hung forward, hiding her face and making her look like a little lost child. He wanted so much to take her in his arms. It was all he could do to keep from doing so.

"I don't want you doing this, either."

She looked up and gazed at him, and he could see the desperation and the fear in her moist eyes. He wanted to tell her that he wouldn't rest until she came back to him.

She sighed brokenly. "Promise me this won't take very long."

"I promise."

She watched him and he could tell she was trying to read his expression. "Do you really mean it?"

"You know I do."

"Do I?"

"You know how I feel about you, don't you?"

A nod.

"This is killing me, Laurie. I don't want to watch you drive away. I want to take you in my arms and—"

Her hand came up, and her sweet vanilla scent drifted into his nostrils. Her fingers gently pressed against his lips. They were cold. "*Please* don't. I can't think of that…right now."

Once again he wanted to strangle himself for hurting her.

She lowered her arm, but her vanilla scent still lingered deliciously close. "I want you to call me and tell me to come back, and I want you to do it soon."

"I will."

Her big brown eyes stayed on him. "I mean it, now..."

"So do I."

She sighed and ran a hand through her hair. "I probably won't sleep very well."

"Neither will I."

She looked at him and he could see the anger in her eyes.

"I'll make up for it, babe. I promise."

"You've got a lot of promises to keep, you know."

"I intend to keep them."

"*All* of them?"

"Every last one of the little suckers."

She turned to open the door. Before she got in, she stopped moving and looked like she was gazing at the front seat. "Please. Don't watch me leave."

"Can I kiss you?"

She froze and didn't speak for long, tense moments. Then she shook her head. "I would love that...but no. Not now."

"I get it."

"When I come back, okay?"

"Definitely."

"Another promise?"

"That one will be automatic."

She turned and he caught the beginnings of a smile. Then she got in behind the wheel.

He went back up the walk that led to the front entrance.

The Nissan fired up, and a rush of helplessness rocked through him. Then frustration, followed by confusion and self-hatred.

I can't let her go like this! I need her!

He wanted to turn around and look at her one more time. He wanted to rush over to the car and tell her to stop, to get back out. To come back to him. To rejoin his life. To—

You can't. You need to fix this first. Otherwise, your relationship will remain broken.

He forced himself not to turn around.

The sound of the Nissan growing softer as she drove away brought about a sense of regret he had never experienced before.

***

He spent the next two hours sitting in the kitchen, staring at the skillet Laura had placed in the drainer after their breakfast.

He kept waiting to hear the door open. To hear her footsteps, then watch her come in and stand there, looking at him with tears running down her cheeks while saying very softly, "I couldn't stay away."

He could see himself getting up to greet her, stopping just a foot or so from her, and saying, "I never wanted you to go in the first place."

"I had to," she'd reply. "I felt like I'd been intruding."

"How could you possibly feel like you were intruding when there are only two of us?"

"To me, it feels like there are three."

You're an idiot. He reminded himself yet again how stupid he was, letting the best girl he had ever known walk out the door. He knew she'd be back, but all he could think about was walking into the bedroom later that night and sleeping alone in a bed he had shared with her for the last six months. Then waking up the next morning, going through the motions of fixing breakfast, then eating all alone while staring at the empty chair where she should be sitting, smiling at him as she ate.

Then doing the same thing all over again. And again.

And again.

For how long?

He told her he'd fix this soon. And she told him that she wanted him to keep his promises.

How soon would it be?

"I want you to call me and tell me to come back, and I want you to do it soon."

He had no idea how soon it would be. All he knew was that he had to get a handle on this, and he had to do it as quickly as possible. The longer it took, the less chance he had of preserving his relationship with Laura. He knew she loved him, but he also knew that might not be enough to keep them together. She was a beautiful young woman, and beautiful young women, as he'd observed over the years, were not known for their infinite patience. The fact that she was a babe made the situation even more tense. Guys had been hitting on her ever since high school. He knew damned well that the situation wasn't likely to stop just because she'd encountered a bump in her present relationship.

I have to get this done as quickly as possible. Then I need to get Laura back and try to make things how they once were.

But could he? Was it possible?

Or was this obstacle of his much too great to destroy completely?

He had to try. He knew of no other way.

Once again, he saw her image standing in the kitchen doorway, watching him.

He suddenly realized that he couldn't fix anything by sitting here, feeling sorry for himself. He had to go on out there and start using his brain. And that meant leaving the condo and doing what he'd started doing before.

He needed to find the young blonde.

But this time, he had to bite the bullet and follow through.

Instead of fainting the next time he saw her, he had to face the situation like a man.

This meant talking to her.

***

By 8:00, the Paradise Bar & Grill was packed with the Saturday evening crowd.

Bill chose a stool at the bar and ordered a vodka and tonic. The bargirl went to fix it when Chuck came out of the kitchen carrying a mop and bucket. After spotting Bill, he hurried right over.

"'Sup?" He set the bucket on the floor beside him and leaned the mop handle against the counter. "Find that babe you were lookin' for?"

"Not exactly." He didn't want to tell the boy about his fainting episode. It wasn't the type of subject a guy brought up. Guys just didn't mention

116

their shortcomings to other guys. "I did find out that you were right about where she works, though."

"Peterson and Croft, right?" He shrugged. "Then you saw her?"

Bill decided to fudge the facts a little. "A coworker spotted her coming out of the elevator."

"How'd he know it was her?"

"This guy, well, he's kind of a dog, and he told me about this young blond babe he saw. I asked what she looked like, and from what he told me, it sounded just like her."

"Really?" Chuck looked doubtful.

"It's all I have to go on for now."

"Well, I can pin it down for you, if you wanna be sure it's her."

"Whaddya mean?"

"Buddy of mine, he says he might know a little about her."

Bill sat up. "Really?"

"Says she's seein' this guy, works at a place on the Trail. The Lantern—know about it?"

"Not really. Too many places on the Trail to keep track of."

"I've been there once or twice. It's about two miles south of Sand Lake. Anyway, my buddy says this guy's a musician, plays in the house band. Keyboard. They gig there on the weekends. They'll prob'ly be there tonight."

"What's this place like?"

Chuck frowned. "Typical for that area. They score a lot of blow there. White collar guys go there just for the blow. Cops like to keep close, so make sure you're clean if you go there. But if you wanna

117

scope her out, that's a place you might wanna look into."

"Thanks. I just might."

"Like I said, be careful. Don't wanna see ya get hauled in."

"I'll be fine. And thanks again."

***

The Lantern, a one-story block building painted white, sat less than two miles south of Sand Lake Road, on South Orange Blossom Trail.

The packed gravel lot boasted a busy night. Two rows of twelve vehicles filled the lot in the front. Several others, most of them pickups, formed a jagged line near the side of the building.

Bill parked the BMW at the far end of the second row. He sat behind the wheel for the next few minutes, staring at the building while telling himself that he needed to turn right around and drive back to the condo. Being here made no sense. So what if the blonde was inside? What would it accomplish for him to go in there and then spend the rest of the night getting shitfaced because he was too frightened to walk over and talk to the girl?

Because you have to!

This was something he had to do. His future with Laura depended on it. So did his peace of mind. How could he justify wimping out on this and then spending the rest of his life cursing himself for not finding out anything about the blonde?

He couldn't because he knew he wouldn't be able to look himself in the mirror if he didn't.

With a deep sigh, he pushed open the door and forced himself out onto the gravel. His nerves were jumpy as he pushed the door shut, but he took a few deep breaths and told himself once again that he could do this. He realized just how stupid this was, but it had to be done.

He had to know that this girl wasn't Sam, and that Sam was just as dead now as she was when he found out about it years ago. He also had to find out why he went into serious meltdown whenever this mysterious young woman appeared in his crosshairs.

He continued trembling as he approached the building, but he forced his feet to continue moving in the direction of the front door. He tried to resist reaching for the doorknob but was soon spared of that minor inconvenience. A big, tattooed guy in a leather vest, baggy jeans, and cowboys boots stumbled outside and held the door open for him.

***

Inside, the place rocked.

The four-piece band was playing a classic selection from The Eagles, and half a dozen couples moving around awkwardly on the dance floor in front of the stage looked like they'd obviously had too much to drink. Three good ol' boys sat at the bar, arguing with the bartender about whether Willie Mays had been a better long-ball hitter than Mickey Mantle.

Bill sat down at a table about twenty feet from the bar and waited for the waitress to come over.

"What's your pleasure, baby?"

She was wide-hipped, around five-eight, large-breasted, and on the wrong side of forty. Her hair was a sandy blond, tied at the crown with a bright red ribbon, and her face, though still attractive for her age, was covered with too much mascara and lipstick. Her heavy black lashes overshadowed her large gray eyes, and her smile strongly suggested that she liked to flirt.

"I'd like a vodka tonic."

She nodded. "Haven't seen ya in here before, baby."

"There's a good reason for that."

"Lemme guess... This is your first time?"

"You're good."

She laughed again. "You sound like two of my exes."

"They weren't too bright if they're exes, were they?"

"Not even a little." Then she turned and went back to the bar.

The band had stopped playing. The musicians got up from their chairs and went over to the table on the far right, nearest the stage. There were four of them, and they looked fairly young, except for the gray-haired, overweight drummer, who could have been pushing fifty. The keyboard guy was about six feet tall and skinny, with medium length black hair and a full beard. He also wore sunglasses. He sat down at the table, laughed at something the guitarist said, then lit a cigarette.

Something occurred to Bill just then.

It was the keyboard guy. The one Chuck said was the blonde's boyfriend.

The man strongly resembled Bill.

My God. What the hell is happening here? First, I come across a girl who resembles Sam.

120

Then I find out that this girl is hooked up with a guy who looks just like me?

Was this weird or what?

Or something he just didn't want to—

"Here's your drink."

Her voice nearly knocked him out of his chair.

"You all right, baby?" She looked concerned.

"Sure. Why?"

"Ya look like you just saw a ghost."

"I'm okay." He grabbed the glass and downed half of it. Strong. Just what he needed. He sighed, put the glass down, and sat back. He looked up at her and smiled. "It hit the spot, thanks."

She watched him a few moments. He guessed she was waiting for him to do something else that might worry her. "Just yell when ya want a refill."

"You'll be the first to know."

She studied him a few more moments before returning to the bar.

He rubbed his eyes and told himself he'd be just fine. He had no idea why he was here or what he planned to do. He just wanted to observe and see what was going on. He hadn't been prepared for what he'd just seen only moments ago.

Your imagination, he told himself. Trembling, he turned back to the musicians' table.

And sighed in relief.

The keyboard guy was watching the bar. Bill realized right then that the kid resembled him only from the side—not the front.

He turned around in his seat, picked up his drink, had another sip, then put the glass down and turned back to the band members.

And gasped.

The blonde was sitting beside the keyboard guy.

She was looking directly at Bill.

Chapter 12

The room darkened, then blurred.

A loud thumping sound filled his ears.

He struggled to bring reality back, to convince himself he hadn't gone insane. *Close your eyes. Let your nerves relax.*

After taking a few deep breaths, he could feel his blood pressure gradually settling down.

Good deal. Now take another deep breath and try your best to assess the situation. You must analyze it and make sense of it. Only then can you even begin to look at it logically.

The first thing he needed to figure out was how the hell the girl had done that. How could anyone just *appear* like that? One moment, the four musicians were sitting there, smoking, chatting away, and laughing. Acting stupid and crazy. Acting like human beings.

Then…?

The blonde was sitting there beside the keyboard man, staring directly at Bill.

She had just *appeared*. One moment, there were just the four of them. Then there were five. The four guys and the girl.

A girl with supernatural powers, most likely.

Was she real? Or some supernatural being that had taken over Sam's spirit as well as her physical features, and had come back to torment him until—

He was being silly again. She couldn't possibly be a supernatural being. The most logical explanation was that she had probably walked over to the table when he was busy with the waitress. His back was turned; he hadn't even been facing the stage. The restrooms were just ten feet or so away from the stage—a good ten-second jaunt from the room to the chair she was sitting on. It wouldn't take a rocket scientist to figure that out.

Or maybe she came out of the room when he was rubbing his eyes.

That was possible, wasn't it? Ten or twenty seconds to rub his eyes, then another thirty or so for his vision to return. Plenty of time for someone to come out of the restroom, walk over to the table, and sit down.

Get a grip, Nathan. Nothing supernatural about her. She's flesh and blood—just like you.

He reached for his glass with a shaky hand and managed to finish his drink without spilling it in his lap.

He had planned to have only one drink, but after what had just happened, he decided that one more certainly wouldn't hurt. He turned toward the bar to signal the waitress, but she was already heading in his direction with another drink in her hand.

"You're a lifesaver," he said.

"You looked like you needed another one, pretty quick."

"You're also a mind reader."

She shook her head. "Just someone who can see the signs. Comes in handy when you're peddlin' drinks." She went back to the bar.

Sighing tiredly, he sipped the drink just as the band returned to the stage and started another number, this one from Foreigner.

He turned back to the table.

The blonde had come over. She stopped when she reached his table and looked down at him.

"Aren't you the guy who fainted in the Centre Building when I got out of the elevator?"

He found that he couldn't speak. All he could do was stare at the girl's face.

Sam's face. He was looking at Sam's face. Sam was dead, but she was standing right there. Just a few feet away. And she was definitely real.

This was *way* the hell beyond weird.

"You okay?" She was watching him as he steadied his half-empty glass.

He knew he had to pull his hands away from it. He just didn't think he could manage well enough right now to do it without making an embarrassing mess.

"I'm…fine." It took him three tries to get his voice working. The loud volume of the band wasn't helping.

Neither was his brain. He just couldn't accept the fact that he was talking to Sam. He had to force himself to believe that this *wasn't* Sam, but someone who looked like her.

Looked like her? Hell! his inner voice told him. *This girl even* sounded *like Sam!*

"You have a heart condition or something?" Concern showed clearly in her big blue eyes.

125

He took a deep breath and tried to regain whatever control he had of himself. *Take it easy, now. Baby steps…* "No. Why?"

She shrugged a shoulder. "You fainted."

"I was having…a bad day, I guess…"

She raised a brow—just as Sam would have done. "You guess?"

He couldn't stop thinking how similar this girl's voice was to Sam's. Even her facial expressions were similar. This was getting spookier by the second.

"You're having a bad day, wouldn't you know about it?"

"You'd think so, wouldn't you?"

She laughed. "You're funny."

"I've been told that before."

"Well, hope you feel better." She started moving away, then stopped. "You don't faint a *lot*, do ya?"

He reddened. "That was my first time."

She nodded but said nothing.

"I always like to try new things."

She laughed again, this time louder. "You really *are* funny." She gave him a little wave as she moved away.

Something about that wave…

Panic set in. He couldn't have her walking away. Not yet, anyway. He needed to find out things. And find out about her. And talk to her. And look at her.

Because looking at her was just like having Sam back all over again.

"You work at Peterson & Croft, right?"

She stopped and came back. "How'd you know?"

Idiot. Now you've gone and done it.

"Just a wild guess." His thoughts turned chaotic, digging up details he could use to appear less suspicious. "I think I might've seen you with someone who works on the third floor."

"Really? Who?"

He could tell he was sweating. He just hoped he didn't *look* like he was. Thank God the room was dark.

His thoughts continued racing as he went back to the other night, when he first saw her at the Paradise.

"Some guy I bumped into. A short while ago. I...I never really met him, just shared the elevator with him once or twice. Big guy? Maybe three hundred pounds?"

She smiled. "Jim Fields. Yeah, he's pretty important. He and Joanna Croft went to college together. He handles tons of accounts."

"Does he work for you?"

She laughed. "I wish! I just do errands and correspondence. I get to do research occasionally when they need an extra hand. I also answer the phone. You take it easy, okay?"

She hurried over to the bar.

While Miranda chatted it up with the waitress and the barman, Bill struggled to think of some way of continuing the conversation.

As his thoughts continued spinning wildly, he couldn't get over what was happening to him. At first he thought it was his reacting to the similarities

127

between Miranda and Sam. However, when other details came at him, he began thinking that something else was happening that he hadn't counted on.

The way she stood, for one thing. Keeping her hands together in front of her—which was something Sam used to do—especially when she was talking to him or wanted to ask him something. The way she jerked her head occasionally to flick some of her hair away from her cheek.

How about that little flicker of a wave she gave him while moving away?

He was being silly again. Many women did those things. Amy, one of his many ex-girlfriends, did similar things with her hands when she was talking to someone. The hair flicking gesture was very popular with women—especially when they were flirting or feeling playful. And, like it or not, he had to admit that he had known many women who waved the same way.

Why was he overdoing this?

Was he deliberately looking for things that would convince him that Sam had not died at all?

You're hoping she's come back. You know she hasn't, but part of you wishes she has, and you're not quite sure why you're hoping you're right about this. You're also not sure how you'll react if you find out that she really is Sam.

But she can't possibly be Sam! If she was, wouldn't she have aged just a little during the last twenty-plus years? How many women have you ever seen who look twenty when they're in their forties?

And, more important, wouldn't she tell you who she was? Or where she's been? Or what she's been doing all these years?

Why would she continue such a cruel charade? Would she still be pissed about her father? Or maybe she actually did want you to fix the damned rocking horse? Or maybe—

He had to get over this.

He'd just talked to this girl. She was very nice, very easy to talk to. And she had helped him. Now it was time to move on.

He was a grown man. He'd been around the block several times—shouldn't he know by now when it was time to call it a day?

He was turning an innocent encounter into something weird, and if he didn't nip it in the bud right now, there would be hell to pay.

But he had no idea what he should do.

Forget about her? Drive home? Call Laura and tell her to come back?

It seemed the simplest solution, but he just couldn't do it right now.

He had to find a simple solution before he could even think of asking Laura to come back.

A simple solution. Why did it seem impossible that he could even begin to find one?

Was it the girl? The situation? The Sam thing?

What was it about this girl that had him so damned obsessed that he couldn't do a simple thing like—

"You didn't go to the hospital, did ya?"

Her voice jarred him out of his thoughts.

129

She was standing just a couple of feet away, holding a mixed drink in her left hand. "When you fainted. There was this guy coming in off the street. He rushed right over and checked you out. I asked if he was a doctor. He said he'd been a medic in Iraq and that he'd take care of you. Well? Did he?" She laughed. "Well, duh... You're here, aren'tcha? And you're okay, so I guess he wasn't lying, was he?"

"That was Steve Waterson. Yeah, he works with me, and I believe he was deployed in Iraq. He checked me out as best as he could. He didn't see anything wrong, so…"

She nodded. "That's good. I'm really glad you're okay. You looked awfully pale when I went over to you."

"I guess I did look pretty bad, didn't I?"

"Well, ya look fine now, so…" She turned.

"I'm Bill. Bill Nathan." He cursed himself the moment he'd blurted it out.

She turned back around and smiled. "Miranda Resnick. Hi."

He found himself staring helplessly again.

"Something wrong?" She reached up and pushed some hair away from her cheek.

"I'm sorry, but…there's something…very…familiar…about you." He could feel his heart racing as he forced out each word.

"Whaddya mean?"

His heart raced and his palms had become sweaty. He struggled to keep his mouth shut but knew he couldn't. Not now, anyway. It was too late for that. He'd already ventured into forbidden waters. "You...look like someone...someone I once knew."

She nodded and was silent for a moment. Then she smiled. "I get that a lot. Everyone tells me I look like my mother."

A chill raced up his spine.

"Your...m-mother?"

"She's dead. She died before I was one, so I never really got to know her."

He fought hard to ignore the shaking in his limbs.

"Her name was Samantha Lewes. Did you really know her? Or just someone who looked like her?"

He couldn't reply. His blood had suddenly turned ice-cold.

Chapter 13

"Bill? You okay?"

The room had turned hazy.

"My mother. I look like my mother. She's dead. I never really got to know her. Her name was Samantha Lewes. Did you really know her?"

"Bill?"

The voice. Her voice. Sam's voice.

Did you really know me, Bill? Did you?

The room had grown hot. The song the band was playing had become softer, dimmer. Soon it had turned into a hushed silence, as did the room, the clinking of glasses, and the chattering of voices at the bar.

This same thing had happened before. Not very long ago, either. At the Paradise.

The face of the young woman staring at him grew hazy…and for a moment he thought Sam had come back from the grave…

"Bill, why didn't things work out for us? If only Daddy hadn't seen us. If only you and he had gotten together and put your differences behind you. If only you hadn't upset him so much that he couldn't handle his driving the next day, when—"

"Bill?" A gentle hand touched his forearm, and he suddenly felt as if he'd just been poked with a cattle prod.

Everything exploded in light and sound—the room, the glass clinking sounds, the chattering, the face in front of him…

The face moved closer.

Sam?

No, it couldn't be. It was—

Her daughter...what was her name...is this really happening?

"Bill, it's me. Miranda." A gentle nudge. Her face drew even closer, and he could smell vanilla in her hair and a slight hint of alcohol on her breath. "You're not gonna go zombie on me again, are ya?" Another nudge.

Wake up, you idiot! Get out of this before some idiot decides to be a good Samaritan by calling 911.

C'mon, dammit! Wake up!

"Bill, do I need to call someone?" Another nudge.

Fight this! Fight this right now!

He opened his eyes and shook himself. And surveyed the scene.

She was watching him closely, her right hand resting on his left forearm. Worry showed prevalently in her bright blue eyes.

Those eyes... Sam's eyes...

The waitress had already come over, looking very worried and frightened.

Say something, dammit! Get yourself out of this!

But what can I possibly say that will—

Bluff, you idiot!

"Damn..." He reached up and rubbed his temples. "These long days have really caught up to me." He squinted at Miranda. "Did I zone out again?"

She was still watching him closely. For a moment he didn't think she believed him. Then she nodded. "When was the last time you had any sleep?"

He rubbed his eyes and forced out a short laugh. "What day is this?"

She shook her head. "You really need to go home and get some sleep. If you stay here any longer, you could fall asleep driving on your way home and kill yourself, ya know."

"I know. And you're right." He sighed and got up. "I think I'd better call it a night." Two of the band members had come over and were standing a few feet behind her, watching him. The keyboard guy looked puzzled. Up close, Bill was pleased to discover that he'd been right in his assessment. The boy didn't really resemble him much at all.

"You don't live that far away, do ya, babe?" the waitress asked.

"Maybe fifteen minutes."

The waitress nodded and went back to the bar.

"You're *sure* you'll be okay?" Miranda sounded concerned.

He gave her a reassuring smile. "I'll be fine, thanks."

Just as he turned and began walking away, he heard her say something. He turned around. "What was that?"

"You never told me if you knew my mother."

His nerves began tingling again.

Fight this!

"A long time ago." It took him some effort, but the words finally came out.

134

Miranda's eyes lit up. She looked like she wanted to say something.

Before he could give her the chance, he waved, turned toward the front door, and hurried out of the place.

***

He spent the next half hour sitting in the BMW in the parking lot, staring at the block building.

After a while, he closed his eyes, and strange shadows from his past appeared, causing the building to vanish.

Sam in her waitress uniform, smiling at him. Joking with him. Smiling. Pouting. Flirting.

"You have any other moles I should know about?" she'd asked that same weekend, after he'd picked her up at the eatery and taken her to the closest motel.

"I've got three or four more," was his reply.

"Where are they?" She'd stopped inspecting the one on the side of his neck and kissed his cheek.

Bill just smiled.

"Are you gonna tell me? Or do I have to go on a treasure hunt?"

"Knock yourself out, baby."

Blackness.

Then…Miranda's voice:

"I look like my mother. She's dead. I never really got to know her. Her name was Samantha Lewes. Did you really know her?"

Yes. I really knew her. I knew her very well. For six wonderful months, I lived with her, shared my bed with her, loved her, dreamed of her, and made her every wish my own. She was the first girl I

135

ever truly loved. And since then, I've never been able to love any other girl nearly as much.

Did you really know her? his inner voice asked.

She was my soulmate. My spirit. My life.

It wasn't just a physical thing?

I would have died for that girl, and it tore my heart to pieces when we broke up. It took years for the pieces to come back together, but they never seemed to fit as well as they had when I was with Sam.

Why was this?

Sam had made off with too many important pieces. Pieces that I feared I would never get back.

Life was never the same. *He* was never the same. His destruction had been too much. Sam had taken away his very spirit when they parted, and he was never able to fully mend since.

Twenty-one years sounded like a long time while you were facing it, but not so long at all once it had passed and you were looking back at it in retrospect.

Twenty-one years had passed since he and Sam had parted ways, but as he sat there, staring at the building and seeing only his dark past creeping toward him, he knew that even though he and Sam hadn't been together very long, hardly a day had passed without a small portion of his memories bringing back that last afternoon, when he'd walked away from her forever.

Much had happened since that fateful afternoon, and he decided that even though Sam hadn't lived very long after that day, she'd continued living her life just as he had. She'd mothered a child—which meant she had met someone else. Sam was beautiful; guys immediately turned into zombies whenever they saw her. It couldn't have been very long at all before someone else had fallen for her gorgeous smile, her beautiful, sparkling blue eyes, her bright personality. She might have died just a year or so after he'd left her, but it had obviously been enough time for her to give birth. She was not quite twenty when he'd last seen her, but—

His thoughts stopped when something in his brain began gnawing at him.

What was it?

The time element? The circumstances?

The sudden appearance of Miranda and what she'd told him?

"She's dead. She died before I was one, so I never really got to know her."

Before I was one...

Miranda was what? Twenty? Twenty-one?

When did he and Sam have that argument?

He vigorously rubbed his temples as the dates flew wildly in his head.

It didn't take long at all for the terror to begin smothering him.

He and Sam had parted sometime in July, twenty-one years ago. If Sam died when Miranda was one, that would mean Miranda had been born—

Oh my God...

He sat bolt upright in his seat. His hands closed into tight fists. His heart felt like it was about to thrash out of his chest.

137

No. This *couldn't* be. This could not *possibly* be!

But the strange voice inside him told him it could very well be true.

Miranda might actually be his own daughter.

***

Despite the storm raging inside him, he made it home without incident.

He spent the evening on the living room couch, drink in hand as he gazed numbly at the white drapes covering the front window. As he stared, he couldn't help seeing a hazy image of Samantha's face.

"What the hell happened to us, Sam?" he whispered to the blurred image. "We were so much in love…and then we weren't."

He poured more vodka from the bottle. Then he sat back and sighed heavily. "Everything was so perfect. We were obsessed with each other, couldn't get enough of one another. You could turn me on with a look, and all I had to do to turn you on was touch you. Anywhere. Your cheek. Your mouth. Your hand. A simple kiss on the neck, or a gentle stroking of your hair, and we were ripping each other's clothes off." He shook his head. "Sometimes I feared for my life. You were so turned on, so wild, that I thought you were gonna kill me."

Daddy…

The whisper was barely audible, but more than enough to bring it all back.

The Colonel had seen them. Her father had driven over to bring Sam some mail that had been delivered to the old address. Since their parking

138

arrangement had been limited, her father parked the pickup along the curb in front of the duplex and walked down the drive to enter the building through the rear door, which led into the kitchen. He'd reached Bill's car and, hearing moaning sounds coming from the open windows, moved closer.

And saw them.

Daddy saw us, Bill!

He saw something no *father should* ever *see his little princess doing!*

That was the end.

"It was so...so *wrong*," he told himself as he raised his glass. He placed it gently in his lap, sat back, and stared at the dark ceiling. "It should've never happened," he told the ceiling. "He should've never been there. He should've called, should've let us know he was coming. He shouldn't have gotten so close to the car!"

You shouldn't have been doing it in the car, the soft whisper came back. He didn't know if it was what he thought Sam would say or his own conscience telling him how badly he'd messed up.

"I know," he whispered back, and finished the drink.

He debated with himself if he should finish the bottle. He decided that it was much too far away to bother with. He was comfortable sitting here like this, his head back, his eyes focused on the ceiling.

Besides, he'd had enough. Tomorrow was a workday; there was no reason for him to not go in. The best thing for him to do right now was sit here and listen to whatever Sam chose to whisper to him.

But he heard nothing else and decided she had nothing to say.

This was all right. He no longer wanted to talk, either. It would be fine and dandy to just sit here and stare at the ceiling. His eyelids had been getting heavy. He decided to close them and imagine he was looking at the ceiling anyway.

The couch started swaying, telling him that he'd had too much to drink. That was all right, though, because he wasn't in the mood to finish the bottle. He'd just sit here like this and rest.

Just as a comforting wave of warmth swept through him, he heard himself whisper, "It should have never happened."

The warmth disappeared and was immediately replaced by another whisper, this one sounding just like Sam, who said, "But it did, Bill…it did happen, and now it's too late for anything good to come of *any* of this…"

Chapter 14

The next morning, Bill opened his eyes and had the strange feeling he was dead.

As his senses gradually floated back, he decided that he only *thought* he was dead, and the moment he tried sitting up, he decided that he *wished* he was.

A glance at the half-empty vodka bottle on the end table told him the full story, and he immediately cursed himself for being so stupid. He hadn't drank that much in a long time. The last time he'd done something that idiotic was in college, when he was nineteen, full of himself, and was challenged in one of those stupid macho games young guys delighted in playing amongst themselves. Idiotic, all right. And very dangerous.

And if it had done so much damage to him twenty-plus years earlier, why would he insist on a repeat performance? What in heaven's name would possess him to do it now?

There had to be a good reason for it, right?

Sam.

The answer couldn't have been simpler.

However, what had happened in the last twenty-four hours made that simple answer infinitely more complicated.

Miranda.

Just hours ago, he had come across a young woman who could possibly be his own daughter, and he had no idea what he should do or how he should react.

She needed to know.

Did she? Or was she better off, *not* knowing?

You don't even know. Not for sure, anyway.

For all he knew, Sam could have fallen for a guy just days after Bill had walked out on her. And if she had acted just as she had with Bill, this new guy would have wasted no time whatsoever getting into her drawers.

However, that was just a guess.

The girl's last name wasn't Lewes. It was Resnick. And unless Sam had married and divorced, there was no other reason he could think of that would get her to drop the Lewes.

But you don't know, do you?

That didn't matter. The element of doubt was in his favor, and he told himself that he could live with the possibility.

He had to, didn't he? He had his own life. Why make it more complicated? He'd been sharing his life with Laura for months and saw no reason to compromise the situation. Laura made him happy, and he was reasonably certain that she was happy as well. He wanted her back but knew that if he found out that Miranda was his daughter, Laura might not want to come back. Laura hated complications just as much as he did. Why would she choose to stay in a relationship that had just turned impossibly complex in the short span of a few days?

He had no idea how she'd react to this latest development, did he? No one knew how anyone would react to anything nowadays, and he just didn't want to take the chance with Laura.

"Miranda is *not* my daughter," he told himself. "Once I left, Sam found another guy, fell for him, and got pregnant. End of story."

He consulted his watch. 6:52. It was time to get ready for work. Despite remnants of his hangover, work would be the best thing in the world for him. It would take his mind off Sam, Miranda, and his messy past, and he could concentrate on things that would distract him with unpleasant matters that could easily send him running off to the nearest shrink. Besides, Laura would be there, and if she couldn't provide a pleasant distraction, nothing else in the world could, either.

After taking several deep breaths, he forced himself off the couch and plodded unsteadily down the hall, to the bathroom. He sincerely hoped that a heavy stream of warm, pulsating water would coax him back into the world of the living.

***

As lunchtime approached, Bill found that he was unable to concentrate on anything.

The uncertainty of having a daughter in his life troubled him, and he soon realized that he couldn't go on like this much longer. His mind wouldn't let go of the concept, and each time he struggled to concentrate on something work-related, Miranda's image drifted right back. It was driving him insane, and the only option he could think of was that he had to find out everything he could about Miranda.

But how could he do this without invading her life and asking her all sorts of questions that would freak her out?

He knew he could not possibly waltz into the Peterson & Croft offices, ask to see her, then take her aside and ask her personal questions that would upset her and possibly get her fired. He also knew that it wouldn't be very bright to approach her at the Lantern.

What were his choices?

While the last two Tylenol he'd taken gradually deadened the remnants of his hangover, he wandered around like a zombie, his coffee cup in hand while desperately trying to appear like he was actually working.

At around 12:45, he found that he had wandered into the lunchroom and was gazing at the coffeemakers and the microwaves sitting on the table and wondering when he'd come into the room. Or why he'd come into the room in the first place.

He realized that he was so damned distracted that he wouldn't have been surprised if he'd found himself standing out there in the middle of Robinson, waiting to be mowed down by passing traffic.

Get a grip, damn you!

Sighing deeply, he focused on keeping his brain functioning. He approached the table and began staring at the coffee brewing from the two coffeemakers sitting beside one another. Should he have a refill? He'd already downed at least ten cups, and there were still four hours to go until quitting time. At this rate, his nerves would be short-circuiting like crazy. However, the coffee seemed to help soften portions of his hangover, so he decided to have another cup. Judging by the other cups he'd had, it wouldn't be very palatable, but it would be strong, and would keep him going until four o'clock, when he went home to face another lonely night.

He went over to the table, put down his cup, and grabbed the pot. A moment later, he heard Laura's soft voice close behind him.

"You don't look so good, babe."

He filled up his cup and replaced the pot. He wanted to tell her that he felt like shit, that he wanted her to come back to him in the worst way, and if she did, he'd feel and look *much* better. But he'd set the ground rules. Now he had to abide by them.

He turned to face her.

And once again felt like the world's stupidest man.

Laura looked tired and very sad. Her hair and makeup were far from perfect, telling him that she'd been just as distracted as he was. Her outfit—light blue crepe blouse under her form-fitting black business suit—didn't seem quite as fetching as usual. His decision was taking its toll, and he knew that if she chose to end their relationship right now, he couldn't blame her one bit. Even so, he wanted to take her in his arms and hug her tightly.

You need to fix your problem first...

"Rough night," he said, sugaring his coffee. "You gonna be okay?"

145

Once I get you back, I will, he wanted to say. He had to settle for, "Eventually, I guess," and hoped that would suffice.

She moved closer to him and whispered, "I miss you, babe."

Once again he realized that he hated himself for his latest decision. Her smell, plus the delicious closeness of her, was making him dizzy. And when she added, "Especially last night," he realized right then that he had to close the deal on this present problem one way or the other.

"Me, too, Laurie."

She sent him a quick glare. "Fix this soon, now..."

"I will."

"You promised, remember?"

"Yes, baby. I remember."

"This is hard for me."

"Me, too."

She turned and walked out of the lunchroom.

He wanted to ask her where she was staying but knew better. He'd already agreed not to and promised himself to honor that agreement.

He left the room a minute later.

The moment he sat down at his desk, something finally clicked in his perplexed brain and he realized his next move.

He had to find Sam's sister Eileen.

That seemed the simple solution. If he wanted to find out what he needed to know about Miranda, he had to go right to the source.

He had to confront a woman who hated him.

***

That evening, he drove to a residential area in Casselberry.

Using the company's databanks, as well as a quick scan through an online people locator app, he had found the latest address listing for Eileen Garrison, who was also known as E. K. Lewes and E. K. Resnick.

The area was located just one mile east of Semoran Boulevard, not far north of Red Bug Lake Road and down a maze of subdivisions and condominium developments extending north of Wilshire Drive.

The Garrison residence, a spacious one-story brick ranch house, sat among professionally maintained flowers, palmettos, and well-cared-for plants spanning halfway down the block. The front yard appeared as perfect as any golf course. Two vehicles sat in the driveway in front of the two-car garage on the east end of the building. One was a black Audi, the other a maroon Cadillac SUV.

Bill parked along the curb and sat behind the wheel, his heart thumping erratically as he watched the house and thought about what he had to do.

Get out of the car. That would be the first step, wouldn't it?

Then you need to walk up the drive. Turn left and follow the walk to the front door. Stand in front of the door and ring the buzzer. When the door opens and you see her standing there, start talking and make sure you toss a few key details at her before she has the chance to slam the door in your face.

Simple, wouldn't you say?

He knew right off that *simple* wouldn't begin to cover any of this.

For one thing, he wasn't sure the woman was home. For another, if she was home and happened to be the one answering the door, he wasn't sure she'd recognize him. It had been more than twenty years, after all. A person's physical appearance changes drastically in twenty years. He was thirty pounds heavier, for one thing. His face was fuller, his hair much shorter and lighter, and he carried himself much differently than he did in the old days, when he weighed a hundred and thirty pounds as a skinny punk kid with long hair, some peach fuzz on his chin, and a pronounced Adam's apple. He wasn't quite sure if a woman he'd seen maybe half a dozen times more than twenty years ago would know who he was.

If she did recognize him, he didn't think she'd open the door. She'd hated him back then. What would be different, now that her father and Sam were dead? Wouldn't she still hate him? She'd always blamed him for their father's sudden death, so what would make him think that she'd choose to be civil with him after all these years? The rest of the family felt the same, so why would he assume that any one of them would treat him with any sort of decency?

It doesn't matter, his inner voice told him.

This has to be done.

Did it? Did it really?

Do you want Laura back with you? If you do, you know damned well what you have to do.

Yes. I just don't think I'm up to it.

Are you up to living without Laura?

And with this last thought filling his head, he forced himself out of the BMW, squared his shoulders, and marched down the walk.

149

Chapter 15

"What the hell are *you* doing here?"

Hands on hips, Eileen Garrison stood in the doorway, glaring at him.

Though still a good-looking woman at forty-five, she'd gained quite a few pounds, mostly in the breasts and around the middle, and was trying to hide it with an oversized gray sweatshirt—something she would never have worn when she was young and obsessively flirtatious with every man she ever met.

Back then, she resembled Sam in the mouth, nose, and jawline. However, the years had changed her features with cracks, creases, and a great deal of wattle beneath the chin. She always lacked Sam's fine features and elegant neck, and her eyes were not as alluring or inviting. She also lacked the warmth and the vitality that Sam had had in abundance. Eileen was a very cold, arrogant young woman of twenty-five when he'd entered Sam's life. He wasn't surprised at all to see that the coldness hadn't gone away—or even diminished—over the years.

He could sense that she was trying to convince herself that he was someone else. Denial was written all over her face. Bitterness and bad vibes emanated strongly from this woman. He did not want to be standing here at all and would have preferred engaging in something much less stressful, such as dodging bullets, or wrestling a hungry boa constrictor.

But he had no choice.

"Eileen, I have to talk to you about something." He had to struggle to get the words out. A lump in his throat had developed, making the simple act of speech complicated. He didn't know if it was due to abject fear of this woman or the simple fact that he had re-entered a phase of his life that he had been avoiding for the last two decades and knew that nothing but the same hatred and hurt emanating from it before was about to slam him again.

"I've got nothing to say to you." She'd said it softly, but the words—as well as her tone—were very similar to the low growl of a predatory beast just moments before it would leap onto its prey to rip it apart.

"I really didn't want to come here at all."

She shrugged. "You're here. You're standing out on my front porch, and I don't like it. I don't like it at all. In fact, I *hate* it."

He knew right then that he had to tell her why he was here before she slammed the door in his face. This sparring was getting him nowhere. He hoped that by getting to the point quickly, he could leave this horrible woman's world immediately so he could start breathing normally again.

"I met Miranda the other day."

The woman froze. Her right eye began twitching in the haze of the hall entrance lighting.

"Did you know about her?"

Silence. The woman's glare grew in intensity.

151

"I'm sure you're aware that I didn't know anything about her."

Still glaring, Eileen remained standing there in silence.

"I was hoping that you could tell me—"

"You leave that girl alone, you bastard..."

"All I want to know is—"

"You wanna know who her daddy is, don'tcha?"

He struggled to keep from losing his composure. His pulse hammered.

"Who do ya *think* the bastard is?"

His face grew warm. His nerves began to quiver.

"Go ahead, take a wild shot at it. Maybe you'll get lucky."

The inside of his mouth had turned dry. He had to clear his throat so he could talk. "A-Are you saying—"

"I'm not telling you *anything*, you bastard. You wanna know anything about that girl? Ask her yourself. Or ask someone else."

"But—"

"You heard me. If you wanted to make this easy for yourself, you've come to the wrong house." She reached for the door.

"Eileen, I didn't come here to cause trouble."

She pulled the door a few inches toward her. "You've already done it. My daddy's dead because of you." Her eyes filled the sockets. "My sister's dead because of you. Have any idea how much I'd like to see you lying in a box in the ground as well?"

152

Sam dead because of me?
What the hell did she mean by that?

"Well? *Do* ya?"

The woman began shaking.

He suddenly felt some anger building up within him. "I've got *some* idea..."

"Then you'll do the right thing by getting your disgusting carcass off my front porch. I'll need some time to hose it down and—"

"What did you mean...when you said Sam is dead...because of me?"

She kept a tight grip on the door. The hatred oozing from her made him tremble. "You really are stupid, aren'tcha?"

"Eileen, *please* tell me—"

The door slammed shut. The porchlight went dark.

Inside, he heard her voice yell, "Rot in hell, you bastard!"

He glared at the door another minute or so. His limbs were shaking as he turned around and walked unsteadily back to the BMW.

***

"My sister's dead because of you..."

The phrase haunted him constantly as he drove back to the condo in the heavy Semoran evening traffic.

What the hell did Eileen mean by that?

How could she possibly blame him for anything when he'd walked out of her life more than a year before her death?

Was Eileen's statement simply the result of twenty years of persistent, unresolved rage? The

153

resentment she'd felt for his leaving her sister so soon after their father had died?

Eileen knew exactly what was going on. Although she and Sam had their differences, they were sisters, after all, and confided in each other. Sam might have told Eileen much of what had happened between her and Bill. Eileen had obviously concluded that Bill couldn't cope with her sister's grief over losing their father. Since Eileen had always considered him selfish and self-centered, she expected him to have bowed out of the relationship in favor of less stressful circumstances.

Was this the case? Was it simply a matter of her being spiteful?

Or was there something else she was talking about?

He could never forget the day he was been told by his mother that Sam had died.

Despite his hectic schedule at the bank, Bill called his folks once or twice a month and visited them at their home in Winter Park whenever he could. He didn't do it as often as he'd wanted to because he and his father hadn't gotten along since Sam's father had told them what he'd caught his son doing with Sam. Since Bill's parents were strict Catholics and did not approve of reckless behavior, his dad quite naturally soured when hearing the news. His mom, though slightly more flexible, chose to remain the devoted wife and sided with her husband. It was not surprising that tension burst out in full force whenever Bill paid his folks a visit.

The day his life changed forever was the same day he'd gotten his second promotion at the bank. It had only been a few weeks after his move to a different floor of the bank and more than a year since he'd broken up with Sam. He was setting up his account portfolio in his new cubicle when the phone rang. It was his mother, whom he hadn't heard from for more than a month.

"Did you hear the sad news?"

"About what, Mom?"

"About Samantha, honey."

"What about her?" he asked uneasily.

"She's dead," she'd told him softly. "She died three days ago."

The news caught him unawares, and he gasped. It took him a little while before he could get his voice working. "Are you serious? Sam's *dead*?" That last word got caught in his throat and came out painfully, like a splinter of glass.

"I just read it in the *Sentinel*, honey. Apparently there was some sort of accident, and she died before they were able to get her to the hospital."

"Did they say what happened?"

"Something about a freak accident. They said she was at home when it happened."

He slumped forward in his seat. He was suddenly warm and had to unbutton the top three buttons of his shirt. He felt faint and took a few quick breaths. "Damn. That's…that's really…really *awful. Damn!*"

"I'm sorry, honey. I knew you loved her."

"I would've married her if…if—"

"I know, baby. It just wasn't meant to be, I guess."

"I guess not. This really sucks."

"She was so young, too."

"She'd just turned twenty-one. She was less than two years younger than me. Her birthday was just a couple of weeks ago. I wanted to send her a card, but I didn't think I should, and…"

"That really makes it tough."

A freak accident.

And she was at home when it happened.

"My sister's dead because of you."

Because of me…

Eileen's own personal revenge. She had always been a cold-hearted, arrogant bitch.

But he knew he had to find out what she was talking about.

I have to do this. I really need to find out.

And I need to find out about Miranda, too.

He had to face the frightening fact that it would drive him to the brink of insanity if he didn't find out exactly what happened.

Chapter 16

The next day, Bill took the day off to have a face-to-face with Eileen Garrison.

Eileen worked as an executive manager in the Valet Services Office at the Royal Palazzo Hotel in Disney Village. Bill had learned of Eileen's employment situation through a series of phone calls to several clients he handled at the brokerage. One of them, Kay Atkinson, acted as an insurance agent for the limo service at two of the Village's hotels and recognized the name from her employee contact list. The whole process had taken less than an hour, and by 11:00, Bill was pulling the BMW up the long, winding drive leading to the front entrance of the Royal Palazzo.

After parking in one of the few available spots in the guest parking lot facing the huge, twelve-story building complex, he got out of the BMW. For the next few minutes, he faced the many rows of tinted windows while trying to convince himself that what he was about to do had to be done.

Something very bad had happened twenty years ago. All he knew was that it involved a young woman he'd once loved, a middle-aged woman he'd never cared for, and a young girl who could very well be his own daughter. Like it or not, it was something he owned and, according to Eileen, something he had caused. The bad part of all this was that he had to deal with the woman face to face.

157

He had to somehow endure her wrath and then decide if what she told him was the truth.

Nothing else mattered. He had to know what happened after he'd walked out on Sam.

His legs felt like they were made of solid concrete as he squared his shoulders and began crossing the road.

Valet Services operated at the far end of the huge, cathedral-domed foyer. The area was abuzz with groups of wandering tourists, screaming kids, and harried workers, but he eventually found his way to the window, where a skinny young brunette wearing the hotel uniform leaned against the counter, watching him curiously as he approached.

"Help you?"

"I need to see your boss."

She huffed and shrugged a shoulder. "Which one? I've got three, sometimes four. This week? I think it may even be five."

"Eileen Garrison."

She frowned. Her bright chestnut eyes clouded over.

"She's here, isn't she?"

The girl jabbed her thumb behind her. "She's at her desk. Who should I say—"

"Just tell her an old friend wants to see her."

She turned around and disappeared behind the doorway.

About a minute later, Eileen, dressed in her uniform, appeared, took one look at him, and froze. Her eyes filled the sockets. Her chins quivered. Her body trembled.

"Hello, Eileen." Bill suddenly felt less tense. He knew right then that he had made the right decision in coming here. She couldn't possibly treat him as she'd done at her home—not without consequences. "Got a minute?"

"I'm *busy!*" That last word came out softly, but venomously.

"Too busy to take off a few minutes to talk to a friend?"

"*Friend?*" Her eyes bulged. "You call yourself—" She looked around and lowered her voice. "Get *out* of here, you bastard."

He returned her gaze with a sudden glare. "I'll get out. Right after you tell me a couple of things."

"I told you to get—"

"What did you mean when you said Sam was dead because of me?"

"I thought it was self-explanatory." Her painted brows mashed together as her glare intensified. "Even an idiot like you," she added softly, "should be able to figure *that* one out."

The brunette appeared. Eileen turned around. She must have sent out quite a convincing glare. The girl stopped cold, backed up, glanced at him, then disappeared again.

Eileen turned back to him.

Bill held his ground. "Well, it seems like even idiots like myself need a tad more of an explanation, because—"

"Why don't you just find a hole in the ground and—"

"I would love to," he replied quickly, "but then I'd have to wait for someone cold and vile, such as

159

yourself, to waddle on over and dig one just for me."

A tense silence.

A skinny young guy in a chauffeur's uniform appeared and reached for a key on the peg from the wall on Eileen's left. He snatched it up, spun around, and hurried away.

"I'm not leaving until I get an answer from you," Bill said. "And not just any answer, either. I want the truth this time. The truth—get it? You've heard of it, right? It's like a lie, only just the opposite."

She kept glaring but didn't reply.

"I mean it, now," he added softly.

The brunette came back, checked out the situation, then hurried away again.

He crossed his arms over his chest. "I can stand here all day if I have to."

Her eyes began twitching.

"Five minutes of your time. Then I'll be out of your life again, this time for good."

Silence.

"I wouldn't be here at all if I hadn't bumped into Miranda the other day."

She groaned. "I'll meet you out front," she whispered harshly. "Give me five minutes."

"If you're not out there in five minutes, I'll come right back, and we'll have to continue this one way or—"

"Five minutes, dammit!"

He gazed coldly at her. Then he consulted his watch, gave her one last glare, turned, and crossed the foyer.

As Bill watched the water of the lavish fountain cascading down the stone wall, he experienced a refreshing inner warmth.

The man-made fountain had somehow calmed him. Nothing else made sense. The drive to the hotel had been stressful. So had the walk across the foyer to the Valet Services desk. Lastly, the exchange with Eileen—not to mention the brief sparring at her front door the previous evening—had been among the most stressful encounters he had faced in the last few years.

He confronted tough, arrogant, bull-headed investors every day of his life. He talked to people who had just lost hundreds of thousands of dollars and, undoubtedly influenced by his communication skills and positive attitude, had been able to convince them to invest even more of their hard-earned money. He was able to keep clients even after many of their investments had gone bust.

But none of them had ever been one-tenth as irascible or as impossible to connect with as Eileen Garrison.

The times Eileen, dressed in tight shorts and halter top, had come over to visit would never entirely fade from his memory. Images of her turning, twisting, and bending over at crucial moments when she thought he might be watching, leaped to the front of his consciousness. He could never forget the times she'd asked for his help carrying heavy objects, then turning cold and resentful when nothing physical resulted from them.

Eileen was not the type of woman a guy could trust. He had no idea—nor did he care—what had happened in her life once he'd left Sam. All he cared about was what had happened to Sam and why Eileen had said what she'd said.

Would she tell him the truth?

He had no idea. He did, however, possess the rare gift of being able to sense when someone might be lying to him. This was something that helped him considerably in his career, and he hoped it would help him with Eileen.

Eileen finally came out of the building.

He glanced at his watch. Fifteen minutes since he'd left her. He'd expected her to make him wait, but at least she hadn't forced him to play out his hand by going back inside and seeking her out again.

She walked right over to him and stopped about five feet away. She held out her arms, scowled, and said, "Well, here I am. You happy now?"

"I can see that you're here. And no, I'm not happy."

A scowl. "Then I guess you'll have to get over it, won'tcha?"

"I'll work on that on my drive back home. Right now, I'm interested in a totally different subject."

She didn't reply. She just crossed her arms and stared at him. And looked bored.

"You know what I'm talking about, don't you?"

No response.

"Tell me what you meant."

"Just like I said before. My sister's dead because of you."

"I know what you said before. I just want to know why you said it."

"Because it's true. Anything else you wanna know?"

"Kinda. First of all, *why* is she dead because of me? I was gone more than a year before she died. Unless you're accusing me of coming back to do her in—"

"Oh, I know you didn't do *that*…"

"How do you know?"

"I had someone check."

He studied her expression and decided she was telling the truth. It didn't make him feel better. "Now who would *that* be?"

"Doesn't matter now."

The image going through his mind began making him nauseous. "Don't tell me you *hired* someone…"

"All right, then. I won't."

"You actually *hired* someone to find out if I was there when she had her accident?" He couldn't believe the hatred living inside this woman.

A smirk. "You told me not to tell you."

He shook his head. Now she was being insulting. "And of course you do everything I tell you—right?"

A deep sigh.

"Then since you know that I wasn't there, you also know I had nothing to do with her death, correct?"

163

Her glare grew deeper, darker. "You ripped our relationship apart, you bastard."

"Why? Because we fell for one another and decided to share our life together? And without your interference?"

Her chuckle sounded more like a cough. "I never could understand what my sister saw in you..."

"Sure you did. Otherwise, you wouldn't have done everything but pull down your panties and spread your legs every single time you came over to see her and I happened to be in the same room."

Her face glowed red and she trembled. "You bastard...I *never* liked you *at all*—"

"Your body seemed to have other things to say about that."

The trembling grew. "Why couldn't you just stay away and leave my family in peace?"

"Because a beautiful young girl looking very much like your sister, who I once loved very much, stumbled into my life the other day and I haven't been able to think about anything else."

Her brows mashed together; her eyes filled the sockets. "You need to stay the hell away from her!"

"Listen, Eileen...if she's my daughter, I'd really like to know."

"You'd better not have *any* intentions of—"

"I need to know if she's my daughter. And while you're standing there, I also need to know about Samantha."

"You know everything about my sister, and it's gonna stay that way."

164

"Eileen, I don't want to cause any trouble with you—"

"You've already done that. It's because of you that my father is dead and it's because of you that my sister is dead. If I could find *any* way of proving what you did—"

"What the hell did I do?"

"You know damned well what you did!"

"If I knew, why am I standing here, taking all this abuse from you?"

No response.

"How did she die? Tell me. *Please…*"

She didn't speak for the longest time. She continued trembling and glaring. A few moments later, she sighed heavily and said in a soft voice, "She was leaving the kitchen, getting ready to get in her car…"

"Okay…"

Tears gathered in her eyes. "She fell and hit her head."

"Fell?"

A nod.

"Where?"

"Outside. On the slab."

"She left the kitchen, went outside, and fell? Or tripped?"

"There were three steps—"

"I remember. The steps took you into the Florida room, then into the kitchen."

Another sigh.

"You're telling me she tripped on the steps?"

"She tripped, fell, and hit her head on the concrete. The guy living with her, Donnie, found her when he came home from work. He came home more than an hour after she'd fallen. She was lying there, out in the hot sun. He called nine-one-one, but it was too late. She had a brain bleed, and they couldn't do anything to bring her back."

"How is this my fault?"

"It couldn't have happened like that and you know it. And I know it as well!"

"Eileen, how is this my fault?"

"Sam was in terrific shape—"

"I know."

"She jogged, did Pilates—"

"I remember. She even lifted light weights when she couldn't do her morning jog around the block when it was raining."

"There was no way a girl as coordinated as Samantha could've fallen down those steps and hit her head like that."

It took him only a moment to realize what the woman was accusing him of. "You're trying to say *I* did that to her?"

No reply.

"I *loved* her, Eileen!"

"She told me you had a bad temper. You yelled, tossed things, slammed doors…"

"I *never* got physical with her!"

A groan.

"She *never* told you I *ever* got physical with her, did she?"

"I don't know how you did it, but—"

"I didn't *do* it, Eileen! Why can't you get that into your head? I loved Sam, dammit!"

"She *knew* those steps were there…"

166

"So did I. Accidents happen!"

She didn't reply. The tears continued running down her cheeks. She stood there another minute or so, scowling at him.

"Eileen, I didn't—"

"If I'd found *any* proof you'd been there that day…"

"I *wasn't there*, damn you!"

She continued trembling. "Go to hell. And leave me the hell alone. For good!" Then she turned and stomped back to the building.

Chapter 17

Bill spent the afternoon agonizing over what Eileen had told him about Samantha's fatal accident.

He sat near the kitchen window, sipping coffee while staring at Laura's garden, hoping that the sight of fresh flowers basking in the sunlight would calm him, cleanse his spirit, and make him feel less—

Less what? Guilty? Responsible?

What should he feel guilty about? Sam's accident? Her death? The fact that she'd died so senselessly?

Or should he feel responsible because he wasn't anywhere near Sam when it happened?

Could he ignore the nagging feeling that Sam wouldn't have died if he'd been with her? That he would have at least been there when she'd fallen and hit her head, and would have immediately driven her to the hospital in time to save her life?

Was he letting Eileen win by accepting her claim that it was his fault Sam had died? Did he actually agree with the bitch in her claim that Sam would still be alive if he hadn't walked out?

Or was he feeling guilty that the woman he had once loved so much was dead simply because he had walked out of her life and hadn't been with her when she'd needed him most?

"Sam was in terrific shape..."

He remembered how conscientious Sam had been. How proud she'd been of her condition. Of how she looked in her clothes. How upset she became whenever she'd discovered a gain of a single pound from an occasional binge. How she'd gone on a starvation diet and a strict program of vigorous exercise until she'd lost that cursed pound or two and regained her tremendously tight, slim figure.

He smiled at the memory of her morning jogging around the block. Her exercising in front of the widescreen on Saturday and Sunday afternoons in her leotards, scolding him immediately whenever he came over to give her a gentle pat on her toned butt...or planted a quick kiss on the back of her neck while she was doing pushups.

"She knew *those steps were there..."*

That was another thing that was so troubling.

Sam was coordinated. She rarely lost her footing, or balance. Whatever had happened to cause that fatal accident was something that seemed illogical, something that had been growing increasingly suspect...

He began wondering about the guy she was involved with when she died. A guy named Donnie. A guy who, according to Eileen, came home more than an hour after her accident.

A guy who, according to Eileen, wasn't with Sam when she'd fallen and hit her head.

But despite all this, Eileen didn't suspect Donnie—not at all.

She didn't suspect Donnie. She suspected Bill.

"If I'd found any *proof you'd been there that day..."*

But she didn't. She'd brought in someone to make sure he hadn't been.

"You actually hired *someone to find out if I was there when she had her accident?"*

It was Eileen's accusations that got his blood surging hotly through his veins. So hotly, in fact, that he finally realized what he had to do.

***

Half an hour later, he sat in the BMW across the street from the duplex in the Conway area he and Sam had once shared.

His nerves jumped around wildly as he stared at the familiar place. The ghosts came from out of nowhere, unnerving him, but he ignored the sensations as he pushed the door open, got out, and crossed the street.

It was about an hour before dinnertime, and it occurred to him that he could be intruding on whoever was living there. There were two cars parked in the drive beside the building but that didn't seem to matter. He needed to find out a few things, and from his viewpoint, much of his discovery hinged on his returning to the scene of the accident.

If, of course, it had been an accident.

He walked down the drive, until he came to the corner of the building. And froze.

He was staring at the pavement between the building and the garage. The area where Sam had fallen. Where she had hit her head. Where her brain had bled, causing her death. And where the man

170

living with her had found her much too late to take her to the hospital to save her life.

A wave of nausea swept through him. He wanted to get down on his knees so he could get a closer look. He saw no blood but didn't expect to. Twenty years tends to wash away most everything.

But it can't wash away memories. And as he gazed numbly at the area, he realized that time also managed to bring most of them back.

What happened, Sam? he wondered, focusing on the concrete. *Was it really an accident? Or did something else happen?*

The image of Sam in her jogging outfit blipped brightly. He could see her standing there in the kitchen doorway, stretching her arms and shoulders as she always did before a workout, smiling her bright, dazzling smile and asking him in her little girl's voice if he wanted to join her.

Not this time, he'd always told her, admiring her trim figure.

You always say that, she'd replied. *What's wrong? Don't you wanna look streamlined, like me?*

One streamliner in the family's enough for me.

You're silly.

And you're so damned sexy, you're lucky you're not in the bedroom right now, fighting me off.

What makes you think I'd even consider doing something as silly as fighting—

"Help ya?"

The husky voice behind him destroyed his thoughts.

171

The woman standing on the top step was about fifty, tall and very slender, and gaunt looking. She was smoking a cigarette while looking him up and down. Her thick dark brown hair could have been a cheap wig. Her neck, judging by the tightness beneath her square chin, looked like she had had a facelift. She was wearing skintight blue slacks and a loose fitting long sleeved yellow blouse with the first two buttons undone, showing off her freckled cleavage.

Bill felt uneasy, scolding himself for coming. The two vehicles parked in the drive meant someone would be home, so he knew he had to deal with this.

He decided to try to explain this as best as he could without alarming anyone. He didn't know this woman and realized how radical people could get if they felt threatened. "I'm sorry to bother you, but I used to live here."

"Really? When?"

"About twenty years ago."

She nodded and blew some smoke in his direction.

"I was just wondering if someone named Donnie still lives here."

She shook her head slowly. "Just me'n my boy toy, and his name's Jake. And my two Dobermans." She grinned at his startled reaction. "Don't worry, they're locked up."

"Good to know."

The woman blew more smoke his way. Her gaze slowly wandered downward. Bill began growing even more uneasy.

"Twenty years ago, eh?" She fluttered her lashes.

Bill nodded restlessly. Coming here hadn't been such a good decision after all.

"Jake and me, we moved in six, maybe seven months ago."

"Then I guess you wouldn't know anyone who lived here before you." He smiled and gave her a friendly wave. "Sorry I bothered you."

She seemed to be thinking things over. "When ya lived here, who'd ya pay rent to?"

"It was a realtor, but I can't exactly remember the people who managed it."

"Name Bradley sound familiar?"

"Not really. Is that who's handling this now?"

She nodded. "Got a place on Primrose, not far from here. Got a sign out front, says Bradley and Company, Limited. Tom's his first name."

"And that's who's been taking your money?"

She laughed. "And they do it real good, too."

"I'm sure they've had lots and lots of practice. Thanks for your help."

"Sure."

He turned to walk back to his car.

"Like a drink?" she called after him. "Got some good Kentucky whiskey I just picked up at the liquor store. Jake won't be back till Friday. Got business in Panama City, does work for the County up there every now'n then."

"Thanks, I'm good." He hurried back to the BMW.

***

"Hello, I'm Tom Bradley."

173

"Mr. Bradley, I'm Bill Nathan."

"Mr. Nathan. Please. Call me Tom." The man shook Bill's hand and invited him in. He was about five-seven and around two hundred pounds, with short gray hair on the sides and nearly bald on top. Bill guessed his age at around sixty.

The living room was small, but comfortable and warm. The burnt orange walls were covered with small, elaborately framed family photos, along with larger shots of the ocean and sunset scenes. A large, frayed, L-shaped sofa rested against the far wall. A padded brown armchair faced it. A large widescreen was attached to the front wall of the room, and an ancient rolltop desk sat in the corner.

Tom Bradley gestured for Bill to sit in the armchair facing the sofa. "Should I know you?"

Bill lowered himself into the chair. "We've never met."

Bradley nodded in relief. "Glad of that. Sixty-seven's hitting me kinda hard in the ol' memory banks lately."

"No problem." Bill adjusted his frame in the chair while the other man dropped his sizeable butt onto the couch with a grunt. "Forty-one can be a bitch sometimes, too."

Bradley laughed. "You'll long for these days when you're my age." He shrugged. "So…how can I help you?"

"I used to live in one of your units around twenty years ago and was wondering if you could possibly find someone for me who also lived there."

"Is this a friendship type thing? What I mean is, were you two living there at the same time, and

174

you're trying to find him—or her—for legal or financial—"

"This is something different."

Bradley looked confused. "Are you from the Government? Or—"

"Nothing like that. Apparently this person knew someone I once knew, and I'd like to talk to him about a very sensitive, highly personal matter."

Bradley nodded. "I understand. Where *is* this unit? My wife and I own three."

"This one is in the Conway area, just two roads north of Curry Ford Road. It's a duplex—"

"Gotcha." He pushed himself up and went over to the rolltop desk, where piles of paperbacks and folders covered the hard wooden surface. He picked up a pair of reading glasses and slipped them on. "We acquired that unit about ten years ago, as I recall." He went through the piles and pulled out a black, leather-bound journal. "If he was living there when we acquired it—"

"He most likely wasn't."

The man stopped what he was doing and turned around. "If he wasn't living there, I can't possibly—"

"I understand. I was just playing a hunch."

Bradley was silent for a few moments. Then he opened the journal and rifled through the pages. He pushed his reading glasses farther up his nose and brought the journal closer to his face. Then he shook his head. "Looks like there were only two tenants living there at the time, and both were well into their seventies." He closed the journal and shook his head. "I'm sorry, but—"

Bill's heart sank. He knew he didn't have much to go on. But he figured it was worth a try. "It's all right. It was just a long shot."

Bradley put down the journal and stood there a moment. Then he held up his index finger. "You know what? I might know the man who was one of the big realtors in that area back then. He's retired now." Bradley pulled a cell phone from his shirt pocket, flipped it open, and scanned the address book. "Lemme see if I can get hold of him."

"That would be great."

A few moments later, Bradley said, "Lou? This is Tom. How ya doing, you old bandit?"

A pause, then Bradley laughed. "Same here, same here! Listen. I've got a gentleman here, would like to find someone who rented out one of your units twenty years ago, and—"

Another pause, and Bradley laughed again. "Yep, me, too. Anyway, he'd like to look up one of your old tenants to—"

A pause.

Bradley turned to Bill. "Would you by any chance have a specific date in mind?"

The last time Bill had seen Sam was in September, but since he'd completely cut all ties from her and her entire family, he couldn't pinpoint anything after he'd left. "All I can think of is that this would be twenty-one years ago. I believe the man's first name would be Donnie, or Don. Maybe Donald. He was living with a woman named Samantha Lewes. Samantha was living there before Donnie, so her name could be the one on the lease."

Bradley turned his back and began talking into the cell. He stopped talking, then laughed, said something else, and went silent again.

About two minutes later, he turned back to Bill. "His records show that a woman named Samantha Lewes was sharing the unit with a Donald Falco. Miss Lewes listed her occupation as waitress while Mr. Falco listed his as master auto mechanic."

Bill's heart raced. He finally had the portion of the puzzle he needed. For the first time since Laura had left, he began feeling optimistic.

Donnie Falco. Master auto mechanic.

Orlando employed hundreds of mechanics, but one thing he'd learned about them over the years was that they all seemed to know one another. He also knew that reputations rang paramount with auto mechanics.

"Will that help?" Bradley held the cell against his left ear.

"Would your friend happen to have the man's age available?"

Bradley lowered his voice. "Lou, did these two people provide their ages?" A moment later, he nodded and turned back to Bill. "Miss Lewes put down her age as twenty, Mr. Falco, twenty-five." He raised his bushy gray eyebrows. "Will that do it for ya?"

Greatly relieved, Bill stood up. "You have no idea."

Chapter 18

That evening, after doing research on his laptop, Bill found that Donnie Falco lived in Altamonte Springs and worked at the Grand Auto Depot in Fern Park, off 17-92 and just a few minutes from 436.

It took him less than half an hour of fighting the heavy southbound dinnertime traffic to reach his destination, and before he realized it, he was sitting in the BMW in the crowded parking lot of the shopping complex, staring at the two open stalls of the two-story brick building on the other side of the lot.

Was he insane to have come here?

He had to find out, didn't he?

He was determined to find out everything he could about Sam's death. Something about it just didn't make any sense.

He kept thinking of what Eileen had said

("my sister's dead because of you")

and even though he knew otherwise, he had to know why she'd said it and why she continued thinking it after more than twenty years.

He knew nothing about Donnie Falco. There was no reason why he should know. He had completely closed the book on Sam and their life together the moment he'd walked out. In his view, there was no longer a reason for him to stay. She'd closed the book on their relationship the day her father died. When Bill walked away from their life

178

together, he had also walked away from all the hurt and resentment that had been hurled his way since Sam's father's funeral.

There was no reason things could have ended differently. Once hurt and resentment consumes love and affection, there really isn't anything left. Nothing good, anyway. There was no reason why he should know anything about Donnie Falco or anyone else Sam might have been associated with after their breakup. Keeping in touch with someone under such circumstances would have been downright stupid as well as ridiculous. You don't keep the lines of communication open with someone who has hurt you so much and turned their back on you. Even if you wanted to, you knew what a colossal mistake that would be.

All he knew about Falco was that he was living with Sam when she died. According to Eileen, Falco was the one who'd called 911 after he came home and found her. He was also a master auto mechanic and, according to what Bill had learned through some research, worked in the two-story brick building that was sitting just a couple of hundred feet away, on the opposite end of the parking lot.

That was it in a nutshell. He didn't know what the man looked like, where he lived, what he did for entertainment, or how many skeletons were gathering dust in his closet.

According to Eileen, no one else had been within earshot when Sam had fallen onto the concrete. This told Bill that any number of things could have happened.

Water under the bridge.

In a sense, it boiled down to that. But since Sam had given birth to a daughter, Bill knew he couldn't stop his investigation until the very end. He had to know what happened to Sam so he could decide what to do about Miranda. The girl was just a year old when her mother died. That simple fact made him feel guiltier than anything else he had ever done in his life.

But why should he feel this way? Sam hadn't bothered to contact him to tell him she was pregnant. A full year had passed from the time of Miranda's birth to the time of Sam's death. There had been plenty of time for Sam to get in touch with him. He hadn't moved out of state or changed his name. She knew where he worked as well as what he planned to do once he'd left the bank. There was no reason in the world why she couldn't have told him what was going on.

So why didn't she?

Was it because she didn't want him to know? Was she afraid he'd want to come back to her if he knew they had a daughter together?

It was the only thing he could think of. In his view, there was no other legitimate reason.

That last thought angered him, and he knew he had to find out. Struggling to keep calm, he got out of the car, slammed the door shut, and started walking toward the big brick building.

***

"Wanna talk to Donnie?"

"Is he available?"

180

"He's out there, somewhere. Prob'ly workin' on that Caddie. Help ya with somethin'?"

The boy was about twenty-five, long limbed and skinny in his dark blue, stained uniform. His face was covered with black smudges, and he smelled of grease and machine oil. He wore his turquoise baseball cap a little cockeyed, mashing down his greasy black hair.

"It's a personal matter." Bill scanned the huge area behind the large window separating the office from the bay. Two mechanics were busily at work underneath a Ford pickup and a maroon Cadillac SUV, both up on lifts. "If he's too busy, I can leave my cell phone number—"

"Hang loose. I'll go get 'im." The kid jumped up. He was about six inches taller than Bill, and wiry. His waist was tiny, and his partially opened shirt revealed a protruding collarbone above a generous smattering of curly black hair sprouting from his sunken chest. He pushed open the back door and was gone in a flash.

Bill took a deep breath to calm his nerves. He desperately wanted to turn around and leave, but each time he considered it, he reminded himself why he'd come here. He had to face this guy and find out what happened to Sam, even if it meant finding out that Falco may have somehow been responsible for her death.

What if this were the case?

That very thought unhinged him, and he caught himself gawking at the front door again.

What would he do if he found out that Falco had murdered Sam? How would Falco react to someone accusing him of murdering a young woman twenty years after he'd done the nasty deed? Would Bill want to be in the same room with the man? What would happen if Falco went crazy and attacked Bill for threatening him with incriminating questions?

Bill considered himself in fairly good shape for being a white collar executive who did very little exercise. He ate moderately and indulged himself only in well-balanced meals. His only vice was his drinking, but he tried his best to keep that to a minimum and overdid it only on weekends or holidays. Or, as in this case, severely stressful situations.

Even so, he knew he was no match for a mechanic. Nearly all the mechanics he'd known were strong. It took considerate brawn—as well as a fair degree of agility—to handle heavy equipment, manipulate and stack tires, and lift engine parts.

What would he do if he found out that Falco had been responsible for Sam's death? Would he want to pursue this legally? Would he be able to overcome his own rage to handle this through proper channels? Would he be able to dial 911 if he was forced to? Would Falco—

"I'm Donnie Falco."

The low-pitched voice startled him.

The man standing in the doorway was about four inches taller than Bill, with wide shoulders and large, muscular arms. He would have been considered fit-looking if not for the spare tire creeping over his belt buckle and hips. His dark hair was combed back, with a heavy lock of it splitting from the rest and falling over his forehead. Flecks of gray and white dotted the sides and around the temples. He was handsome in a rugged sort of way, with thick black brows, dark-brown eyes, a broad nose that had obviously been broken, and a softening jawline. Two short white scars extended from the bottom of his left cheekbone and a long jagged one marked his square jaw.

The name *DONNIE* was stitched in white scrawl over his shirt pocket.

Falco was wiping his hands thoroughly with a large, stained white towel. Black smudges peppered his cheeks, forearms, and the side of his thick, corded neck.

"Mr. Falco..." Bill struggled to keep calm. His heart was racing, but he couldn't think of any way of getting it to slow down. "I'm Bill Nathan."

"Call me Donnie. Bobby said ya wanted to see me."

"Is there somewhere we can talk?"

He pointed to the hall to his right. "Follow me."

Bill followed the big man into the second room on the left. It was a small room, with nothing but a square metal desk, a folding chair facing the desk, and a single filing cabinet shoved against the opposite wall.

"Have a seat."

"Thank you." Bill sat while the other man closed the door.

Donnie circled the desk and sat. "Now...what's this all about? You're not a lawyer, are ya?" He appeared very cautious.

"I'm an investment broker."

183

Donnie shrugged. "Hope you're not here for *that*. Got most of my cash invested in this setup, really don't have anything extra for—"

"I'm here," Bill said uneasily, "to talk about Samantha."

Donnie didn't reply. His hands stopped working on the towel. He seemed to be studying Bill.

Bill suddenly felt very uncomfortable and thought once again about leaving.

"Samantha…Lewes?"

Bill wondered for a moment if the man was having trouble with his memory. "You know who I'm talking about, right?"

After a few moments, the man nodded. "You mean Sam, right?"

Bill nodded.

"She's dead, died a while ago."

"Yes."

Donnie went silent again.

"You remember her, don't you?" Bill was having trouble understanding the man's confusion. It made him wonder just how involved the two of them had been. "You lived with her—"

"Right." Another nod. "Yeah. I remember." He frowned. "Damn! That was, what? Fifteen, sixteen years ago?"

"Twenty-one, to be exact."

"Seriously?" He frowned again, then nodded. "You're right. Twenty-one years. Wow…" He shook his head. "I was a kid then. So was she, wasn't she? Yeah, we were both damn young. I just come outa mechanic school and was havin' trouble

184

findin' work. I'd done a shitload of engine and body work on my own Chevelle when I was in high school, so I thought I'd try my hand at—" He stopped talking and stared at Bill. "What's this all about? Yeah, we were livin' together. That duplex. Two bedrooms, two baths. South Conway area."

"Yes. I know."

He shrugged. "We were only together maybe a year or so when she had that bad accident."

Bill nodded. So far, Falco had the timeframe right. Now was the time to get down to the details. "Could I ask you a personal question?"

"Sure. Go 'head."

"How involved were you two?"

"Involved?" He sat forward. "Well, like I said, I'd only been livin' there a year or so. I was givin' her half the rent, and—"

"How well *did* you know her?"

"Not as well as I wanted to." He chuckled and lowered his voice. "Listen. You're a guy, you'll get this. I met Sam at the grocery and we kinda hit it off. She was gonna have a kid in a couple months and was havin' trouble with the rent. She asked if I needed a place to live, and could I afford half the rent, so I said, yeah, sure, I could do that. So I moved in." He shrugged. "That was about it."

"Then you two weren't close?"

He shook his head. "Her head just wasn't into anything like that. She had her kid and was kinda over her head with other things, so I figured, why get involved—especially when I got my own problems? 'Sides, she had a thing goin' on with some other guy, said he just moved out one day.

185

Anyone could tell she never got over him. It was written all over her face. You know. A babe like that? Not interested in guys or even other babes? I tried once or twice to get it on with her, but you could tell she wasn't into it. Between workin' and havin' her sister come in and take care of her kid? She didn't seem to have time for anything else."

"Her sister took care of her daughter?"

"Sometimes that sister of hers would grab the kid, then take her to their brother, or some other relative. The sister was workin', too, so it was kind of a hassle, dumpin' the kid on each other all the time. But that's what they had to do, I guess."

Bill shrunk in his seat. He was beginning to feel as badly as he'd felt that day he'd walked out on her.

"I decided to leave her be. I was busy back then, workin' at Jiffy Lube. Then I got some gigs at Auto Mania and was able to sock away some cash for this place." He shrugged. "But like I said before, she wasn't really into me, so…" He held out his hands.

"Then you two weren't physical at all?"

"Like I said, she just wasn't interested. Too bad, though." He shook his head. "She was quite a looker, even got her figure back right after she dropped her kid. Anyway, I had other things to worry about, tryin' to start up my own company."

Something about all this struck him as odd. It just didn't sound reasonable, for some strange reason.

"Somethin' on your mind?" Falco asked. "Ya look confused."

He knew better to ask, but he also knew that he'd kick himself if he didn't. "Then you weren't the one who got her pregnant?"

"Me?" He chuckled. "Hell, no! Like I said, she was already pretty far along when I met her and moved in. And as far as the messin' around went, we didn't get chummy at all. It was nothin' more than a business deal. She sublet half the place to me. Nothin' else."

"Then it was that other guy's baby?"

"Had to be. She never seemed to be interested in anyone else—not even me." He chuckled. "Shame, though. Like I just said, she sure was one firecracker of a babe. Got all my cylinders crankin'—if ya know what I mean."

Bill said nothing.

"But that guy she was bonkers over, he sure had her right there." He held up his thumb. "He left the scene for some reason, but anyone could tell she was expectin' him to come back."

Bill sat forward and rested his elbows on his thighs. He rubbed his eyes and hoped the sinking feeling that had taken over would leave him alone.

This all happened in the past, he reminded himself. *There was no way it could be undone. As awful as it was, it happened the way it was supposed to.*

"You okay? Ya look kinda—"

"Did she ever mention…the guy's name?"

Falco took a moment. "Can't really remember—wait, I think…yeah, it mighta been…Bill? Yeah, Bill—" He stopped suddenly. His eyes grew. "You?"

187

Bill nodded.

Falco groaned. "Listen… Hey, I didn't mean—"

"It's all right."

"I sure wouldn'ta opened my big mouth if I knew you were the guy who—"

"I asked, didn't I?"

He nodded.

Suddenly tired, Bill sat back in his seat. *It's almost over,* he told himself. *In just another minute or so, you'll be back in the BMW, driving back to the condo, where you can pour yourself a drink, stretch out, and try your damnedest to relax.*

"I need to ask you about one other thing."

He nodded.

"Tell me about Sam's accident."

Falco froze in his chair. The expression on his face suggested something bad had just entered his mind. It took him a little while before he could speak. "What exactly do ya wanna—"

Bill had to clear his throat before he could use his voice. "How did you…find her?"

Falco sat forward. "Sure ya wanna know?"

Bill felt a sourness in his gut. "I'm sure."

"Some of it's a little fuzzy, now…"

"Sure. It's been over twenty years."

"But most of it's still pretty damn clear. Things like that? A guy doesn't forget easy."

"I can imagine."

"That was a pretty damn badass day…" Falco sighed deeply and dropped his elbows on the table. His face had lowered; he appeared to be gazing at the pens crammed in the plastic cup on the table. "I

188

came home and there she was, lyin' on the cement slab about twenty feet from the garage." He shook his head. "I panicked, then I went over to her and checked her neck for a pulse. There was one, but it was weak. I mean barely there. I didn't know if I should give her mouth-to-mouth or try that chest-thumpin' thing ya see in TV shows, so I called nine-one-one and told 'em what happened. They told me to do the chest compressions till they got there." He shook his head, sat back, and sighed tiredly. "She was already gone by the time they showed up."

"It was a brain bleed?"

"I can't remember exactly what they said, I was so fucked up by the time they got there." He shook his head and ran a big-knuckled hand through his hair. "I tried, I really did, but—"

"I think I understand." It was difficult watching the man as he went through the nightmare again. He seemed genuinely upset even though the event had happened many years earlier. Bill was looking for signs of guilt but didn't see anything suspicious. He decided that the man was either innocent or a very good liar.

He chose to believe the man's innocence. He didn't want to go through the agony of suspecting anyone of murdering Sam.

"They picked her up and put her on that gurney thing, and all I could do was stare at the bloodstain on the slab. I wanted to freak out, but I knew I shouldn't do anything stupid. They might think I needed to be brought in, too, so I just stood there off to the side, outa the way, while they got her ready for the trip to ORMC."

189

"You followed them to the hospital?"

He nodded. "I figured I oughta be there. You know, just in case somethin' weird happened, and they could bring her back. They seem to know how to do that sorta stuff nowadays."

"But nothing happened?"

He shook his head slowly. "She was gone."

"Then what did you do?"

A shrug. "Nothin' else, really. I just talked to one of the doctors. There was a cop there, too, takin' down everything. He asked me a few questions, then told me to go back home and get some rest. That's what I did."

"So you went straight home?"

"Well, I cleaned up the slab a little. I hosed down the blood first. I didn't know if I could do it, I was so fucked up, but it was really freakin' me out, so..." He shrugged. "Then I picked up her hammer and took it into the garage so—"

"Hammer?" Bill felt something catch in his throat.

"There was a hammer lyin' there on the slab, about three feet from her head."

"A *hammer* was lying on the slab?"

Falco nodded. "Sam mighta been workin' on somethin' when she tripped and hit her head."

"*Working* on something?" He didn't remember Sam being interested in carpentry. Sam was all about good health and sunshine and exercise. He didn't recall ever seeing her use a hammer.

"Every once in a while, she'd wander off into the garage and do some work on a piece of furniture she'd just bought." Falco stopped and tilted his

190

head. "Didn't you know she liked doin' that sorta thing?"

"It must've been something new. When we lived together, she was big into working out. She loved jogging—and lots of exercising."

Falco nodded. "Yeah, she was really into stayin' in shape. It got harder for her when she was pregnant, but she kept at it. Now that we're talkin' about it, she hadn't done any furniture work for quite a while. When I first saw that hammer layin' there, I wondered why it was there in the first place."

"What...kind of hammer...was it?" Bill was having trouble visualizing what had happened.

"Nice-lookin' Stanley hammer. Why? Was it yours?"

Was it yours?

Bill swallowed. This was not right. Not at all. It couldn't be. "Do you remember...if you ever saw her using it before?"

"Nope. Matter of fact, she had her own hammer lyin' there in the kitchen drawer, used it every once in a while whenever she needed to fix somethin' in the house. You know, minor home repairs. Made me wonder about why she was usin' somethin' different. It also made me wonder what she was doin' with it, since I didn't see anything in the garage she coulda been workin' on."

Bill didn't speak for the longest time.

This could not possibly be real. This could only be something horrible coming from a dark place in his imagination.

"Somethin' wrong?" Falco was watching him.

191

Bill shook himself. "Wrong?"

"Ya look…well, messed up."

"It was tough…hearing about it," he managed weakly.

"I can imagine. Sorry it turned out that way."

"So am I."

"Ya don't mind my askin', how long were you two, well, I guess I shouldn't ask, so—"

"We were together about six months or so."

"She was different back then, I bet."

He remembered how bright and bubbly she'd been in the mornings. How she could make him forget a horribly bad day at work with just a smile or a kiss. How she could make him feel as if he'd gone off to Heaven by coaxing him into bed and making him feel like the world's greatest lover.

"You two were tight, huh?"

"I loved her." For some reason, he didn't mind telling Falco how he felt.

Falco shook his head. "Tough, ain't it? Somethin' like that really messes ya up."

"Yeah. And you're never the same." He got to his feet and had trouble steadying himself.

Falco got up and went to the door. "I guess that was all ya wanted to know, then."

Bill nodded as Falco pulled open the door.

"Thanks for your time."

"No prob." Falco scratched the back of his head and frowned. "By the way, I just remembered somethin'."

Bill stopped cold.

"It probably won't matter to ya, but just a few days before Sam died, we had a tropical storm come through from the Gulf."

"I vaguely remember. Can't remember the name of it, though."

"Yeah, we get so damn many."

Bill waved as he slipped through the doorway. He crossed the office and was about to open the front door when Falco said, "Remember somethin' else, too."

Bill kept his hand on the doorknob.

"That hammer I found on the slab beside her?"

Bill immediately grew tense. "W-What about it?"

"It was rusty, and the handle was all mildewed and green. It had obviously been left outside in the elements. Who the hell would do that? It was a nice one, too. Those suckers don't come cheap."

Bill didn't reply. His thoughts began spinning.

"Couldn't see Sam messin' around with a hammer like that. Too big for her hand. She was no neat freak, but her own hammer was clean and much easier for her to—"

"It was mine," Bill heard himself say.

"What happened? Ya forget it when ya moved out?"

"Something like that." He was having trouble breathing and needed to be out in the fresh air.

Falco shook his head. "Guess we'll never know what happened, huh? Anyway, sorry about everything. Take 'er easy."

Bill didn't even remember walking back to his car.

193

PART TWO - RETURN OF THE PAST

Chapter 19

A sharp tap on his side window.

Startled, Bill opened his eyes.

A big blue blur...

He shook himself and rubbed his eyes. When his vision cleared, he had another look.

A cop was standing a couple of feet from his side window, watching him. The man was tall and broad, his face slightly distorted by his helmet visor. The nametag on the man's shirt pocket said, *HAINES*. Bill caught an image of a motorcycle in his side mirror.

Confusion set in and he wondered what he was doing, sitting behind the wheel of the BMW at night.

What the hell happened? Had he zoned out? Did it have something to do with his talk with Donnie Falco?

Another tap.

Bill rolled down the window. "Yes, Officer?"

"You all right, sir?" The man sounded concerned.

Bill sighed tiredly. His thoughts raced. He gazed at the big building on the other side of the parking lot. Nausea gradually set in.

Nighttime. The shopping mall. Donnie Falco. Sam lying on a concrete slab, her life slowly draining out of her. Her fall. An accident.

A hammer.

"The handle was all mildewed and green..."

Sam. With a hammer.

"Sir? Have ya been drinking?"

"Uh, no...no. I haven't had anything to drink."

But you need one right now. As soon as you get home, you need to break open the seal on one of those bottles you've got waiting for you in the kitchen cupboard.

The cop moved closer and aimed a small penlight at Bill's face. Bill could tell that the man was checking for the smell of booze.

Bill frowned and turned away from the beam of white light. "Officer, I've had a really bad day today."

"Sorry to hear that."

"Me, too. *Very* sorry, in fact."

"You realize it's one in the morning?"

"No! Really?" He brought his wrist closer. The digital display on his watch registered 1:03. *"Dammit..."* He'd been sitting here for hours and didn't realize it.

He thought of Sam again. And, of course, the damned hammer.

"You gonna be okay, sir?"

If you really want to know the truth, I'm never gonna be okay ever again because...

Because why?

195

All I know is, Donnie Falco told me something that really freaked me out, and if I don't find out what happened—

"Sir? You need medical attention?"

"No. Thanks. I'll be leaving now."

"You're sure?"

"I'm able to drive, thanks."

"Where d'ya live?"

"Winter Park. About twenty minutes from here. Seriously, I'm okay to drive."

"Be careful, then."

"I will. And thanks again."

***

Half an hour later, he was sitting at the kitchen table, finishing his glass of vodka.

His mind had gone off into another overload the moment he walked through the door. Before he realized it, his thoughts had taken him back to the duplex, during those last weeks of arguments with Sam.

What were they about, anyway?

Daddy, of course. Everything had been wonderful until the day Sam's father had seen them going at it in Bill's ten-year-old dark blue Camaro.

Then?

Chaos. And tension. And many, many intermittent periods of stone cold silence. Glares for no apparent reason. And moods—shitloads of them.

The arguments broke out constantly, usually over nothing, and grew in intensity in just seconds. To make the situation even worse, the atmosphere of foul hatred filled the air, shrouding their lives in a cold darkness.

But did that explain the most important issue about all this? The one thing that brought the hatred and the darkness back the instant Falco had uttered that single blood-chilling statement?

"There was a hammer lyin' there on the slab, about three feet from her head."

Why couldn't he get that disgusting image out of his head?

How could he possibly think the damned thing had stayed on the roof—from the time he'd tossed it up there—until it decided to slide down? How could he imagine that it had come down at the most unfortunate moment, whacking Sam in the head and causing her to drop to the slab, where the concrete cracked open the back of her skull?

How could he possibly think that Eileen could have been right about him after all?

"The handle was all mildewed and green..."

So what? That meant nothing.

Didn't it? Or are you just trying to convince yourself that Eileen was totally off base about the whole thing?

He poured more vodka from the bottle, got up, and went into the living room. He collapsed on the sofa and began staring at the white curtains covering the front window. Beyond it, darkness pushed its way in. The wall clock said 1:55. He was beginning to feel a heavy ache in his joints and back.

He had another sip of vodka and settled into a more comfortable position. His thoughts went wild again. He needed sleep. Not just another zone-out,

197

as before, in the BMW, but a few hours of deep, uninterrupted sleep.

"Eileen's a bitch," he muttered, "and she's wrong. Totally wrong."

There was no way in hell he had anything to do with Sam's accident. No way in hell. It was an accident. It was something that wasn't supposed to happen but happened anyway, because that's what an accident was.

"You're a bitch, Eileen," he told the widescreen. "You're pissed off at me because I never wanted to jump your bones, and you're tossing bullshit at me because it's the only thing that can make you happy these days."

Eileen was wrong.

Why else would she be blaming him for her sister's accident?

Prove her wrong.

How the hell am I supposed to do that?

Find a way.

He closed his eyes and tried to relax, to empty his mind. To somehow convince himself that Eileen was wrong—that Sam had died because she'd tripped on the step, fallen, and hit her head on the concrete.

"*I know you didn't do it on purpose,*" a soft, muffled, low-pitched voice said just a few feet from him.

He sat bolt upright and scanned the room. "W-Who's there?"

Silence.

His heart pumped furiously as he sat there stiffly, frighteningly alert.

"Sam? Is that…*you*?"

Silence.

"*It was an accident, baby*," the voice said moments later.

His skin stood out in gooseflesh, and he shivered.

"Sam?"

Silence.

"I'm drunk, and now I'm hearing things." He scowled at the empty glass in his hand and put it on the end table.

With a deep sigh, he leaned back and closed his eyes. "She'd understand," he muttered to himself. "If Sam really was still alive, she'd know I'd *never* do anything to hurt her."

Then, of course, Eileen's voice slithered into his head: "*My sister's dead because of you.*"

"Fuck you, bitch."

"*Because of you.*"

"Go to hell."

"*You yelled, tossed things, slammed doors…*"

He dozed off, waking up every now and then and seeing an image of Sam standing in front of the living room window, looking at him.

"*Tossed things…*"

I didn't do it!

He finally fell asleep and managed to make it through the night without nightmares.

When he awoke, it was past eight o'clock, and he knew the moment he'd opened his eyes that he had to drive back to the duplex.

It was vital to see if his worst nightmare had really happened.

***

An ancient Dodge pickup from the seventies was parked in the drive next to the two-story duplex.

Bill sat in the BMW, staring at the place. Remembering things. Events. Remembering Sam— how she looked, how she dressed, how she smiled, how she cried. How she had changed so drastically in just days.

What in heaven's name was he doing here?

Why had he come back?

Was it because of what Eileen said? Something she'd accused him of doing even though he knew she was wrong?

Or was it because he didn't know for sure if she was wrong about any of this and desperately needed to see for himself?

You had nothing to do with Sam's accident.

He knew he was right. He had walked out of Sam's life, period. He hadn't once looked back. Hadn't called, hadn't gone to any lengths to see how she was doing. He didn't *want* to know how she was doing, how her family was doing. If she'd finally gotten over her grief for the loss of her father. If she forgave Bill. If she wanted him back. That chapter of his life had snapped shut the day he left, got into his car, and drove away.

Why in heaven's name was he agonizing over this?

Was it because of Miranda? Was it because he had just learned that he could be the father of a beautiful young girl? And if he really *was* her father, this meant that he had been totally absent from the girl's life since the day she was born.

He didn't know which he felt worse about—Sam's accident, or the fact that Miranda might be his daughter.

But first, he had to find out something that had been grinding away at him ever since he'd spoken to Eileen. This was something that needed to be addressed, to be eliminated from his long list of things to feel guilty about.

Once and for all, he had to find out if Eileen was lying to him. He knew that he couldn't live with himself if he found out that she wasn't.

Hopefully, she was just using her resentment and her anger to get back at him. He sincerely prayed that she had nothing to base any of her accusations on.

Either way, he had to find out.

***

"Back again?"

The woman appeared on the top step of the rear porch the moment Bill reached the concrete slab. She was wearing a red V-necked tee shirt and tight jeans with the cuffs rolled up. Her hair was pulled up and back and held tightly in place with a brown barrette. Jade jewelry adorned both slender wrists, her neck, and several fingers. The spiked heels made her look ridiculous. She was obviously trying to look younger and sexy. She was smoking a cigarette. Bill could see her gaze moving southward on him as before.

"I had to come back to check out something."

She carefully descended the steps and sashayed over, stopping a couple of feet from him. Her smile made him uncomfortable. "And what would ya wanna be checkin' out, honey?"

Oh boy...

He decided to make this visit as quick as possible. "When I lived here, I left something on the roof and just wanted to see if it was still there."

"How long ya say it was since ya lived here?"

"Twenty years."

She scowled. "And ya think it could still be up there?"

The way she'd said it made it sound silly. It also made him feel like an idiot. But he had to find out.

"I know, I know. But it's important, and I figured I ought to find out for sure."

Her gaze lowered once again. "Ya sure *that's* why ya came back?"

He held back a groan. *This woman's too much.* "You wouldn't by any chance have a ladder lying around somewhere, would you?"

She puffed on her cigarette and pointed to the garage. "Go knock yourself out, honey."

An aluminum ladder lay on its side against the concrete wall of the stall. He grabbed it by its end and slowly dragged it out. Luckily, it was light in weight and easy to handle. He hauled it over to the rear wall of the duplex, positioned the square metal feet on the slab, and carefully pushed it straight up. He lowered it slowly until the top section rested on the aluminum gutter running along the length of the building. He was about to climb it when she said, "What is it you're lookin' for, honey?"

He turned. She was standing just two feet away, smoking her cigarette. The smell of the smoke, mixed with her strong perfume, was making him nauseous. Good thing a warm breeze was drifting by.

"You wouldn't believe me if I told you."

She grinned, showing stained teeth, and blew some smoke directly at him. "Lemme hear it and I'll letcha know if I believe ya."

He frowned at the memory. "I got very angry one day and lost my temper."

She shrugged. "So? What's that gotta do with the roof?"

"I had a hammer in my hand at the time."

"Ya threw it up there, didn'tcha?"

He nodded.

"And ya think it's still up there?"

"Maybe."

She looked pensive. "Had a boyfriend a while ago, did shit like that. Had helluva temper, always throwin' things, punchin' the walls, the door…"

"You yelled, tossed things, slammed doors…"

Ignoring the irritating thoughts, he turned back to the ladder and began climbing.

"You do that much, honey?" she called after him.

He stopped and looked down. She was standing less than a foot from the ladder, looking straight up at him.

"Do what?"

"Throw things? Punch the walls?"

203

"Not anymore." He resumed climbing. She said something else, but he didn't care enough to stop climbing so he could ask her to repeat it. He had more important things on his mind.

He reached the roof. He was able to see the portions of the red tile that hadn't been covered with stray globs of Spanish moss or clumps of pine needles dropped from the trees hovering less than thirty feet from the property. He carefully knelt on the bottom tiles, above the gutter. Then, struggling to remember where the hammer had landed on that fateful day, he scanned the area. And groaned.

There was no hammer.

About halfway up, several small chips in a small section had marred the otherwise smooth surface of the tile about five feet down from the roof peak. He could also see green smudges of what was probably mildew between the tiles, as well as several scratches extending downward and stopping just a few feet from where he knelt.

The back of his neck grew warm.

He'd thought of that hammer several times since that horrible afternoon, mostly wondering why he hadn't gone back to retrieve it. He'd thought of it only because it had been an expensive hammer. He never went back because he didn't want to confront Sam again. Not once had he thought that the damned thing wouldn't stay up there but might slide back down one day and drop onto someone's head.

Not once did he think that it would come down and kill Sam...

"Ain't up there, is it?" the woman barked.

"Not anymore," he muttered to himself.

"Prob'ly fell down from one of those damn storms we always get in the summer."

Bill struggled to keep from losing control. Not up here, anyway. That could come later, after a few drinks, then a staggered walk out into the middle of Semoran during rush hour to end the nightmare forever.

"Good thing ya tossed it up there that long ago," the woman said. "Damn thing coulda slid down, dropped, and smacked me or one of my main squeezes on top of the head."

Bill closed his eyes tightly shut, bit his lip, and told himself not to scream.

"Those damn things are heavy. They'll kill ya, they whack ya on the head."

Shut up, dammit!

His eyes remained tightly shut as he slowly descended the ladder.

***

He spent the evening in some dive just off Semoran that he'd found on his way back to the condo.

It was past dinnertime, but he had no desire to eat. He also had no desire to drive back to the condo.

He'd spotted the dive while waiting at the red light at the last intersection. It looked like an old block building someone had bought cheap and turned into a bar. It sat next to a garage, separated by stacks upon stacks of truck tires crammed next to old, beat-up pickups on blocks. The neon sign attached to the roof said, *DRINKS*. In his present mood, it was much too convenient—and inviting—to pass up.

After finishing his third vodka tonic, he found that he wanted to keep drinking. And forgetting. And trying very hard not to hate himself.

How can you forget something like that? he asked himself.

I don't know. I have to try. The voice in his head rang crystal clear.

Good luck.

I'll need more than luck.

You'll need to go back in time and undo what you've already done.

I can't do that...can I?

You know the answer to that.

"Another round?"

He nodded. The short, hazy blur moving somewhere off to his right picked up his empty glass and quickly disappeared.

Bill lowered his face, closed his eyes, and willed himself to go back in time.

You can't do that.

I've got to try.

It won't work.

I don't care. I've got to do it.

The damage has been done.

There's got to be some way of fixing it.

Idiot. You can't fix the past. In fact, you can't fix anything.

His refill came. He picked it up, drained it, found some bills in his pocket, dropped them on the counter, and got up to leave.

Outside, he could think clearly, then get in his car and—

You really think you can drive, ace?

It's the only way I can get out of here.

That won't work, either.

Why not?

You're drunk.

I still have to try.

You'll end up dead.

So what?

Let me guess. You don't care.

Right. I don't.

Because of Sam?

Right again.

What would she think of this?

I honestly don't know.

How about Laura?

What about her?

She's the one you're sharing your life with now. The one you say you love. How do you think she'll take it if you end up dead?

She'll get over me—just like Sam did.

Sam never got over you.

He stopped moving outside the front door and felt his heart sputter. *How could you possibly say that?*

I didn't say it. Falco said it. You should know. You were there, weren't you? Weren't you paying attention?

He closed his eyes and willed the voice in his head to stop tormenting him. *It doesn't matter. Nothing matters. Not anymore.*

Go ahead. Feel sorry for yourself. Say hell with Laura and your life together and your career and—

"I don't fucking *care!*"

He opened his eyes. He was standing outside in the front lot, just a few feet from his car. The bar was right behind him. Sighing heavily, he began reaching for his keys when he heard the crunching of the gravel behind him.

He turned and caught an image of a tall, broad figure moving toward him. He was in the process of trying to bring the man's face into focus when the tip of his shoe connected with something hard.

There was a brief flicker of the man's dark features before something large, hard, and smelling of something foul

(machine oil?)

smashed into the left side of his face.

The last thing he remembered was his keys flying in the darkness just seconds before something large and solid jumped up from the ground and slammed him in the forehead.

Chapter 20

The darkness thinned, turning gray, then silver.

The silver grew into a solid object.

A ladder lay propped up against a concrete wall.

"What are you doing?"

It was Sam's voice.

Sam's voice? What the hell?

Startled, he spun around.

Standing with her hands on her hips, she watched him from the open door of the duplex. She wore those tight jeans that he always liked and that light-blue tee shirt that showed off the brightness in her beautiful blue eyes.

She was also wearing her angry face. He'd been seeing it entirely too often these days. He didn't like it but knew why she'd been wearing it so much. He was the reason, and this told him that he was the only one who could get her to stop wearing it. He believed he could do it, but it would take time.

Even so, she was entirely too sexy to be standing there like that. Under other circumstances, he would have walked right over, picked her up, and carried her inside.

But not now. She was pissed, and when Sam was pissed, romance just wasn't anywhere on the table.

"I thought you left."

He was still trying to figure out why he was here. And why Sam was standing there like that.

Something was very wrong. Last he remembered, something else had happened, something horrible, but he couldn't recall the details. He guessed that it had something to do with his hammer.

Whatever the issue, he knew that it was very important that he climb up to the roof and get it.

"Well?" Sam was waiting for an answer. "Didn't I watch you walk away?"

"You did."

"For good—right?"

"You could probably tell by the way I left."

"But you're back."

"I guess I am."

She sighed. "*Why* are you back?"

"What's it look like?"

"From here, it looks like you're getting ready to do something with that ladder."

He began dragging it out. "I had a feeling something like that wouldn't get by you."

"You still haven't told me why you came back. I thought you walked out on me. Just closed the book on us altogether."

"I came back to get that damned hammer off the roof."

"You should've never tossed it up there in the first place."

"I know, and I feel badly about it."

"You do?"

"Of course. It was stupid and childish."

"I thought so, too. But you did it anyway."

"I was pissed. You were there. You remember, don'tcha?"

210

"Of course I remember. For a second I thought you were gonna hit *me* with it."

He groaned. "You know better than that."

"Do I?"

He couldn't believe she'd said that. He had *never* laid a hand on her. He had never laid a hand on *any* woman.

Whatever would give her such a ridiculous idea?

"Did I *ever* hit you? Slap you? Do *anything* with my hands that you didn't want me to do?"

Another sigh.

"Can't think of anything, can you?"

"I just wanna know why you came back to get it. It's not exactly an heirloom…"

"I came back for it so it doesn't slide down off the roof and smack someone on the top of the head."

"How very thoughtful."

"I've always been a thoughtful kinda guy."

She watched as he brought the ladder over. "It's nice of you to do this, you know." Her voice lacked the cold edge it had just moments earlier.

He shrugged. "I shouldn't've tossed the damned thing."

"But as you said, you were upset."

"I was, wasn't I?"

She watched him curiously. "You're not *still* upset, are you?"

He suddenly felt no anger. Whenever she looked at him like that, she turned right back into the Sam he'd fallen in love with, and whatever had

211

angered him moments earlier just evaporated. "No. I'm not."

She dropped her arms to her sides and descended the steps. "What will you do after you get the hammer?"

"Drive back to my apartment, have a few drinks... I'm not sure."

She was giving him another of her suggestive looks.

"Got something in mind?"

A smile slowly took over her features. He'd seen that same smile a hundred times before and knew what it meant. He knew right then that coming back for the hammer had been a smart decision after all. "Are you thinking the same thing I'm thinking?"

"Probably."

"Then why don't we go inside and—"

"We can't." She sighed tiredly. Her smile quickly vanished.

"We can't what? Go inside? Or go inside and have one of our fun parties where we play rock, paper, scissors to see which one of us gets to take off your clothes?"

"We can't do either."

"Why not?"

"I don't know." She looked around.

"What are you looking for?"

"Something's...not right."

He'd felt it, too, but didn't want to say anything. He didn't want anything to spoil the mood. He had just had a nightmare about killing Sam and didn't want to go through it again. In it, he'd stared at the back of her head and wondered how it would look after he'd whacked her with the hammer.

Good thing that had just been a nightmare…

He wanted to retrieve the hammer so it wouldn't slide down the roof and hit someone on the head. His nightmare had really frightened him and he knew that if he didn't get it down, something very bad would happen.

"What's not right?"

She walked around the slab, glancing at things. "I don't know. Something just…doesn't *feel* right."

"What is it? The duplex? Me? The ladder? The hammer? Pick one."

She stopped glancing around and gazed at him. Her face turned dark, and he could sense a cloud of gloom emanating from her. "I don't think…I'm supposed to be here, baby…"

"Whaddya mean?"

"I think I'm…supposed to be…somewhere else."

"Where are you supposed to *be*?"

"I have this feeling. I think I remember being…somewhere very far away…from here…"

"Where?"

She went silent. She seemed to be looking past him. Then she shivered and said in a little girl's voice, "Daddy's marker."

He took a step in Sam's direction.

She began fading.

"Sam?"

Then she was gone.

He was all alone. The only thing he could see now was the opened stall door of the garage building. "Sam?"

Suddenly unsteady, he began walking toward it. As soon as he got within a foot of it, the stall opening grew darker and larger, and began moving toward him. It quickly consumed him, and he found himself engulfed in complete darkness.

"Sam?"

Distant muffled whispers growing louder and closer.

The darkness dimmed.

Figures in white hovered over him.

A flurry of masks and white gloves.

A strong whiff of antiseptic.

He knew he was lying down but couldn't figure out what was going on. One of the white figures was doing something to his left arm. He tried to see the figure, but the darkness prevented him from recognizing any details. He could tell by how the figure was touching him that it was a woman.

A nurse?

Another figure applied something wet and cold to his forehead. He could feel pain, but it seemed far away, somewhere off in the darkness.

The darkness dimmed somewhat, and he could see the figure's eyes. The mask hid most of her features, but the eyes were visible. They were large, heavy-lashed green eyes. A woman, all right. A nurse, most likely. She was watching him closely while applying gauze gently to his forehead.

More voices, but they were still too soft for him to hear.

However, he did hear one word, and it made him shudder. And when he shuddered, the nurse wrapping his arm said, "Movement."

Someone else said, "Reflex?"

The nurse said, "Could be a contraction."

"Involuntary," someone else said.

All he could do was concentrate on the first word he'd heard. Someone standing over on his right had said it, and it sounded like a man's voice. He had said only one word, but it was something he did not expect—or want—to hear.

The man had said: "Comatose."

The darkness returned very quickly.

***

When the darkness lifted, he found that he was surrounded by gravestones in an open field.

Dressed in black, Sam faced one of the markers. She suddenly dropped to her knees, lowered her head, and whispered something. When she got to her feet and turned around, her eyes were wet.

"I'm really sorry, Sam."

"I know."

"I honestly don't think I was responsible."

A deep sigh. "You weren't."

He wondered if he'd just heard her correctly. "Then why do I *feel* responsible?"

She sniffed and carefully wiped away a tear. "Because of me. And my sister. And my mother. My whole family blamed you."

"But why would they *do* that?"

She shrugged. "It was easier than accepting the truth."

215

"What *was* the truth?"

"His heart."

"He had a heart condition?"

A nod.

"Why didn't you tell me?"

"There was no need for you to know. Things were going well for us. He even approved. I didn't think he would because he hadn't liked anyone else I'd brought home. And you weren't exactly his ideal choice. But I'm pretty sure he eventually grew fond of you. If only…if only he hadn't seen us—"

"I know."

She went silent for a few moments. Then she shook her head. "Why'd we do it, Bill?"

He couldn't believe what she'd just asked him. For one thing, it had been her idea. For another, they were young. And totally in love. "You know why."

She reddened, then lowered her head.

"We couldn't keep our hands off each other, Sam. You know that as well as I do. We were both obsessed with one another."

She raised her head. "But…in your *car*? In the *driveway*? And with the *windows* down?"

He shrugged. "It was a hot day. Florida. In the summer. Both of us were hot and sweaty. Literally dripping in sweat. And, to make the situation even worse, hornier than hell. What else can I say?"

She suddenly broke out in laughter.

He wanted to wrap his arms around her and hug her. He wanted to kiss her. And rub her back. And kiss her chin…and then her neck…and move farther down, until—

216

But he couldn't. He couldn't because of two reasons. The first one, of course, was that that they were standing just three feet away from her father's gravestone.

The second was because…

He didn't know. He suddenly discovered that every time he wanted to touch her, a strange coldness came from out of nowhere and inched its way up his spine, making him shudder. He had no idea what this strange cold feeling was. All he knew was that some weird force was telling him not to touch her at all.

"I've always loved you, Bill."

"I've always loved you, too, Sam."

"Even when I was so angry at you that I wanted to kill you. Even when we began drifting apart. And when we had that last argument. And when you tossed your hammer on the roof and walked away from me. From us. From what would have been our own private, wonderful world."

"Even then?"

She nodded. "Especially then."

"Why?"

"That was when reality slapped me in the face and told me how much I'd messed up."

"Messed up?"

"By letting you go."

"I really didn't want to go, Sam. Not ever."

"I didn't want you to."

"I didn't think I had a choice. The pressure was getting to me. Your family—"

"My family." That last word sounded more like a cough. She groaned and shook her head. He could tell by her expression that she felt badly about everything. "They made me believe things that I didn't really believe or feel, and I ended up saying things to you I never meant to say, and I regretted saying them the moment the words left my throat. I hated my family for treating you the way they did. Especially my sister. Eileen and I never talked much after you left. I hated her for how she treated you."

"I wasn't too wild about her, either."

She smiled. "I could tell."

"Tell me why you didn't stop me, Sam."

She was silent as she gazed at him. He had the feeling she was confused.

He was feeling confused himself, and suddenly the issue of his leaving evaporated from his thoughts. His newfound confusion had something to do with the hammer, and he had the strong urge to hurry back to the duplex and get it down off the roof.

"Sam, we've got to get back to the duplex."

"After I pay my respects."

"To your father? I thought you just—"

"To someone else."

"Your mother?"

"My mom's still alive. She's living with my brother Dean and his wife in Altamonte. Mom couldn't handle living in that big house all by herself—all those memories. She moved in with Dean and Janice. She cooks for them and does the wash, even watches their kids whenever they wanna have some privacy—"

"Who, then, Sam?" That odd cold feeling had come back.

218

Sam stared at him. Her cheeks were wet with tears. She sniffed and said, "Someone else." She turned and pointed to the marker sitting just five feet or so next to her father's marker.

"No." The cold feeling had turned into an urgency he had never known before. He couldn't see the marker because Sam was standing in front of it, but something inside him told him he didn't *want* to see it. He only knew that there was some important reason why he shouldn't see the name on the marker. "Sam, we need to leave. Right now."

"After I pay my—"

"No! Now! We need to leave *now*!"

"But—"

"*Now, Sam!*" The urgency had become as painful as a red hot poker in the gut.

"I'll feel just awful if—"

"Sam! Come with me! We need to get away from this place!"

She turned, took one step toward the marker, and he could almost make out the first letter on the—

"No!"

Another step—

"No, Sam, *no*!"

He reached out for her—

And the darkness thundered right back, consuming him again.

Chapter 21

The darkness drifted away.

When everything cleared, Bill found that he was standing in the doorway of a hospital room, staring at himself as he lay in the bed, his head covered in bandages.

Was he dead? How could he be standing in the doorway if he was lying in the bed?

Had he left his body? Had he become a spirit?

What the hell was going on?

Where was the cemetery? The duplex? The ladder? The hammer?

Where was Sam?

What were those bandages?

He reached up and felt nothing but empty air. No bruises, no bandages. Nothing.

A nurse was standing beside the bed, studying one of the monitors hooked up to his body.

Bill walked over to see what she was doing. Just as he was about to look over her shoulder, he heard a woman's soft voice behind him.

"He has visitors, Lil. They'd like to hear his status."

The bedside nurse walked over to the other woman, who was standing in the doorway. Both were tall and slender, and probably somewhere in their late thirties or early forties.

The bedside nurse whispered, "Who are they? Family?"

"Both are from his brokerage firm. One of them is his partner. The woman says her name is Laura Winston and that she's his girlfriend. She's been insistent for the last several hours. I wanted them to speak to Doctor Richards—"

"He's not here."

"Should I page him?"

She shook her head. "He's at the clinic all day."

"These people should be given an update. I could—"

"I'll talk to them."

"Thanks, Lil."

They walked out of the room.

He followed them.

Laura and Ted Albright were in the waiting room. Laura stood in the center of the big, brightly lit room, obviously tense and upset. She had on frayed jeans. Her red crepe shirt wasn't tucked in, and she wore her lightweight blue windbreaker over it. She'd obviously dressed in a hurry—which was rare for her. He guessed that she'd only recently been told about him.

She was gripping her sides as if she were trying to keep herself from coming apart. Her face was streaked with mascara. She'd been crying.

He wanted to take her in his arms.

When she saw the two nurses, she hurried right over.

"*Please* tell me how Bill's doing," she said breathlessly. "I'm Laura Winston. I'm—"

"We know," the bedside nurse said.

221

Ted came over and stood beside Laura. "What's the verdict?" he asked softly. "Bill gonna make it?"

"I'd really like to know what happened," Laura said. "No one has told me."

"No one?" The bedside nurse looked surprised.

"All I was told," Laura said with difficulty, "was that Bill had an accident...outside some bar...on the Trail. That was all. No one told me why he was there in the first place, or if...he was alone...or—"

"Apparently Mr. Nathan was brought in by ambulance as the result of a nine-one-one call. I believe the call came in last night, sometime around ten, and—"

"Ten *o'clock*?" Laura's eyes filled the sockets. She glanced at the wall clock on the wall behind the nurse. "That was *thirteen hours ago*! Why was I only informed about this two hours ago?"

"Ma'am, I'm very sorry, but I can't give you a satisfactory answer to that. I just don't know. All I can tell you is what was relayed to me."

"What did happen?" Ted asked. "I heard someone say something about a blow to his head. Was this some sort of accident? Or something else entirely?"

"From what we were told, Mr. Nathan had a bad fall in the parking lot outside the bar. He either tripped or lost his footing, then hit his forehead when he fell."

"What...did he hit it on?" Laura asked softly.

"From what the paramedics told us, it was the side mirror on one of the vehicles parked outside the

222

bar. There was also a large, square bruise on the left side of his face, at the cheekbone. That might have been made by another vehicle. The vehicles are parked very close together, so that could be a deciding factor. We determined that he'd had at least two drinks before he left. He either tripped or lost his footing, then fell forward and whacked himself before he landed."

Laura covered her mouth with her left hand. She took a breath, lowered her hand, and said, "Are you saying he was falling down drunk?"

"We're just saying there was alcohol in his bloodstream. We have no idea what condition he was in when he tripped."

Laura sighed brokenly. "How bad...is his injury?"

The nurse took a moment before replying. "The paramedics said Mr. Nathan was unconscious when they found him. I'm afraid he's remained unconscious since he was brought in."

"Oh my God..."

"Are we talking concussion here?" Ted asked.

The nurse nodded. "Mr. Nathan was already given an MRI, but we haven't seen the results yet."

"Have you checked him for...bleeding?" Laura asked in a whisper.

"He's been checked for hematoma, but we don't think there will be a problem in that respect. The same with hemorrhage. We're confident that in this case, it was simply a concussion brought on by the blow to his head."

"But...he's unconscious." Laura kept her hand close to her mouth.

"We're monitoring him constantly and will let you know the moment there's any change."

"He's comatose, then?" Ted asked.

"Yes, sir."

"And you have no idea how long he'll stay that way."

"No, sir. But as I just said, we'll let you know the moment—"

"I wanna see him." Laura lowered her hands and kept her gaze steady on the nurse. Her eyes were wet, but she was holding herself together.

Bill smiled with pride. When Laura wanted something, she usually got it.

"He won't know you're there," the nurse warned.

"Yes he will," Bill said, moving closer. "I mean, I already know."

"I still wanna see him. Please?"

The nurse smiled. "Follow me, then."

"I'll be here when you're ready to go, Laura," Ted said.

"Thanks." Sniffing and wiping her eyes with a Kleenex, she followed the nurse down the corridor.

***

They slowly approached the bed.

Laura trembled as she stared down at him. The tears drifted down her cheeks.

Bill wanted so much to tell her he was standing right beside her.

"You can get closer," the nurse said softly.

Laura didn't respond.

"I'll be right outside the room if you need me."

Laura continued staring at Bill as the nurse left the room.

After about a minute or so, Laura took two slow, cautious steps closer to the bed. She then stood perfectly still, gazing down at him.

He wanted to take her in his arms and comfort her. He felt badly that she was forced to come here. None of this would have happened if he hadn't spotted Miranda at the Paradise. Everything had been great with Laura. Their life had been perfect. They spent all their time together, had fun together. Living with such a terrific woman was wonderful. In his view, there was nothing better, and it was as close to being in Heaven as was possible in this world.

Laura placed her right hand on his as he lay in the bed. "Why'd this happen to us, baby?" she whispered. "Why couldn't fate just leave us alone?"

He moved closer. "I'm sorry, babe. I just—"

"*Please* don't leave me, Bill. *Please* don't. I *love* you. I don't want to spend the rest of my life without you!"

"I'm really sorry I caused all this, Laurie…"

"Moving out was unbearable for me, baby. I haven't been able to function. My work sucks at the office because I can't concentrate on anything but you. I can't sleep at all. Not without you lying beside me, touching me, kissing me, whispering sweet things to me…"

The familiar images awoke a stirring in him. "I miss that, too, Laurie. More than ever."

"*Please* don't die, Bill!"

"I'll try my best not to, baby."

225

She let go of his hand, moved her arm, and lightly stroked his hair. She took a breath, then touched his right cheek. "I love you, Bill. So very, very much…"

"I love you, too, Laurie."

"*Please* come out of this for me…for *us*."

Watching this was tearing him up, making him feel even guiltier. He turned away just as Laura said, "You were gonna fix this for us… *Please* don't fix it by dying. If you die, I…I don't think I'll…be able to…to go on…"

He gazed longingly at her hair. "All I wanted to do was find out about Miranda. I *had* to find out. I couldn't live with myself if I didn't at least try. Now that I know who she is and what happened, I *still* don't know what I should do. Even if I did know, I don't know if I'll be able to—"

"*Please* come back to me, Bill…"

"Laurie, if I could, I'd come back to you in a—"

"Do you *really* want to go back to her?" asked a familiar voice directly behind him.

He spun around.

The hospital room had suddenly vanished.

***

He and Sam had returned to the duplex.

She was wearing the same outfit she'd worn during their last argument. Standing just three feet away, glaring at him,

"What's going on?" He had a feeling he knew what this was all about. "It's about the hammer, isn't it?"

"Good guess."

"Sam, I wanted to get a ladder and—"

"But you didn't, did you?"

"Well, no…"

She continued glaring.

He could tell she wanted him to know all the details. "What happened to it?" he asked softly.

"Whaddya think? *You* didn't climb up there to get it, so *I* decided to do it."

"*You* climbed up there? *You* grabbed the hammer?"

She shook her head. "Didn't have to."

He was afraid to ask. "Whaddya mean?"

"It saved me the aggravation."

He swallowed. "You mean it just…it…*slid* down?"

Sam nodded. "Yep, just came right on down."

He didn't reply. He was afraid to say anything.

"Wanna know what happened after that?"

He suspected she was about to tell him.

"It came right down and made a tiny crack in the pavement."

"Really?"

"Why would I lie?"

"Then…the hammer *didn't* kill you?"

"Actually, the concrete slab killed me."

"You tripped?"

"Not exactly…"

The darkness in her eyes made him tremble.

"Tell me what happened, Sam."

"As I just said, the hammer didn't kill me. The concrete did. And no, I didn't trip."

"Then how—"

227

"I had help, Bill." Her eyes had become fierce slits. "I was pushed."

He gasped. "*Pushed*? You were *pushed*?"

"Yes, Bill. Donnie and I were having an argument. It kinda got out of hand."

He swallowed a lump in his throat. "*Falco* was the one? The one who—"

"Yes, Bill. That idiot has a really *horrible* temper—*much* worse than yours."

"What were you arguing about?"

"Hell, what *weren't* we arguing about? He moved in with me to help me with the rent, but he tried hitting on me from day one."

"But when I talked to him, he said—"

"He's a liar, Bill." She shook her head. "That jerk lied every time he opened his mouth."

This was incredible. He had just spent half an hour with the man who had murdered the first great love of his life. He wanted to scream. Most of all, he wanted to find Falco and rip his head off.

"Don't do it," she said suddenly.

"What?"

"I said, don't do it."

"Don't do what?"

"I've seen that look before, Bill. Don't try and fool me. He'll kill you. He almost did it already."

He cringed. "Did *what* already?"

"I saw him, Bill. He was right there. Outside, in the parking lot. You were coming out of that bar. He was waiting for you, and—"

"*He* was the one who hit me? And made me slam my head into someone's car?"

"He's an animal, Bill. He comes across as a nice guy—that is, if you don't know him. But once you see what he's like—"

"And he *lived* with you!" He felt the anger building up.

"He was okay if you gave him space, but if you got in his way or didn't give him what he wanted…" She shook her head.

"Tell me he didn't punch you and knock you down."

"He didn't *punch* me, but I could tell that he really wanted to. He did push me, though—which was why I fell and cracked my head open."

"He must have pushed you pretty hard."

She smiled. "It was a dandy. Good thing the slab broke my fall."

He didn't share her humor. "He told me he found you like that and called nine-one-one."

"Did he also say Eileen showed up?"

The back of his neck grew hot. "What did *she* have to do with this?"

"She showed up when he got back to the duplex after he left the hospital."

It started making sense. "She probably saw the hammer and wanted to blame me."

"Of course she did. She wanted to blame you for everything."

"Sam, I'm *so* sorry about all this. And I'm sorry about tossing that stupid thing."

"You were pissed."

"I know I shouldn't have tossed it. I knew it the instant I let it fly."

"It doesn't matter now, does it? You let it fly. It landed on the roof. And stayed there. But it didn't really matter in the end, did it?"

"*Dammit*!" Once again he couldn't believe how everything had fallen apart.

"We both know who's buried out there beside my father, right?"

He couldn't reply. He had never felt worse in his entire life.

"You knew, too, didn't you?"

He still couldn't reply.

"It was a shock." Sam's expression turned sad. "It takes a lot out of you, you know—finding your own headstone. I freaked. If I'd still been alive, I would've probably died of a heart attack right there. I needed to talk to you, but when I turned around, you were gone, and I was all alone. That made it worse, Bill. *Much* worse—"

"Dammit, Sam, how can I fix this?"

"Are you serious?" She gave him a strange look. "You couldn't even fix whatever that was with your latest girlfriend—what's her name?"

"Laura."

"What were you trying to do for her, Bill?"

He hesitated. "I needed to find out...about Miranda."

"What about her, Bill?"

"I had to find out who she was."

"Why would finding out about her accomplish anything? She has nothing to do with this."

"She's not my daughter?"

"What do *you* think?"

"I think you're playing with me."

230

"I think you know, Bill. I think you know the answer to that."

"I think I know, too."

"Then say it."

He suddenly felt lightheaded. "I...don't know if I can."

"Say it. You need to."

"Why?"

"Because you won't be able to deal with *any* of this if you don't say it."

"But I *know* it. Isn't that enough?"

"No."

"Why isn't it?"

"You need to *say* it."

"Again, why?"

"For yourself. And especially for *me*."

"For you?"

"Yes."

"But you already—"

"I need to hear it. If you hadn't tossed that hammer on the roof, I wouldn't have been forced to get it. Things would have been very different. I wouldn't have had to sublet half the place to a guy who turned out to be a dirtbag and spend the next year dodging him until he just got so fed up that he caught me out in front of the garage, right after I'd snatched up the hammer."

His jaw dropped. "You had the hammer in your hand when he confronted you?"

"I was gonna clean it up and put it in my toolkit."

"I didn't even know you had a toolkit. Falco said you did, but—"

231

"It was your toolkit, Bill. You didn't come back for it."

His heart sputtered. "I'd totally forgotten about it."

"I'd always hoped you'd come back for it." A pause. "And for a few other things."

"Dammit, Sam…" He was afraid his heart couldn't take much more.

She was silent for a few moments before she spoke again. "Just a few days before my accident, I had convinced myself to look you up and tell you about Miranda."

"No!" The words were like a knife to his gut. "Don't *say* that. *Please*!"

"It's true. I was gonna tell you about her."

"Oh my God…my God…" He clutched himself. He wanted to throw up. This was awful. The worst thing he could ever think of.

"I'm sorry, Bill. I guess it just wasn't meant to be."

Once the nausea eased up, he took a few deep breaths and straightened. Through his tears he could tell she was sincere.

"Yes, Bill. I truly *am* sincere."

He groaned. "I know."

"Then say it."

"She's really mine, isn't she?"

"She's really your what, Bill?"

He took a deep breath. The nausea had gone, but he felt faint. Even so, he was determined to trudge on. "Miranda…she's…my daughter."

"Yes, Bill. She's your daughter."

Idiot, he told himself. *A fit of temper. Your ridiculous fit of temper altered two lives—not including yours. Only two—not three. Because in this case, yours doesn't count, does it?*

Sam was watching him. Her eyes were moist.

"And now that I've said it?"

"Now you can deal with this."

"Just because I said—"

"You've acknowledged her. That was step one."

"Step one?"

"Step two would be fixing things with *me*."

"And how can I possibly do *that*?"

"Figure it out, Bill. And when you've done that, I'll know."

"But—"

"Figure it out."

"I don't think I can."

"Try."

"I'm drawing a blank."

"You'll never be free as long as this hangs over your head."

"This could take a long time."

"How long, Bill?"

He had no answer.

"Let me help. How's this? As long as it takes. Will that suit you?"

He still could not speak. He had entered a different dimension, where time had somehow ceased to exist. He glanced at his watch and noticed that it hadn't budged since his accident. He'd reached timelessness and could not progress until he'd accomplished what Sam asked him to do.

233

"This could take eternity," he finally said.

"Will you be able to rest peacefully if this isn't fixed?"

"No…"

"Then double down. Get busy."

"You mean right now?"

"You got something else going on right now?"

"Not exactly…"

"Okay, then. Get busy. *Do* it. *Fix* it."

"How will I know when I'm finished?"

"I'll know. Then you'll see me again."

"Really?"

"Yes, Bill. Really." Then she turned around and walked away.

The darkness swallowed her up.

Chapter 22

The darkness cleared.

Bill had returned to the hospital.

Laura was sitting on the couch in the waiting room, holding a cup of black coffee in her lap with both hands. Ted Albright was standing just a few feet away, looking down at her.

"Laura," he said in a soft, caring voice, "you really need to go home and—"

"I'm staying here."

"You've been here all day."

Laura didn't reply. She didn't even seem to be listening to him.

"You haven't eaten."

"I'm not hungry."

"But if you'll at least—"

"I have to be here when he wakes up."

Ted went silent. He was obviously trying to think of another good argument. "But what if it takes—"

"Takes what?"

"It could be weeks before—"

"*No!*" She shook her head. "I don't wanna *think* of that! Not for a *second!* No. He's gonna wake up. I know he is."

"How can you possibly think that that'll—"

"I just do."

"He's suffered a major concussion. He's lucky there was no brain bleed."

"He'll pull through." She was watching the window that opened up to the hall leading to Bill's room. "I know he will."

"Laura—"

"He *has* to, Ted!" She was on the verge of tears. "He *has* to pull through!"

Ted said nothing. He obviously knew he had met his match. When Laura's mind was made up, no one could change it. Everyone who knew her was aware of that.

As Ted went over to the coffee machine, Bill drifted over to Laura and lowered himself beside her on the couch. A mix of her lavender perfume and the vanilla scent of her hair made him want to stroke it. And wrap his arms around her and tell her how much he loved her.

But he couldn't. He had to set the record straight with Sam before he could do anything else, but he knew that Laura wouldn't wait very long. Laura was mortal and still bound by time. For Bill, time had mysteriously stopped. But even so, he knew that Laura would wait for him until there was no longer any reason for her doing so. Despite his feelings for her, he hoped she wouldn't. Life was much too short. She would end up wasting her life for someone who could no longer be there for her.

He couldn't permit her to do that. He couldn't let the woman throw away the rest of her life for someone who might not ever come back to her.

"Babe," he whispered very close to her ear, "you have to let me go. I don't know how long I'll be like this or if I'll ever be able to come back. It just wouldn't be fair. You're a beautiful, caring person, and I love you, but I can't in good conscience let you waste your life waiting for me."

Laura sighed, pushed some hair away from her face, and continued watching the doorway.

"I know I told you I'd handle this," he whispered, "but I had no idea the damage I'd done. This involves more than just you and Miranda, and it can't be fixed while I'm not here with you. I can't promise you how long it'll be before I can come back. I can only promise you that I will not rest until I find a way, but I can't possibly ask you to wait for me while I look for one."

Laura just sighed.

"I wish I could kiss you, babe." He stood and stared at her for the longest time. He remembered how they'd met. Their first date. Their first kiss. Laura was the first woman who had ever made him forget about Sam. The first woman who had made him feel comfortable with a woman other than Sam. The first woman he had ever wanted to spend the rest of his life with since the day he'd met Sam.

Now he had to walk away from Laura just as he'd walked away from Sam. But in this case, he had every intention of coming back to her.

He only hoped she'd still want him when that time came.

His heart was heavy as he bent and made the move to kiss her on the top of her head. He felt nothing but was almost certain that she'd flinched the tiniest bit when he did it.

"I promise I'll find a way to come back to you, babe," he whispered, his mouth very close to her cheek. Then, struggling to ignore the sadness growing within him, he disappeared.

***

He'd returned to the cemetery.

It was getting dark. He turned, cringing when he saw that the markers of the two people whose lives he had changed forever were only a few feet away.

He could not feel the ground beneath his feet as he slowly approached Sam's father's marker. The flowers that had been placed in front of the stone had long since died. The family members obviously hadn't visited the grave in quite a while.

"I'm sorry about what happened," he said, staring at the marker. "I'm sorry you saw something you shouldn't have seen and that it changed your relationship with Sam. But it shouldn't have changed anything. Sam loved you and continued to love you even though you turned your back on her."

He heard nothing, of course, and wasn't surprised that he felt no different after what he'd just said. He knew that you couldn't go back and change the past. The past was dead and, in this case, buried.

So how did Sam expect him to change anything?

He moved to the next marker. Seeing her name on the stone unnerved him. He shuddered when he thought that he would be forced to spend eternity trying to set things right. The problem was that he had no idea what he had to do and would be doomed to remain in darkness.

238

But what about Laura? He loved her, didn't he? He loved Sam, too.

Yes, he loved both, but Laura was still alive. And he knew she'd wait for him as long as she possibly could.

Sam was dead and so was his life with her. He still had strong feelings for her but knew that the chapter had closed. He now belonged to Laura, and unless he came up with some solution, he would lose her as well.

"Sam, I don't know what to do," he told her marker. "I'm not guilty of causing your death, but I still feel remorseful, and I'd give anything to be able to go back in time and undo what happened to you. For a moment I thought I might be able to do it, but now I know I can't."

No matter how hard he tried, he could find no answer.

He had to keep trying. He didn't want to spend eternity like this. He'd always thought eternity would be a wonderful thing. He'd never thought it would be a state of constant doubt, self-hatred, and a nagging guilt that would never go away.

"I've already apologized to you," he told her marker. "I loved you and would have never done anything to hurt you, but I never thought you'd want me to spend eternity feeling guilty for an accident I wasn't even responsible for."

He closed his eyes and cursed himself.

Once again, the approaching darkness came for him.

***

239

From his kitchen doorway, he watched Laura pouring coffee from the coffeemaker.

Barefooted, she was dressed in her oversized gray sweatshirt—her usual outfit for the evenings.

He was glad that she'd finally left the hospital.

Her suitcases sat on the living room floor beside the couch. She'd apparently decided to come back to the condo. He found that he had mixed emotions about this. He was pleased that she'd returned, but the sight of the suitcases made him angry with himself again.

Laura took her cup into the living room and sat down on the couch with her legs curled up—her normal couch position. As always when watching her, he felt his juices heating up and cursed himself for not being able to sit down next to her and comfort her.

She sat quite still, her eyes fixed on the widescreen even though it was turned off. The remote lay on the cocktail table in front of her, yet she made no effort to reach for it. Sadness, fear, and uncertainty emanated strongly from her.

Just then, she picked up her cell from the end table and pressed the call option. A voice came on. Laura said in a soft voice, "This is Laura Winston again. Is there any change in Bill Nathan's condition?"

The voice said something short, and Laura sighed deeply. "Thank you." The voice said something else. "Thank you, I appreciate that." She put the cell back down, leaned her head back, stared at the ceiling, and said, very softly, "Come back to me, Bill. *Please* come back to me."

He moved closer and saw the tears gathering in her eyes.

"I don't care about anything else, I just want you back. I want you here. Beside me. Holding me." She sniffed. "God, Bill, I really miss you holding me...kissing me...making love to me..." She sighed brokenly. "If only I could—"

Just then, her cell hummed.

She scooped it up and brought it up to her ear. "Y-Yes?"

A woman's voice.

Laura sat up sharply and nearly spilled her coffee. "*Who* did you say?"

The reply was short.

"No...I don't think I know a Miranda Resnick."

Bill cringed at the name.

Laura carefully placed the coffee cup on the table. "Can you please describe her?"

This reply took longer.

Laura immediately grew tense. She reached up with her free hand and shakily pushed thick strands of black hair away from her face.

When the voice stopped, Laura said in an unsteady voice, "D-Did she say how she knows Bill?"

Another long reply.

"Please, *please* do me a favor. Ask her to stay there until I can get there, okay? I *really* need to talk to her. I mean, this is very, *very* important!"

A short reply.

Laura jumped up and looked down at herself. She shook her head and groaned angrily. She

241

brought the phone up to her ear. "I can be there in…in fifteen, maybe twenty minutes."

Another short reply.

"Yes. Thank you *so* much. If she asks, please tell her who I am. I need to speak with her. Tell her I'm on my way." Laura dropped the phone, picked up one of her suitcases, and ran down the hall to the bedroom, carrying it as if it weighed nothing. She tossed it on the bed, flipped it open, and frantically grabbed some clothes.

***

Bill sat in the back seat of Laura's silver Challenger as she tore down the highway at nearly double the speed limit.

Judging by how she was driving, he feared she would either be pulled over by a cop or kill herself slamming into someone.

He edged forward, until his face was only inches from the back of her head. He didn't think she'd hear him, but he knew he had to try anyway. "Babe, you'd better tone it down a tad. The cops'll pull you over in a heartbeat. Or some moron who's had a little too much to drink will do something stupid at the perfect time. Slow down, Laurie. Don't worry, we'll get there."

He wanted to drop his jaw when she suddenly eased off the gas.

He sighed in relief. Then, as he sat back in the seat, he realized what was about to happen.

Laura was on her way to the hospital to meet Miranda.

The thought of it brought chills to his spiritual form.

242

She's on her way to meet Miranda.

No matter what he made of this, he feared it wouldn't turn out well. Laura was extremely upset and would ask all sorts of personal questions. This would freak out Miranda, who had no idea who Bill really was.

His mind went berserk with insane images. Why was Miranda there in the first place? Was it to look in on him? Why would she even want to? She had no idea who Bill was. Hell, they'd seen each other just a couple of times, and under very strange circumstances. All she knew about him was that he fainted a lot and mentioned something about knowing her mother—which could confuse Laura, causing her to ask even more irritating questions.

This was *not* happening. This was just *not* happening.

I've got to do something about this, he told himself. *I've got to prevent the two women from meeting one another.*

But how could he?

And even if he could, what would it accomplish?

Wouldn't it make things even worse?

Fix this, Sam had told him. And so had Laura.

Fixing things did not seem possible if you did something to mess them up even worse, did it?

He wanted to scream, but he was no longer in his body. He couldn't do much of anything right now. The only thing that seemed to be working was his brain, and he wasn't even sure if that was functioning to his advantage.

The only thing he could do was follow Laura inside and watch what was left of his existence crumble before his very eyes.

He just hoped it wouldn't be as bad as he feared it might be.

***

Miranda, looking nervous and confused, was watching her from the doorway of the Waiting Room.

As Bill followed Laura down the hall, he felt like a man on his way to the gallows.

Miranda was wearing a long-sleeve silk shirt, gray knit slacks, and open-toed sandals with two-inch heels. Her hair was brushed back; her makeup looked fresh. She had obviously come directly from work.

Laura approached her and smiled. "Are you Miranda?"

"Yes…" Miranda smiled uneasily.

"I'm Laura Winston. Thank you for waiting. I hope I didn't inconvenience you."

Miranda shrugged. "No problem. Please tell me what this is all about."

"I will, but if you don't mind, I'd like you to tell me why you're here."

Another nod.

"Why don't we sit down?" Laura gestured to the room behind them. "This might take a little while."

"Really?" Miranda asked softly.

"It's very important."

They went over to the couch on the opposite side of the room. No one else was in the room.

Miranda sat near the far end while Laura sat in the middle, facing her. Both looked uncomfortable and nervous.

"Do you know Bill?" Laura asked.

Miranda shook her head. "Not really. I met him at a bar on the Trail. The Lantern. Before that, I saw him in the lobby of the building where I work on East Robinson. The Centre Building. He'd just fainted, and I ran over and—"

"I remember. You mentioned the bar. Can you please tell me about that?"

"Can I ask *you* a question?"

"Of course."

"Are you his wife?"

Laura smiled. "No. Bill and I live together."

Miranda nodded.

"Now…what happened at the bar?"

Miranda sat forward and rested her forearms on her thighs. "It was the strangest thing. I was with this guy I've been seeing. He plays the keyboard for the band, Mellow Mood, and when they're performing locally, I go there and spend about an hour or so with them. They're really nice guys—for musicians." She laughed. "I knew some musicians when I was in high school, and they were real jerks. But not these guys. Anyway, I was there with them, and when I turned around, I saw Bill sitting by himself at a table, watching me. I didn't recognize him at first, then I remembered him, so I went over to see if he was the same guy."

"Okay…"

"We started talking, and I knew right off that he was very nice. He is, you know. I know a lot of assholes out there, excuse my French."

Laura smiled. "Yes. He is. He's one of the good guys."

Bill just sighed.

"Anyway, I could tell something was on his mind. It was the way he kept staring at me. It wasn't one of those, you know, pervo things. He didn't seem that kind of guy. He told me that I looked really familiar to him, and that's when I knew why he'd been staring at me like he was."

"What else did he say?"

Miranda paused for a moment. "That was the strange thing. He said I looked like someone he once knew."

"Did he say who it was?"

"No, but when he said that, I told him I get that a lot. And I do, I really do. Everyone tells me I look like my mother, and that's what I told him."

"Your...m-*mother*?" Laura sat back and paled.

Bill cringed.

"Are you okay?" Miranda's eyes grew.

Laura didn't respond. She seemed to be struggling to pull herself together.

My God, Bill thought uneasily. *She knows about it now. She knows about everything now.*

"Laura?"

Laura remained silent. She was obviously struggling. Trying to figure things out. To decide what to say, how to say it. After a while, she took a deep breath and let it back out slowly.

"Something I said?" Miranda asked.

Laura forced a smile. "Just a little lightheadedness. I'm fine now."

"You're sure?"

Laura nodded.

"You looked just like Bill did when—"

"Please go on with your story."

Miranda took a breath. "This is when things got *seriously* freaky. As I just said, Bill looked like he'd just seen a ghost when I told him about my mom. And when I told him that she died when I was just a year old, he looked just like he did when he fainted in the lobby of the Centre Building. I asked him if he was okay, but he didn't say anything."

Laura grew quiet again.

When nearly a minute had passed, Miranda said, "Are you gonna tell me what this is all about?"

Laura nodded. "Just tell me one other thing first, okay?"

"All right…"

"Why are you here?"

Miranda didn't speak right off. A strange expression had taken over her face, giving Laura the impression that she was lost in her own thoughts. Then she pulled herself out of it. "A couple of hours ago, I was in the Centre Building, getting in the elevator. And when I got in, that same guy was in there already. He was the guy who'd helped Bill that time he fainted in the lobby."

"That was Steve. He's a mutual friend."

"Anyway, I asked him how Bill had been doing, and he said that he'd had an accident and was rushed to ORMC."

"Really? He *told* you?"

247

"He sure did."

"And *that's* why you're here?"

"That's the weird part of all of this. I felt bad for him, but I didn't know if I should come here to see how he was doing. I'm not working with him or anything, and he doesn't really know me. It's not like we're family or anything, is it?"

Laura didn't reply.

"Weird, huh?"

Laura nodded. "That *is* weird, your meeting up with Steve."

"The weird thing was that even though I didn't think I should come here, something inside me kept telling me I should. I was curious, for one thing, and worried. As I told you, he's a super nice guy, and I like him."

Laura was smiling again. "I like him, too."

Bill wanted to take her in his arms.

Miranda blinked. She suddenly looked embarrassed. "I hope you don't think...that is, I don't have any ulterior motives or anything—"

"It's all right. I don't think that at all."

Bill smiled. It was Sam. He had no idea what she'd done or how she'd done it, he just knew that all this was because of her.

"Doesn't that sound crazy to you?" Miranda asked. "You don't think I'm crazy, do you?"

After a few moments, Laura smiled. "To your first question? Yes. To your second? Definitely not."

Miranda shook her head. "It sure was creepy, though..."

"Miranda, may I ask you a personal question?"

248

"As long as it's not *too* personal…"

"How did your mom die?"

"She was going out to the garage, probably to drive to the store, when she tripped and fell on the concrete. She hit her head so hard that she had a brain bleed, and by the time the guy she was living with came home and found her, she was already gone."

"She…hit her head?"

"On the concrete. Why? Is there something—"

"Miranda, may I ask you another personal question?"

"Okay, but I gotta say this is getting really freaky."

"I know, but this is necessary, believe me."

"Okay, then."

"Who raised you?"

"My Aunt Eileen. She's my mom's older sister. She works at Disney. Valet Services. She—"

"Did she happen to tell you anything about your father?"

Miranda sighed. "Whenever I brought it up, she always changed the subject. I kinda got the idea that she didn't think he was very nice. Like I said, she didn't say much about him, and I sorta figured that she didn't want him around. My guess is that he probably hit on her. Back then, everyone was. At least, that's what she kept telling people. It could be true, though. She's been married four times, you know."

"I didn't know."

Miranda smiled and lowered her voice. "To tell you the truth, I kinda think she made up a bunch of stuff. I mean, she was pretty hot when she was young. Growing up, I saw slews of pictures of herself on the walls. But she wasn't nice at all. She's got this awful temper, and when she's pissed, she gets shrieky, and you've gotta cover your ears. She was nice to me and all, but she always seemed to be in a bad mood. Know people like that?"

"Unfortunately."

"They bring everyone down, don't they?"

"They tend to."

Miranda went quiet and watched Laura, who continued sitting there, looking down at her hands.

Bill could tell there was something she wanted to say. He only hoped she wouldn't say what he thought she would.

It was Miranda who broke the silence. "Is that all you wanted to know? I mean, I don't know him or anything, but like I said, he's a super nice guy, and I hope he comes outa this okay. I feel strange being here. Something like this has never happened to me before, and—"

"Miranda, I think there's something you should know."

Oh my God… Bill could feel his spirit form shaking.

"About what?"

Laura sighed deeply. "It's about how your mom died, and—"

"Whaddya mean? Are you trying to tell me—"

"I'm trying to tell you what really happened to your mom."

Miranda's eyes narrowed. "How would *you* know? And what's *really* happening? And why do I feel so strange? This is really—"

Bill didn't hear the rest.

The warm blackness came from out of nowhere. He closed his eyes and surrendered to the pleasant sensations.

The warmth quickly subsided, and the darkness drifted away.

He opened his eyes.

He was lying in a hospital bed.

Chapter 23

A blond nurse was checking his monitors.

"Welcome back!" The nurse noticed that he was awake and smiled brightly.

Confusion set in. Last he remembered, he was getting drunk at a dive on the Trail. He had just left the bar and was about to get into the BMW. He couldn't remember where he'd intended to go, just that he was in a hurry to leave the bar. But as soon as he squeezed between the BMW and another parked vehicle, he slipped on something, lost his footing, and tripped, whacking his head on something hard.

That was about it—except for the fact that he vaguely recalled that he'd been drinking because he was depressed.

And that he'd seen movement somewhere on his left the moment he tripped.

He couldn't remember how many drinks he'd had. Was it three? Four?

Why so many?

How depressed was he? He couldn't remember. He couldn't even remember where he was before he'd driven to the bar. He vaguely recalled talking to someone earlier. Someone important.

They were talking about Sam.

The moment it started coming back, the image of a face blipped in his head before vanishing into the darkness.

Then he remembered.

252

The man had been living with Sam when she died. He'd been the one who found Sam. He'd found her on the concrete slab, lying on her back, blood from her skull staining the concrete. Her blood and—

His hammer.

The hammer he had tossed onto the roof of the duplex. The hammer he was using when Sam confronted him about something that had made him angry enough to toss it before walking out of her life.

What was the argument about?

He couldn't remember that, either. All that registered was what Donnie Falco had told him.

"There was a hammer lyin' there on the slab, about three feet from her head."

Was I the one responsible for Sam's accident? Had the hammer come down off the roof when she—

No. It *didn't* happen that way. Not at all.

How did he know?

He wasn't sure; he just knew. At that moment, a strange dialog started up in his head, and he realized that he had had a dream about Sam. But then he began wondering about it. Wondering and believing it. Believing it because it didn't *feel* like a dream.

No. *Not* a dream. It felt more like a sort of meeting in a different place.

They'd found each other in another place. In another world. And once they'd found one another, Sam told him what had really happened to her.

"The concrete slab killed me."

253

Falco had killed Sam. He hadn't meant to—it just happened. Sam had mentioned something about an argument. And how Falco often lost his temper. And how he'd been hitting on her. But Sam hadn't wanted him and told him so. This made Falco angry. Very angry. He wasn't thinking clearly. Push literally came to shove, and Sam went down, hit her head hard on the concrete, and died.

It hadn't been my fault at all.

All this time he thought he'd been the one responsible, but it hadn't been—not at all.

He'd tossed the hammer, but it hadn't killed Sam. It took another man to do that.

Somehow, this didn't change what he wanted changed, and he found that he had mixed feelings about the whole thing. He'd walked away from a woman he'd once loved, not knowing that the woman was bearing his child.

Fate had intervened, showing him the young woman who had been the product of the love he had shared with Sam…

Just then, he noticed two figures standing at the foot of the bed.

Groaning with the effort, he raised his head just a few inches.

"No sudden moves." The nurse frowned, adjusting his pillow. "Not yet. You've been immobile. You need time to let your body accustom itself to—"

"I have to see…" His voice was weak—a mere whisper.

"Just give it time."

He raised his head another inch. And groaned.

254

Laura and Miranda stood beside one another, watching him.

Laura, the woman who had walked out on him.

Miranda, the young woman who was his daughter.

Oh my God...

They knew. He could tell by their expressions that they knew what had happened.

He wanted to freak.

Laura suddenly hurried over and bent over the side of the bed. She kissed him gently on the mouth and very carefully touched the bandages covering his forehead. Tears filled her eyes. She was obviously very happy. "You're...you're back?"

"How long...was I out?"

Laura turned to the nurse, who said, "About twenty-eight hours."

"Damn. What...happened?"

Laura blinked in confusion. "You...don't know?"

"I...hit my head. Didn't I?"

"That's *it*?"

"All I can remember..."

"Nothing else?"

He groaned weakly. "A bar? Too many drinks?"

She shook her head. "Nothing more than that?"

He lay back and sighed. His eyes closed even before he'd realized it.

He heard the nurse say, "I'm afraid he's exhausted. You'll have to let him rest."

"Just a moment. Please?" Laura's soft voice.

The nurse didn't reply.

"Honey?" Her voice had grown much closer. "You don't remember anything else?"

Her voice began drifting away.

"Miranda. Do you remember Miranda?" Laura's voice sounded very far away.

The nurse said something, but he couldn't make it out.

Laura's voice: "Bill? Can...ear...e..."

The darkness thickened, and its warmth comforted him.

***

Sam was floating right above him as he lay comfortably within the warm, soft cloud. She appeared just as she did before—except for a hazy bright light hovering around her.

"What happened?" he asked. "Where am I?"

"You're in my neck of the woods now." A smile.

Had he died? Had she brought him here?

"I didn't bring you here, Bill. You're not dead."

"How'd I get here, then? And why *am* I here?"

"I fixed things for you."

"You what?"

"You couldn't do it yourself, so I did it for you." She laughed. "I did it pretty well, if I say so myself."

The way she'd said it made him suspicious. But he had no idea what she was talking about, and this frightened him. It frightened him even more than not knowing where he was. "You did *what* pretty well?"

"You'll see."

"I'll see what?"

She just smiled.

"Sam, this is *not* the time to be cute."

"Oh, I think it's the perfect time." She was still smiling.

He cringed at her statement. His rage at Falco returned hotly.

"You're blaming yourself again, aren't you?"

He made no comment. Even in this other place, Sam could read him very well.

She was no longer smiling. "I don't want you doing this, Bill. I don't blame you for my accident."

"But it was my hammer that caused all this. If I hadn't—"

"You didn't toss it up there so it would come back down and kill me, did you?"

"Of course not."

"Why not?"

"Why would I want to kill you? I loved you. I was angry. I was angry at you, your family—everyone. But I still loved you."

"I loved you, too."

"If only I hadn't walked away…"

"Even so, it wasn't your fault."

"Would you believe that I haven't tossed or punched anything since that day?"

"I'm sure it was a wakeup call."

"It cost too damned much. It cost me you…and our future together."

"Let it go, Bill."

"I don't think I can."

"You have to."

"I don't think I *want* to."

"What about Laura?"

257

"What about her?"

"Do you love her?"

He hesitated.

"C'mon, now. You can say it."

"Well…yes…"

"Laura's the first girl you've had a serious relationship with since you and I hooked up. You realize that, don't you?"

He didn't reply. He hadn't thought of that, but the moment Sam had said it, he knew she was right.

"Let it go, Bill. If not for you, do it for Laura. She's a wonderful girl. You two make a great couple. You're terrific together."

"We were a great couple, too."

"We were. Once. A long time ago."

"Until…"

"Until we weren't. And now I'm dead and you're still alive. Know what that means?"

He didn't reply.

"You've got the rest of yours to live. That's thirty, maybe forty years. You'd better do it with her. Otherwise, you'll regret it."

"She really is special."

"She really is, Bill."

"But…what about you?"

"What about me? I'm dead."

"I meant—"

"I know what you meant. You've got a terrific gal waiting for you. She loves you just as I did and still would have, had I lived long enough. Don't forget: the two of us made a beautiful baby together. Now she's all grown up, and she's a beauty."

"A beauty I didn't even know about."

"Thank Eileen for that."

"If I could, I don't think I would."

"Forget her, Bill. Concentrate on Laura. And make sure Miranda knows who you are."

"What should I tell her?"

"Tell her whatever's in your heart."

"I'd like to tell her about you. About us."

"That would be nice. But be sure you're subtle about it."

"Whaddya mean?"

A pause. "Don't tell her *too* much of the good stuff when Laura's around. She just might get a little jealous."

He smiled. "When will I see you again?"

"When it's your time, I'll be here."

"I'll miss you, Sam..."

"I'll look in on you from time to time. But you won't see or hear me. You won't even know I'm there."

"Not at all?"

She shook her head. "It's not how that works."

He sighed. "I understand."

"Do you?"

"I'm pretty sure."

"Good." The haziness surrounding her dimmed. "Before I go, remind me what you're supposed to do."

He hesitated.

"Let it go, Bill. Live your life. With Laura. And forget about me."

"Never."

"Oh, you will."

"I don't think so..."

259

"I do."

"Sam…"

"I *am* serious, Bill."

"I know. I just don't think—"

"Go to her. Let it go. Live your life."

The haziness dimmed even more. Sam began fading. "One last thing."

"What's that?"

"Include Miranda in your life."

"I wouldn't know how to go about it."

Clouds appeared, hovering around her. "Learn, Bill. You've got to. She's yours. She'll always be. Never forget that."

"But—"

"No buts. Just do it. And when it's time, we'll see one another again."

"I'd love that."

"So will I."

"And you know something else?"

"What's that?"

"I'll never be able to love Laura completely because there will always be that tiny place in my heart where you'll always be."

"I love you, too, Bill. Now and forever."

He felt the tears gathering warmly in his eyes. "I'll be seeing you again one day, Sam."

No reply.

The clouds had swallowed her up.

Chapter 24

Laura was sitting at the round table near the window, reading a magazine when Bill awoke again.

The bright Florida sun was struggling to come into the room, but the heavily tinted window permitted only a soft, golden haze.

"Laurie?" His voice was weak. A mere whisper.

She jumped up, rushed right over, and bent to kiss him. Then stopped. She looked frightened. "Baby? You've been…*crying*?"

Crying? He'd been crying?

He fought to remember.

Last he recalled, they were asking him if he remembered what had happened to him.

He'd apparently been crying…

He had no idea what she was talking about. But it had to be true. His cheeks felt damp, and his wet eyes had made everything blurry.

What had upset him so much?

A dream?

What else could have caused such a reaction?

"Are you all right, baby?" She grabbed his hand and held it, gently massaging his wrist and forearm. Her thick black hair hung down, swaying just inches from his face. He wanted to reach out and touch it. He also wanted to reach out and put his hand around the back of her neck so he could pull her face down and kiss her.

261

His arms felt incredibly heavy. He barely had the strength to reach across his chest and rest his other hand on hers.

"I think so…" He tried smiling but it was quite an effort. His facial muscles also felt like lead.

"Are you sure?"

"My forehead and cheek hurt, but I think I can make it. Why am I here?"

"Baby, you had an accident."

It took him a few moments to remember. Then he shook himself and tried focusing on Laura.

"Is any of it coming back yet?" she asked.

"Slowly."

"I would like to know why you were crying. Bad dream?"

"I wish I could remember." A flash of Sam blipped in his head, but this didn't cause him concern because he'd dreamed of her so many times before. He also suspected that she might have been talking to him, but he could not remember the details.

"You're telling me your mind's a blank?"

"Feels like it…"

She sighed. "Well, whatever it was must have been a doozy. If it was a nightmare, I'd understand. Every time I ever had one, I blocked it out right after I woke up."

Another flash of Sam flared up. In this one, she was smiling at him.

The image revitalized him, and before he realized it, he'd propped himself up on the pillow. "I don't think it was a nightmare…"

"But if you can't remember anything about—"

262

"Sam was in it."

Laura went silent.

"She was smiling at me."

Laura sighed and pushed some hair away from her face. "You miss her, don't you?"

He wanted to slap himself when he realized what he'd just did.

"Baby, this has nothing to do with you and me."

"You're obviously not seeing this from my perspective."

"I know, and I'm sorry. But I just can't close my mind on my very first love."

"What about ours?"

"I wouldn't trade what we've got for anything."

"You're sure?"

"Absolutely positive."

She touched his cheek. "I really needed to hear you say that."

"If you want to know the truth, the one thing that I just can't let go of is my guilt. If I hadn't tossed that damned hammer…"

Laura gave him a blank look.

It made him wonder if he had told her that part of the story.

"The one I tossed on the roof."

Laura sighed. "You can't change the past, baby. Whatever you did is over and done with. Twenty years have gone by. You've got to let it go."

"I wish I could."

"I think you should."

"It tore our relationship apart, and she was forced to face childbirth all by herself—"

263

"Baby, it doesn't matter. Not anymore."

"How can you say that?"

"Because of what I've learned in life."

"What have you learned that'll justify any of this?"

"It's the cause and effect thing. The fact that what happens whenever you do or don't do something."

He groaned. "My mind must really be messed up, because I can't understand what you're trying to say."

"Here's my take in a nutshell. Whatever you did or did not do brought you to me, and if you could possibly go back, the slightest change would take both of us somewhere else."

"That makes sense, I guess..."

"It's the only thing that should matter, really."

"But what about Miranda? Because of me and what I did, she was dealt a bad hand, and—"

"She still managed to turn out okay, didn't she?"

"I honestly don't know."

"You've talked to her. She seemed just fine, didn't she?"

"Maybe…"

"She's got a nice job, her own car, and her own apartment. She's reasonably happy, gets along with people, knows how to dress and present herself, can speak intelligently, and she doesn't seem to have any mental disabilities or hangups."

"She grew up without a father."

"From what she told me, Eileen's husband treated her pretty well while she was in his care."

"Tell me something, Laurie."

"What's that?"

"Did you tell her about me?"

"What about you?"

"Don't be silly, now. You know what I mean. Did you tell her I was her father?"

She shrugged. "I figured you'd want to do that yourself."

"You figured right—except for one small detail."

"What's that?"

"I don't think I can."

"Why not?"

"Because I'm scared to death."

"I can see how you'd feel that way, but you really shouldn't."

"What if she hates me? Or worse, what if she says she doesn't believe me? Or asks where I've been all her life? Or believes every damned lie Eileen told her and wants me dead? Or—"

"What if none of that happens?"

"I wouldn't blame her if she hated me just a little…"

"You're much too hard on yourself."

"I don't think I'm hard enough on myself."

"I do."

"You only say that because you have to."

She raised a brow. "Why do I have to?"

"Because you're my only ally and you love me, and don't want me wandering off again and acting even dumber than before."

"That's not true and you know it."

265

"You're saying you *don't* love me? Or that you *do* want me wandering off—"

She groaned. "Don't be ridiculous. You know what I mean. As I've said, you're much too hard on yourself, and I honestly think that if you told her the truth, she'd probably forgive you."

"You really think so?"

"Yes. I really do."

"I do, too," said the voice coming from the direction of the hall.

Miranda was standing at the doorway.

He cringed at the sight. At first, he thought he was looking at Sam, but as his thoughts cleared, he knew better. It was Miranda. His daughter. The beautiful young woman he had made with Sam but had no knowledge of until very recently.

She was watching him from the doorway. Watching him with those big blue eyes. Eyes the same size…and shape…and color…as her mother's. It could have been Sam out there, but as his mind struggled to maintain common sense at all costs, he realized that it wasn't.

It was Miranda, and she'd just said something he could not believe.

"*I do, too.*"

Had she meant that? Or had his imagination swooped in at that precise moment to give him some much-needed relief?

"Miranda?" His voice had become a weak whisper.

She continued gazing at him. He could see curiosity in her eyes. And confusion. And a few other things he never expected.

But the one thing he did *not* see was hatred…and this was what baffled him.

His eyelids began getting heavy. Sleep was approaching, and he found that he was much too weak to fight it any longer.

Miranda suddenly smiled. "Dad?"

Warm tears gathered in his eyes.

She entered the room and came closer to the bed. Her eyes glistened in the harsh lighting.

His thoughts swam with wild images. His eyelids had nearly closed, but he fought to stay alert. He had to tell her things. All sorts of things. She needed to know why he'd left. Why her mother no longer wanted him around. She had to know why he'd felt that he had no choice but to leave.

Most of all, she needed to know why he hadn't come back…why he hadn't thought…

If I'd only known, Miranda…I wouldn't have…I wouldn't…

I hadn't known…

Your mother…she didn't tell me… I had no idea. None. If only…if only I had…

"Miranda…"

"Dad?"

"I didn't know…"

The darkness drew closer.

"Know what, Dad?"

"Miranda…can you…will you please…forgive me?"

"Dad—"

"I didn't…she didn't tell me…I was…"

The darkness…so overwhelming…

267

The room…the bed…everything began moving around in different directions.

"Bill?" Laura's voice sounded far away.

Unconsciousness came quickly.

***

Laura was standing over near the tinted window when he awoke, but there was no sign of Miranda.

He tried sitting up but discovered that he was much too weak.

Laura came right over. "Feeling any better?"

He tried to speak, but his voice had decided to hide somewhere in his throat. He could only manage a slight whisper. "Miranda?"

"She had to get back to the office, babe."

"So soon?"

Laura laughed. "Silly boy. You've been sleeping for twenty-four hours."

Twenty-four hours gone.

"Really?" It felt like just a couple of minutes.

"Really."

He lay back and tried to remember what had happened before sleep had ambushed him. What he'd said to Miranda. What she'd said to him. Her voice, her expressions.

For some reason, his memory had decided to do tricks on him again, creating lapses and solid walls of darkness.

However, something very important and wonderful still managed to penetrate his consciousness.

"She doesn't hate me…at all."

"As a matter of fact, she told me she likes you."

"She actually *said* that?"

268

Laura nodded.

"You think she'll come back?"

"Don't worry, babe. She said she'll be back as soon as she can."

"I hope so…"

"I don't think she would've said that if she didn't mean it. Besides, she needs to talk to you. She wants to ask all sorts of questions."

"Questions?" It made his pulse skip a beat.

"Of course. She wants to know things. All sorts of things. Things about you and her mother. She's curious, babe. And you need to tell her."

"What do I tell her?"

"Tell her whatever's in your heart."

Sam's voice again… Or was it just his imagination?

"Tell her whatever she wants to know," Laura said.

"Everything?"

Laura nodded. "If she wants to know everything…"

"I honestly don't know…" He began trembling.

"Don't worry, babe. She's tough. You can tell her what she needs to know."

"I hope I can."

"I know you can."

"How can you possibly know that?"

She bent and kissed him lightly on the lips. "For one very important reason. I know *you*."

Chapter 25

Three days later, after Bill was discharged from the hospital, Miranda came over to their condo on that bright Saturday morning.

Bill and Laura were sitting at the kitchen table, having a late breakfast. Aside from occasional headaches and some spasms in his neck and back, he was feeling relatively fine, but still weak. The brokerage had agreed to let him have some time off, and since he hadn't taken a vacation in the last three years, they told him to come back when he felt well enough to handle his client workload.

However, his health had quickly taken a backseat to the main issue. Miranda had become a major item in his life, and he was determined to right as many of the wrongs he had done by forcing her to grow up without a father.

He still couldn't believe how well things had turned out. Miranda had taken to him very quickly and didn't seem to harbor any ill feelings toward him. Although he knew he couldn't properly justify his absence from her childhood, he did manage to tell her what had happened to cause him to leave.

Miranda understood the emotional turmoil he'd been experiencing and told him that even though she had always wondered about him, she always suspected that there was much more to the story than what Aunt Eileen had told her.

Miranda poured a cup of coffee from the coffeemaker. When she sat down at the kitchen table, Bill experienced a strange feeling of exultation. And as he gazed into Miranda's eyes, he sensed yet again a strong feeling that Sam's spirit lived in their daughter. He even suspected that if Sam were still alive, she would approve of how things turned out.

"Would you like some breakfast? Laura asked.

"No, thanks." Miranda carefully made sure the sugar in the teaspoon was level—just as Sam had always done.

Bill forced himself not to freak.

"Something wrong, Dad?"

He smiled. "Everything's just fine."

Laura got up and took the breakfast dishes to the sink. "I hope you two don't mind, but I need to get some shopping done. I'll only be an hour or so. Then we can visit—that is, if you haven't got any other plans." She smiled at Miranda.

"No. Actually, I wanted to talk to Dad about something that's been bothering me. I hope you don't mind."

"I certainly don't." Laura turned on the tap and started doing the dishes.

Bill could tell something was on her mind. In a soft voice, he said, "Is this about…your mom?"

"Among other things."

"You got the time?"

"I've got all day."

"Hope I have the answers you're looking for."

Miranda had a sip of coffee. "I hope so, too."

He could tell she was nervous. The way she was staring at her coffee cup told him she was struggling for the right words.

"Miranda, you can talk to me."

She nodded but said nothing.

"I really wish you would."

She took a deep breath. "I'd really like to know what happened to my mom."

***

Miranda sat on the couch, deep in thought while staring at Bill.

"You okay?" she finally asked. "You look kinda funny."

"Funny how?"

She tilted her head. "Not funny ha-ha, funny—"

"Funny weird?"

She nodded.

He sighed. "You took me back."

"Back?"

"I just went back there."

"Where?"

"Twenty years."

She blinked. "You mean—"

"What I mean is, you look *so* much like her that…that—" He couldn't finish his statement, so he just shrugged.

"I get it."

"I kinda thought you would." He sat back in the chair.

"You really loved her, didn't you?"

He just smiled and felt the tears gathering.

"*Please* tell me…" She tilted her head. "I know you want to."

"Miranda, I loved your mother more than anything." He fought off the tears. This wasn't exactly the right time. "A giant chunk of my heart

272

stayed with her when I walked away. I honestly believe she grabbed it and held on to it with a death grip, and when she died she took it with her, and I haven't been the same since."

Miranda's eyes were beginning to tear up as well, but she sniffed them back. "I'm sorry things messed up."

"You have no idea how badly I feel about everything."

"I think I do."

"Really?"

"I can see it in your eyes."

He picked up his coffee cup.

"So…tell me what happened."

He started to talk, but she interrupted him. "Before you say anything, first let me tell you what Aunt Eileen told me."

He wanted to cringe at the woman's name. A strange icy feeling crept up his spine, but he managed to ignore it. As much as he hated the woman, he realized that now was the time he should know for sure what Eileen had told Miranda.

"All right," he said. "Let 'er rip."

"First of all, I have to tell you what I think of my aunt. She raised me and took care of me and did all the things I know my mom would have done if she'd been alive, but I really didn't trust her, and even though I loved her when I was little, I found that by the time I was ten or twelve, I really didn't like her very much."

"Really?"

"Yes." Her eyes had suddenly become cold.

"May I ask what changed your opinion?"

273

"The way she talked to people—especially when she was in a bad mood. The way she treated Jack, her husband—especially when he disagreed with her. She was always moody, and whenever someone asked how she was doing, she always told them she was "a little under the weather." I caught her lying to people all the time, and I can't count the number of times she told me things about people that would curl your hair—and these were people she told me she *liked*."

He knew right then that he'd been right about Eileen from the first time he'd met her. This made him feel guilty once again for forcing his beautiful daughter to be brought up by such a heartless bitch.

"So, what did she tell you about me?"

Miranda reddened. He could tell she didn't want to say anything.

"You can tell me."

"She referred to you as "the jerk." You treated both her and my mother like shit, and she couldn't even stand to be around you."

"Did you believe her?"

"No."

"Why not?"

"Mostly because of how she was. How she lied to people. How she always seemed pissed off about something."

"You based your opinion of me on her actions, then?"

"Like I said, mostly."

"What else?"

She hesitated.

"Tell me, Miranda."

"You won't think I'm weird?"

"I won't think you're weird."

"But this...this isn't something I can tell people...without them thinking I'm—"

"You can tell me."

She stared at him again, then nodded. "I really think I can."

"Then tell me."

"I've always had this strong feeling about you and my mom. What you said before? About loving her so much?"

"Yes..."

"I've always felt that she loved you just as much."

He felt more tears gathering.

"It's always felt like she's been in the back of my head, telling me things—even when I was living with Aunt Eileen."

"And you think this is weird?"

"I think other people will."

"Would you like to know my opinion of what others think?"

"I really would."

"Opinions are like assholes. Everyone's got one."

Miranda laughed.

***

Later, after Laura returned from shopping and began preparing dinner, Bill and Miranda sat out in the backyard, where butterflies frolicked in Laura's flower garden.

It wasn't long at all before Miranda repeated her question.

"What really happened to my mom?"

"You never told me what your aunt said about it," he replied curiously.

"Aunt Eileen said you caused it somehow, but whenever I asked her more about it, she changed the subject and we never seemed to get back to it. Instead, she started going on and on about the squabble you had with my grandfather. So, going by what she told me, you not only killed my mother, but you also gave my grandfather a fatal heart attack as well."

He couldn't help smiling.

"It's all bullshit, isn't it?"

"Basically."

She raised a brow. "Basically?"

"I blamed myself for your grandfather's death, too. For the longest time."

"What about right now?"

"Not really, but sometimes I do…"

"You're gonna have to explain that one."

"We were all on fairly good terms until one day, when your grandfather came to see us just a few months after your mother and I moved into a duplex apartment just off South Conway." Not knowing how to keep going, he stopped and tried to think of a delicate way of telling her the rest of the story.

"What happened?"

He suddenly found that he was afraid of what he should say.

Miranda watched him closely. She sat with her legs crossed, her hands in her lap. "We're baring our souls, aren't we?" she finally asked.

"I guess we are."

"Don't you think I deserve to know?"

"Well, you *are* twenty-one, aren't you?"

She reddened. "Are we getting into an adult theme here?"

He couldn't help it; he laughed.

She turned serious. "Dad, I really need to know."

He shifted uncomfortably in the chair. He'd never in his wildest dreams thought that he'd be telling his own daughter what he and her mother were doing that lovely but fateful afternoon. For one thing, he never thought he'd ever have a daughter. For another, he'd never visualized such a strange scenario. "He saw us doing some really wild things in the backseat of my Camaro when he came to the house unannounced."

Miranda's eyes grew. "Wild?"

"Very." He couldn't help smiling at the memory.

Miranda covered her mouth with her hand. She sat very still, gawking at him. Then she lowered her hand. "You mean—"

He nodded.

"You're saying that my grandfather saw my mom slapping boots with my dad? In the backseat of a *car*?"

"Actually, no boots were involved, but you've basically got the picture."

She shook her head and laughed. "Go, Mom!"

"She did. Believe me." He couldn't help smiling.

Still smiling, Miranda went silent.

"What are you thinking?"

She chuckled again. "I'm not thinking, I'm visualizing."

Suddenly embarrassed, he had more coffee and shifted his thoughts to the rest of the story. "And from that day on, that man never spoke to your mother and never had anything good to say about me."

"Really? Just because he saw the two of you—" He nodded.

"But you and Mom…you were in love…"

"It didn't matter. He always treated your mother as his little princess and couldn't accept it when he saw her acting like—"

"Someone in love?"

"That's a polite way of putting it."

Scowling, Miranda shook her head. "That really sucks."

"It devastated your mom. Before that, they'd been very close. I destroyed their relationship."

Miranda went silent again. Moments later, she said, "So tell me what happened to you."

"You mean after I trashed their relationship?"

"No. What happened to put you in a coma?"

He sat back and thought about what he should say. It didn't take him long at all. He suspected it was because he'd been thinking about it ever since Miranda had come to the hospital. "Do you remember when we saw each other at the Lantern that one night?"

"Vividly."

"And do you remember when you told me about your mother?"

278

"This was right after you told me that I reminded you of someone you knew."

"Then you told me her name."

Her eyes grew. "*That's* what happened! And *that's* why you went all freaky!"

"Exactly."

"I *knew* something totally weird was going on! It was just so strange, your reaction and all. At first it made me wonder about you, but you seemed so cool and all, I didn't *think* you were a fruitcake... I guess that's when I was convinced something seriously strange was going on."

"Well, when you told me that your mom was Samantha and that you didn't know her because she died when you were a year old, an avalanche of events came crashing down, and I knew that I needed to find out more about who you were."

"Let me guess... You went to see Aunt Eileen."

"Right again."

"I'll bet *that* went over really well."

"Not exactly."

"I was being facetious."

"I wasn't. She wanted to kill me."

"Sounds like her. So...what did she tell you?"

"For openers, she blamed me for your mom's death. Then she said that if she could have come up with proof, she would have had me arrested for your mom's murder."

"She really *is* a bitch, isn't she?"

"That's kind of a no-brainer. But anyway, she told me about this guy Donnie Falco, who was living with your mom not long after I left the scene."

Miranda sat up. "Aunt Eileen never told me about him..."

"Never?"

"She said my mom had sublet the duplex. Nothing else."

"Falco was a little more involved than that."

"You mean he was *involved* with my mom?"

"He wanted to be."

"What happened?"

Bill felt his pulse accelerating. The story was coming out again, but this time, it involved his daughter, and he knew he had to get everything out as clearly as possible.

"I had a talk with Falco just a few days ago. He told me what happened...and I actually believed him."

"Now you don't sound like you do."

He didn't respond right off. The blurry images that had been floating around in his head since his coma had come back. This time, however, they seemed less blurry. "I don't think I do anymore."

"What changed your mind?"

"I honestly don't know. All I do know is that ever since I came out of that coma, things feel different. *I* feel different."

"Different how?"

"As I just said, I no longer believe what Falco told me."

"What did he tell you?"

"How your mother died."

Miranda went silent for a moment. "Tell me what he said," she said finally.

He told her.

When he'd finished, she said, "What part of that don't you believe?"

"I don't believe that he found her lying on the concrete, bleeding from the back of her head."

"What do you think happened, then?"

"I believe Falco killed your mom."

Miranda gasped.

Laura came outside.

"You heard." He'd seen her standing in the archway.

"I heard."

"How do you know for sure?" Miranda asked.

"I don't."

"Then why do you think—"

"I don't know that, either. All I do know is that I've been feeling this way ever since I came out of that coma."

Laura came over and sat down beside Miranda. "You have no idea where this is coming from?" she asked him.

"Not exactly."

"Then how can you possibly—"

"I'm not sure," he said uneasily. "But some seriously strange ideas have been coming to me ever since I came out of that coma."

***

Later that night, as they lay in bed, Laura said, "Talk to me, baby."

She was lying on her right side, watching him intently. Her hair covered her left shoulder like a dark blanket. She was wearing her pink transparent nightie, which had always turned him on. But not now. Now wasn't the right time for sex.

281

Besides, he didn't think he could manage it.

Even if he could, he had too many other things on his mind.

There was something strange about the whole thing. When he was talking to Falco, it sounded like everything the man said

("I came home and there she was, lyin' on the cement slab...")

made sense.

Since his coma, however, certain things just didn't seem legit.

"All I could do was stare at the bloodstain on the slab."

"I cleaned up the slab a little."

He tried to recall Falco's expression during his explanations. The man sounded upset, but something in his demeanor revealed a kind of deception Bill hadn't noticed at the time. Something about how he'd phrased certain things. It was something Bill couldn't exactly pin down.

Not then, anyway.

However, since his coma, Bill couldn't help noticing certain things he could only view as suspect.

"I hosed down the blood first...it was really freakin' me out, so..."

As he replayed the conversation in his head, he realized that everything Falco had said sounded as if he knew beforehand what he would be asked. As if the last couple of decades had done absolutely nothing to dull the memory.

Despite a span of so many years, Falco had forgotten nothing about Sam's death.

"Then I picked up the hammer…"

"Bill?" Laura was waiting.

He pulled himself out of his mental turmoil and forced himself to pay attention to the woman lying beside him.

"Your explanation," she said. "I'd like to hear it."

"Which one? I've got a lot of things going on up there right now."

"I'd like you to start with what you said about Samantha being murdered by that guy Falco. And especially what you meant when you mentioned those strange ideas."

He lay back and stared at the darkness of the ceiling.

He would have to proceed with his suspicions very carefully. He didn't want to alarm Laura and he sure as hell didn't want her to think he was losing his mind. But he couldn't ignore the fact that he was almost certain he had somehow communicated with Sam while he'd been in the coma. He had no evidence of this and he certainly had no way of proving any of it. All he knew was that strange images about Sam's death had been coming to him ever since he'd awakened in the hospital bed.

"Miranda seems just as skeptical as I do about what you told us," Laura said. "I'm sure you'll agree that when she left, she was kind of perplexed about the whole thing."

Miranda had been very quiet while she helped Laura with the dirty dishes. Although the rest of the evening had been relatively pleasant, particularly

283

when Bill had told her a few amusing anecdotes about her mother, the girl was very pensive and distracted when she left.

"She *was* kinda quiet," he agreed.

"I don't think you scared her, but I'm pretty sure what will be on her mind for a quite a while. I know, because it's on mine, as well."

He knew she was right but thought it necessary to tell them how he felt. They had to know because he was positive about what he'd told them. "I honestly believe that what I said is true."

"You really think you communicated with Samantha?"

The way her eyes had focused on him, even in the dark, troubled him, but he had to be honest. He'd already come dangerously close to losing her just days earlier and didn't want to go there again. "I'm pretty sure I did."

"What are you really trying to tell me, baby?"

"I'm not exactly sure. I only know that I don't have any idea what's been happening to me. Ever since I came out of my coma, I've been hearing voices and sensing things about Sam I never even thought of before."

"Like what?"

"For one thing, I don't think she ever wanted me to leave."

"You actually thought she *wanted* you out of her life?" Laura sounded surprised.

"At the time I did."

"But not anymore?"

"Falco told me things that surprised the hell out of me. For one thing, he said Sam was hung up on me and that she never seemed interested in anyone else."

"Then you're saying Falco told you things—not Samantha?"

"About *that*, yes."

"Then Samantha told you other things?"

"I'm reasonably sure she told me Falco killed her."

"Baby, I don't know what to think about all this. I know you were in a coma, but I have no idea what was happening to you while you were in it. I read a few things about comas while you were in the hospital, but I still don't know much about them. I don't think anyone else does, either. Not as much as we should know, anyway. All I know is that you were unconscious for more than one full day, and Samantha has been dead for more than twenty years. If you think the two of you somehow connected with one another, that's something only you can decide."

"What do *you* think?"

"It doesn't matter what I think."

"It does to *me*…"

"You know I love you, so I'm gonna support you no matter what…"

"That doesn't tell me what you think about all this."

"I don't know *what* to think, baby."

"Tell me you don't think I'm crazy. I really need to know."

She rested her hand on his shoulder. "I don't think you're crazy. I think you might be a little confused. Which is to be expected, judging by what you've just been through." She patted his shoulder. "Does that help?"

"Immensely."

"Good. Now…getting back to this Falco… If you didn't like some of the things he said, you really need—"

"Things he said..." His pulse hastened. Something had raised flags the moment the statement left her lips.

"Baby?" She pushed herself up. "Is something coming to you?"

"He said something about Sam…" The image was becoming clearer by the second.

"From what you told me, he said a lot about Samantha, and this is where you thought she didn't want you to—"

"It was something he said about finding her..."

Laura switched on the nightlight. "*Finding* her?"

"When he came home and found her lying on the slab."

"What was it, baby?"

The image continued coming.

"Baby?"

He closed his eyes and focused.

Falco was talking about Sam. About coming home and finding her. About seeing her lying there. About…about…

The image grew sharper, and Falco's statement flickered just long enough

("*Sam mighta been workin' on somethin' when she tripped and hit her head…*")

for him to catch it.

286

That was it. The topper of them all.

"Tripped. Falco said Sam had "tripped.""

Laura looked confused. "Okay…"

"Tell me something, Laurie."

"Sure…"

"How the hell did Falco know Sam had *tripped* if he hadn't been right there to see her do it?"

Chapter 26

Miranda came to see them the next morning.

She was dressed casually—scuffed jeans, red tee shirt, athletic shoes—and had her hair pulled back and tied at the crown with a blue rope.

"Not going in to work today?" Bill asked.

"I thought I'd take a few days off." Her forced smile told him something was on her mind.

After Miranda and Laura exchanged greetings in the kitchen, Miranda went right over to the coffeepot. "I hope you don't mind. I didn't have any breakfast. I even missed my morning coffee, and that *really* bites."

"Help yourself," Laura said.

As Bill gazed at his daughter, he quickly discovered that watching Miranda fix a cup of coffee was unsettling. Once again, it was just like watching Sam.

I've got to get over this, he told himself angrily. *This isn't Sam—it's her daughter. Our daughter. And the sooner you realize that, the better it will be for everyone concerned.*

Miranda put her cup down and sat facing Bill. She picked up a wedge of buttered toast and started munching.

"Something's really bothering you," he said.

She stopped munching and looked at him, then at Laura. She picked up her coffee cup. "How'd you know?"

"I can tell."

"How?"

"You're like your mom in many, many ways."

"Really?"

"It's uncanny. I have to constantly remind myself that you're not really her."

Miranda frowned. "Is it bothering you that much that I'm here? I didn't realize—"

"Don't feel badly about it, okay? I'll get over it. What I *won't* get over is if you suddenly disappear from my life just days after I found you."

She laughed. "No need to worry."

"You're sure?"

"I'm sure."

Bill suddenly felt relieved.

Miranda had more coffee. "I guess you can figure out that I'm pretty freaked about what's been going on."

"You'll have to be more specific," Bill said.

"Okay. I really need you to tell me more about these strange ideas you've been getting about my mom."

He reached for a bacon strip. "I honestly can't explain it. Some things are coming back, but the process is taking its time, believe me."

"This all started with your coma?"

"I can't recall anything like this happening to me before that."

"Do you think my mother's spirit might've connected with you while you were unconscious?"

"I wish I could tell you that's what happened, but—"

"How else can you explain this?"

289

"As I just said, I can't. All I can tell you is how I feel and what Falco told me."

"Do you think he told you the truth?"

"I don't know. I imagine this depends on what actually did happen. If your mom really did fall on the concrete, then yes, he told the truth."

"You don't think that's what happened, do you?"

"No. I don't."

"Is it because of what you told me last night?" Laura asked.

"Among other things."

"Fill me in," Miranda said, shrugging.

"Falco told me your mom had tripped."

"Tripped?"

He nodded. "How'd he know?"

"How'd he know what, Dad?"

"How'd he know she tripped if he hadn't been right there when it happened?"

Miranda was silent for a few moments. Then she glared. "Damn... That bastard!"

"But that isn't the only reason you've been skeptical, is it, babe?" [1]

"I think it's a combination of how I've been feeling lately. Because of the voices I've been hearing. And because of the dreams I've been having."

"You didn't tell me about these dreams." Laura was frowning.

He had some coffee and thought it over. Since nearly all his dreams had been forgettable, he'd expected most of them to just vanish. But for some

290

strange reason, details of Sam's death remained just as clear to him as they had been in his dreams.

"I keep getting this strong notion that she told me she was pushed."

Miranda's jaw dropped. "My mom said she was *pushed*?"

"That would explain your theory about Falco telling you she tripped," Laura said.

He nodded. "I'm also fairly certain that she and Falco constantly argued."

"About what?" Miranda's glare had returned. "What could have been so bad that he pushed my mom and knocked her down hard enough to kill her?"

"I've got this strong feeling that Falco has a horrible temper."

Miranda remained very still. He could tell what she was going through because he'd experienced similar feelings when he was convinced that his hammer had killed Sam.

"Miranda?" Laura looked concerned. "Are you all right?"

She didn't answer right off. Then she whispered, "I don't think I'm ever gonna be all right ever again."

Bill could feel his body growing warm. Because of a single act of rage, this beautiful young woman had been deprived of her mother. It just wasn't fair.

And Sam's killer was still out there.

"Bill?" Laura was nudging him.

He snapped himself out of it.

"You all right?"

"No."

"Bill—"

"Laurie, I've got to take care of this."

Laura groaned and sat back. "*Please* don't tell me we're going through *this* again..."

He didn't reply.

"What's she talking about, Dad?"

"This is how it all started." Bill rubbed his temples.

"How what all started?"

"This all started when I first saw you at the Paradise and thought you were Sam. I went zombielike and knew I had find out about you. And that led me to Falco. And..." He stopped cold.

"Bill? What's wrong?"

"Dad?"

"I just remembered something else."

"About what?"

A crunch of gravel. Moving closer.

"Just before I fell and hit my head outside that bar..."

"Go on, Bill..."

"Something hit me in the face, which knocked me down and forced me to slam my head into that bumper."

"What was it, Dad?"

The image was unmistakable. "It was someone's *fist*..."

Laura gasped.

Miranda froze. Then she cleared her throat and said, "You're just remembering this *now*?"

He nodded.

"Someone *mugged* you, baby?"

292

"I don't think it was a mugging."

"How can you be sure?"

"They told me when they found me that my wallet was still in my pocket. They also said my keys were lying on the pavement just a few feet away from me, and my watch wasn't taken."

Laura thought this over. "Maybe whoever punched you was interrupted. He might have been getting ready to rob you when he heard someone come out of the bar. This happened right outside the building, so there were probably several drunks wandering around—"

"It wasn't a mugging, Laurie." This time, he wasn't hearing a voice in his head. This time, he was getting a glimpse of a figure he'd seen a split second before the lights went out.

"Is there something else, Dad?"

"Just a moment before I was clipped, I caught the image of broad-shouldered figure approaching me."

"Was it Falco?"

"I don't know. All I can remember was that the figure was large and smelled kind of funky."

"Funky how?" Laura asked.

"I distinctly remember catching a whiff of something."

"Any idea what it was?" Miranda asked.

"I think it was motor oil."

***

Later that morning, Miranda drove Bill to the office of Brooks & Markum Investigations, a corporate agency she knew through their association with Peterson & Croft.

293

The B&M firm operated from the twelfth floor of the Seneca Building on East Robinson, just three blocks down from where Bill and Miranda worked.

As she'd explained to Bill, her company used Brooks & Markum whenever business transactions and mergers involving foreign businesses impacted her company. The agency was run by two corporate lawyers and had affiliates in Los Angeles, Dallas, and Miami. When Bill questioned her about using them, Miranda had said that they frequently engaged in short-term contracts with professional clients on personal matters.

As they rode the elevator up to the twelfth floor, Bill couldn't help wondering if this was a sensible decision. Hiring detectives to investigate a man who had accidentally murdered a woman twenty years earlier? It seemed problematic as well as foolish, and he could see no positive end to it.

He had no idea how these B&M people might handle this. Even if Falco was investigated and found guilty, how could this possibly balance the scales? No matter what new evidence was discovered, Sam was dead and always would be.

By the same token, how could anyone possibly find out that Falco had been the one who had put Bill in the coma unless Falco admitted it? As far as Bill knew, no one else had been out there when he left the bar. The way he remembered that night, he'd gone outside alone, walked over to his car alone, and was about to get his keys out when the lights went out.

If it hadn't been for the sudden flash of a broad-shouldered figure as well as that whiff of machine oil...

"You're awfully quiet." Miranda was watching him. "What's goin' on?"

He shrugged. "Just thinking about things in general."

"I don't think I like the sound of that."

"Miranda, do you really think we should be doing this?"

She groaned. "You're all set to bail on this one, aren'tcha?"

"I just don't want you to get your hopes up."

Her lips tightened. "This isn't about my hopes. It shouldn't be about yours, either. It's about justice, and I think my mother deserves this. And so do you. You don't sound like you agree, but I'm almost positive you're hiding your true feelings. If I'm not mistaken, you're probably hiding them because you don't want me to get hurt."

She was right. This wasn't about them, it was about a killer walking around free. What the man had done might have truly been an accident. However, lying about it to the police and the medical people had turned it into unpremeditated or reckless homicide, which was much worse.

He couldn't help it; he began to smile.

Miranda's brows pushed together. "Why the smile?"

"I was just thinking how proud your mom would be if she could see how you turned out."

"You really think so?"

"Definitely."

She sighed. "Before we go inside, promise me something."

"Depends on what it is."

"Promise me you'll tell me all about her. I mean everything."

"Everything?"

"Every single, juicy detail."

Her smile made him smile as well. Yes, Sam would definitely have been very proud of their daughter.

The elevator dinged to a stop.

"Well?"

He held out his hand. "Promise."

They shook hands as the doors slid open.

Bill continued smiling as he followed her out into the carpeted hall.

Chapter 27

The sign,

Brooks & Markum
Corporate Investigations, Inc.,

stenciled in bold black letters on the glass walls of the office front, displayed a comfortable, softly lit reception area.

A slender brunette in her mid-thirties was sitting behind the desk, taking calls from a wireless headset attached to her left ear.

The nameplate on her desk said:

Janice McCarthy, Receptionist

Her polished cherry desk presented a surprisingly neat appearance. Her laptop, desk blotter, file trays, and complicated phone center all remained within her reach. Aside from a small stack of memo pads, two black plastic cups crammed with pens and pencils, and a large white mug of coffee sitting at her elbow, no disarray was noticeable.

Other than the receptionist's soft voice whispering into her headset, the room was quiet. Bill couldn't even hear anything going on down the hall just beyond the open doorway on the right side of the open area.

Once they'd slipped in through the heavy glass door, the receptionist smiled and held up a long, slender index finger highlighted by a shiny red fingernail.

Miranda pointed to the couch over on the right, and the two of them took a seat.

Moments later, the receptionist turned to them. "Hello, Miranda. What can we do for you today?"

"Hi, Jan. Any chance of seeing Hal today? My father and I need to talk to him."

"Your *father*?" The woman raised both painted dark brows.

Miranda smiled. "It's a long story. Any chance of talking to Hal?"

The woman consulted her laptop. "He's here till four. I believe he's got something in about half an hour, but I'm sure we can squeeze you in."

"That'd be great. Thanks."

The receptionist spoke very softly into her tiny microphone. Then she gestured toward the open doorway. "You can go on in."

"Thanks again, Jan."

"No prob. And nice meeting you, Mr.—"

"Nathan. Bill Nathan. Nice meeting you, too."

***

Hal Markum didn't look at all like an investigator.

To Bill, Markum could have been someone who worked as a *maître d'* at a fancy restaurant. He was around forty, about six-three, long-limbed, broad-shouldered, and slim waisted. His black hair was short, wavy, and brushed straight back. His small dark brown eyes suggested that he was suspicious. Under other circumstances, he would have been considered good looking. However, his

298

shadowy, inquisitive eyes made the picture less than pleasant.

His office was small and cluttered, but bright and cheerful from the Central Florida sun pushing against the large tinted glass window, which made up most of the wall behind the credenza, three rows of filing cabinets, and a large potted plant sitting boldly in the corner.

Markum stood at the window, talking on the cell as Bill followed Miranda inside. He gestured for them to sit in the two chairs facing his large mahogany desk. He saluted her with his index finger as she sat, then quickly concluded his call and dropped the cell on his desk blotter.

"It's been a while, Randy," he said, grinning at her while taking in Bill at the same time. "Still working with George and Lisa?" He sat and pushed his chair closer to the desk.

"Yep. How are you doing? It's been, what, three months or so since we had that shindig at the O-Rena?"

"That might've been last March, I believe." He smiled briefly at Bill. "By the way, who's your friend?"

"Oops...sorry." She gestured to Bill. "Hal Markum, I'd like you to meet my father, Bill Nathan. Dad? Hal."

Bill stood, reached over the desk, and the two men shook hands.

Hal continued staring after Bill had returned to his seat. He shot a confused glance at Miranda. "You said...your *father*?"

She nodded.

"Randy, I had no idea you even knew—"

"It's a long story."

"I have no doubt."

"And it's why we're here."

"This is business?"

"It's about my mother."

"Your mother? I thought—"

"She died in an accident twenty years ago. I know. Everyone thinks that, anyway."

"Thinks?"

"Until the other day."

"Go on…"

Miranda turned to Bill. "Dad? You're up."

Even though he was suddenly put on the spot, Bill found that he had no trouble opening up to a total stranger. "I'm pretty sure Miranda's mom was murdered."

Markum looked shocked.

"And he tried to murder me as well."

Markum leaned forward and rested his elbows on his desk blotter. "I'm still listening…"

"That's about it," Miranda said. "The thing is, we know who did it."

"Let me guess. This is where I come in?"

"Exactly."

Markum went silent. He stared at Bill, then turned to Miranda. "Then you're telling me this is a local matter?"

"The man who murdered my mom owns and works in a garage in Altamonte Springs. Yes, you could say this is local."

Markum went silent again. This time, he turned to Bill. "Mr. Nathan? You said this same man tried to murder you as well?"

"He put me in a coma."

"And when was this?"

"I was released from ORMC just a few days ago. I was in the coma for twenty-eight hours."

Markum winced. "Ouch. How are you doing now? No permanent damage, I hope?"

"They didn't find any. Aside from some muscle weakness in my legs, a little residual neck and back pain, and an occasional headache, I'm doing all right."

"Good. Great, in fact. I'm sure you can understand how confused I am about all this. Everyone I've spoken to about Miranda seems to be under the impression that her father——"

"Split. Yes. I know. Believe me."

"Care to tell me why everyone thinks this?"

Bill sighed tiredly. He knew this would come up; he just wasn't as prepared for it as he thought. "There's a simple reason for that."

"I'd like to hear it."

"The reason is simple because it's true."

Markum didn't reply. His expression turned solemn.

"That, unfortunately, is another long story," Bill added.

"We'll tell you everything about that later," Miranda said. "Right now, we need to tell you about the bastard who killed my mother and nearly killed my dad."

Markum pulled out a notepad and pen and slid it onto the desk blotter. "I'm hoping you've got enough details about all this so we can actually proceed without worrying about—"

"How about the man's name for a start?" she asked.

Markum paused a moment. "That would be *great*."

"His name's Donnie Falco," she said.

Markum's hand froze before he could write anything down. "Did you say...*Falco*?"

"Uh-huh." Miranda's face squeezed into a scowl. "Don't tell me you *know* this guy..."

"He's one of the best mechanics in the area. As a matter of fact, he worked on my wife's Honda about a year ago."

"That shouldn't matter, should it?" Miranda shrugged.

Markum turned deadly serious. "I would never lead you on, Randy. And I would never do anything that would compromise this firm's integrity, or its relationship with Peterson and Croft. This is a serious matter, and I'm a professional. Have you *ever* known me *or* my firm to perform in an even *slightly* incompetent manner?"

"Never."

"All right, then." Markum gave her a wink. His dark eyes immediately shifted to Bill. "I guess you can start this up by giving me everything you've got."

Bill sighed. "I don't know where to start, exactly."

302

"How about if we start with Randy's mother? Specifically, everything we think we know about her death would be just great."

***

Talking to a stranger about Sam turned out to be difficult.

Each time a special memory flickered in his mind, Bill's blood turned cold and the sadness returned. Though most of the memories were warm and happy, he couldn't keep the bad ones—those leading to their downfall and, ultimately, Sam's death—from oozing into his head. This meeting had quickly turned traumatic, but he somehow managed to stay in control. He sensed something warm and comforting around him and couldn't help thinking that it might actually be Sam's spirit drifting into his sphere to supply him with much needed support.

Even so, telling his tale was tough. He was not only talking about how his first love had died, but he was also reliving the rapid, agonizing death of their relationship, for which he still blamed himself.

When he paused occasionally to collect himself, Miranda reached over and placed her hand on top of his, and he relaxed. He smiled at her and once again realized just how strange and wonderful life could be. Even though the love he had once shared with Sam had faded somewhat through the years, the young woman sitting beside him proved him wrong. The love he and Sam had once shared had produced this miracle sitting beside him. Because of this, he knew he should never again consider their relationship a mistake.

303

It was this feeling alone that made him even more determined to see that the man responsible for ending Sam's young life would pay dearly for his crime.

"You seem convinced that Ms. Lewes didn't actually fall on her own," Markum said, pausing in his scribbling. "Care to tell me why you feel this way?"

Bill carefully thought over his reply. He couldn't come right out and tell the man that Sam had somehow crossed dimensions and communicated with him during his coma. For one thing, Markum wouldn't believe him. For another, the man might consider him unstable and would refuse to look into this case.

"It's a very strong feeling I've had for some time," he finally said. "Sam was very athletic. She was extremely coordinated. In my view, her tripping over her own two feet would be along the same lines as a cat falling off a couch and landing on its back. Does that make any sense to you?"

Markum nodded. "I get it. Unfortunately, we can't go strictly on feelings. Not when it involves an investigation of a crime that was originally labeled an accident. And especially since all this is based on an event that happened more than twenty years ago."

"What about his coma?" Miranda asked. "The two could definitely be connected."

Markum shook his head. "That first event happened twenty years ago, which resulted in an accidental death, while the other took place just days ago, which resulted in a coma case. And don't forget the fact that Mr. Nathan had been drinking."

"How is that relevant?" Miranda asked.

"The defense will argue that Mr. Nathan was not sober and might have easily tripped and injured his face and forehead. This raises doubt—which is something we don't want."

Miranda frowned. "Ridiculous."

"You've got to look at this objectively, Randy. For one thing, the police are probably not going to be interested in this. There wasn't even a case, and the hospital records have undoubtedly documented it as an accident. There are no eyewitnesses—"

"Don't I count?" Bill asked.

"You *saw* Falco walk up to you and knock you down?"

Bill just sighed.

"You did see him, didn't you, Dad?"

"Not good enough to provide a definite ID…"

"What *do* you have?" Markum asked.

"I *smelled* him…"

Markum frowned. "Pardon me?"

"I caught a strong whiff of motor oil just before I was—"

"Motor oil?"

Bill nodded.

Markum didn't say anything right off. Bill could tell the man was going to say something he wouldn't like.

"Not enough, right?" he asked.

"Do you realize how lame that could sound to a jury?"

305

Bill's spirits sank. The man was right. "Now I do. And thanks."

"I'm not the enemy here." Markum sat back in his chair. "I'm sure you'll agree that what you've got isn't very conclusive."

"Maybe not," Bill said, "but it's what happened."

"I don't even see a way of working up a good motive here. Why would Falco even bother doing anything to you when he already got away with murdering Ms. Lewes twenty years earlier?"

Bill shrugged. "Maybe he considers me a threat."

"How?"

"By bringing it up after all these years."

"But he doesn't think you actually *know* anything..."

Bill didn't reply. Once again, the man was right.

"In other words, you're not gonna do anything, are you?" Miranda asked.

"I didn't say that."

"What *are* you saying, then?"

"Give me a few days. I'll get with my sources and try working up something here. If we can build a profile on Falco, we might be able to pull up something."

"You think you can?"

He shrugged. "It's been known to happen."

Bill didn't like the sound of that. "That doesn't sound convincing, actually."

"You'd be surprised how often we can find something on someone just by looking at the right

306

files. No one's perfect. If Falco has such an uncontrollable temper, he might have done something in the last twenty years we could nail him for. And who knows? There might even be paper somewhere that could possibly incriminate him."

"Sounds reasonable," Bill said.

***

Miranda was silent as she drove back to Bill's Winter Park condo.

"A penny for your thoughts." He watched her closely as she sat stiffly behind the wheel, her eyes straight ahead.

She seemed to be in a trance. It took her a moment to pull herself out of it. "I was just thinking."

"Obviously."

"Can't help it. A lot of things going on right now."

"You'd better be careful," he warned. "I used to do that when I was your age."

"You mean when you were living with Mom?"

"She didn't like me thinking too much."

"Why not?"

"She said it made her suspicious."

"Suspicious?"

"She was afraid I was fantasizing."

"About what? Other women?"

"About her, actually."

"Was that something she would be afraid of?"

"There was one thing she really didn't want me to ask her to do."

307

Miranda didn't respond right off. He could tell she was afraid to ask.

"Go ahead. Ask."

"All right. What didn't she want you to ask her to do?"

"She didn't want me to ask her to have sex out in the front yard."

"*Huh*?"

He sighed. "It was the only place on the property where we didn't do it, and she didn't want our landlord to see us and kick us out. She really liked that duplex. It was located in a nice area, and just a few miles from where she worked at the time. Shopping was convenient, too. And there was a hair salon just down the block she liked walking to."

Miranda laughed.

"The front yard was pretty small, you know."

She continued laughing.

"Lots of traffic, too. Especially in the evenings. What really put the stopper on it was the church at the end of the block. She didn't want anyone to have a heart attack—especially when I put on my Zorro costume and—"

"*Stop* it! *Please*!" Tears of laughter flowed down her cheeks. The Honda bumped the curb as she reached for a Kleenex from the console.

He smiled as her reaction.

"You're not being serious, are ya?" She sniffed and carefully wiped her eyes.

"What do *you* think?"

"Hmmm…" She sniffed once again. "I think I would have loved being with you two guys when you were both young and acting crazy."

"I would have loved that, too. So would your mother."

Bill began thinking once again of the time he stopped at the eatery and met Sam. The way she'd approached his table. The look in her eyes. The smile on her face. The way that single strand of blond hair refused to stay away from her right eye. The way she spoke to him, joked with him. He knew that every time he went back to that very special day, he would remember every single detail.

"Hal will find something," Miranda said, breaking the silence. "I know he will."

"You sound like you're trying to convince yourself."

"Maybe I am. But he's good. Their firm's the best in the state. Hal worked for the FBI for more than ten years. He knows how to get in touch with the right people."

"I wasn't getting a warm fuzzy when we were talking to him."

Miranda shook her head. "He was just being cautious. He's always like that. He doesn't want to get our hopes up."

"We've still got to face facts."

"What sort of facts?"

"The one that'll tell us that he might not be able to find anything on Falco."

Miranda went silent again. When she finally spoke, it sounded like she was talking to herself. "He'll find something. He has to."

"I'm sure he'll do his best."

"He has to," she repeated softly. "Otherwise…"

Bill didn't like the sound of that. "Otherwise what?"

She continued staring straight ahead. Her voice had turned into a harsh whisper. "Otherwise, something else will have to be done to make this right."

***

That night, as Bill undressed, Laura came out of the bathroom dressed in her nightie. Her eyes stayed on him as she approached the bed.

He unbuckled his belt. He'd known her for nearly three years and could tell when something was bugging her. "What's up?"

She sighed. "I don't want you doing this, baby."

"Doing what?"

"Whatever you're doing."

He hung his trousers over the back of the chair. "You'll have to be more specific. If you want me hanging these somewhere else—"

She groaned. "You know exactly what I'm talking about. I wish you wouldn't try joking about it."

"Joking about what? And why so glum? I'm feeling much better. And you'd better watch it. When I start feeling more like myself, you're gonna be in serious trouble."

"I'm really glad you're feeling better. What I'm talking about is what you're doing with Miranda."

He knew what she was talking about and had hoped she wouldn't make this more difficult. "Miranda and I have more or less been pushed into this, and—"

310

"Baby, I don't want you causing trouble with the same man who tried to kill you just a few days ago."

"We're not causing trouble, we're merely—"

"He's dangerous, Bill. You should already know that."

"We're not putting ourselves in jeopardy..."

"How can you say that? You're sending a professional team of investigators after him. Anyone with any common sense could figure out what's happening."

"How can he know what's going on? This team is good."

"I don't think he's stupid, baby..."

"He probably isn't. After all, he started up his own business."

"This is what scares me."

"What exactly do you mean?"

"He got away with murdering a woman more than twenty years ago, and just recently put you in a coma without anyone seeing him do it."

"Laurie, *I* know he did it. That's what matters."

"What difference does *that* make?"

"The fact that a team of professional investigators are going after him should tell you that he *didn't* get away with it."

"He will if they don't find anything."

"What if they do?"

"And if they don't?"

"As Markum said, everyone has done something in their life they don't want anyone to know about. In our own case, it's nothing worth

311

worrying about because neither of us have killed or harmed anyone. But in Falco's case—"

"Even if they don't find anything, he's bound to discover what's going on."

"He might not."

"He's dangerous, baby. If he knows you tried going after him, he's bound to retaliate."

"I'm sure that if Markum's team can't find anything, they'll let us know right off."

"Then what?" She sat down on the edge of the bed. She looked really worried.

"Then I guess we'll have to work on some other option."

"Like what?"

"Laurie, it's been a long day, and I'm tired." He lay back and sighed. "Come to bed."

"I probably won't be able to sleep."

"We can cuddle…"

She didn't reply.

"Come to bed, baby. I can't promise that I'll have an answer that'll make you feel better, but I can promise you one thing."

"What's that?"

"Markum's team is good. They work with several corporations and have a solid rep. If Falco's got anything on his record that could hurt him or his business, they'll find it."

She lay down beside him. Her expression was dark, and her eyes were moist. He knew she was worried; he just couldn't figure out a way of getting to the bottom of this without it affecting her.

"I just…I don't want him hurting us, baby…"

He smoothed out her hair. Her sweet smell and the closeness of her had already begun arousing him. It told him that he was already back to being his old self. But he realized that Laura didn't need that right now. She needed to be comforted, not aroused.

"I won't let him hurt us, Laurie," he said softly, kissing her lightly on the forehead.

She closed her eyes and smiled. Then she opened her eyes. "Or Miranda?"

"I won't let him hurt Miranda, either."

"Can you stop it from happening?"

"I'll do everything I possibly can to protect the three of us."

"I love you, baby," she whispered, kissing him lightly on the mouth. Then she turned over and flicked out the light.

"I love you, too, Laurie." He watched her as she lay on her back and pulled up the covers.

Before he drifted off, he thought of Miranda and wondered if he really could prevent Falco from hurting them.

Then he remembered what Miranda had said earlier

("something else will have to be done")

and began to wonder if he'd done the right thing by bringing her into this.

Chapter 28

Miranda appeared agitated when she came to see Bill and Laura two days later, as they were having lunch.

"What's wrong?" Bill asked.

Miranda didn't speak as she came into the kitchen.

"Could this be a work problem?" Laura asked, sneaking a peek at Bill.

Miranda shook her head. "I wish…"

"C'mon in," Bill said, gesturing. "Stay a while. We can talk while we finish lunch."

"Actually, it's all about Falco."

Bill and Laura exchanged worried looks.

"Would you mind? Could I have a beer?" She glanced at Laura, then Bill. "I could really use—"

"Sure." He got up. "No problem."

"No. Please sit. I'll find it. Thanks."

Bill sat back down. "Let me take a wild guess. You spoke with Markum."

Miranda closed the refrigerator door and sat down with a bottle of Guinness. "About an hour ago, actually." She noticed the cap and frowned.

Bill went to the counter, opened a cabinet drawer, pulled out a bottle opener, and handed it to her. "Not good, right?"

She cracked open the bottle. "Hal found something, all right. He just doesn't know how long this is gonna take before he can actually do anything about it."

"What did he find?" Laura asked.

Miranda had a slug of Guinness, sighed, and put the bottle down. "They found out that Falco's dirty, all right. They just don't know how to proceed."

"How dirty *is* Falco?" Bill asked.

"Ya know that garage he owns and runs? Well, Brooks and Markum found out that Falco didn't use his own money to finance it."

"Where'd he get the capital?"

"He had a partner."

"Had?" Bill asked.

Miranda had another swig of beer. "This is where things get crazy. Falco's partner had a wife who used to be a stripper. Guess what happened."

"Falco had a thing for the stripper?" Bill asked.

"Good guess."

"Let me take a stab at this one," Laura said. "This arrangement fell apart when the partner found out about the two of them, got angry, divorced his wife, then walked away from Falco?"

"Another good guess," Miranda said, "except for one tiny flaw."

"Let's have it," Bill said.

"His partner didn't walk away."

"Hmmm," Laura said.

"The plot sickens." Bill shook his head.

"Judging by what they found, the partner decided to hand over most of his assets to Falco *before* he and his wife split up."

"That makes no sense," Laura said.

"It doesn't, does it?"

"This can't be how it all ended, can it?" Bill asked.

"It ended not long after that."

"After Falco's partner walked away?" Laura asked.

"As I just said, he didn't walk away."

"What *did* happen?" Laura asked.

"He disappeared."

***

At three o'clock that afternoon, Hal Markum, showing signs of stress, slumped in his chair behind his desk.

"You haven't just given up, have you?" Miranda asked uneasily.

"We don't do that and you know it." Markum straightened in his seat. "In this business, you *can't* give up—not when people are depending on you. People who have paid you a great deal of money and are waiting for you to do what it takes to get their lives straightened out."

"Where are you with this, then?" Bill asked.

"Presently, I have one of our men putting in considerable time at the courthouse, going through every record he can find regarding this case. This man is good. Nothing gets by him. It won't be long at all before he finds some sort of discrepancy that we can use that'll connect Falco to Albert Saucier."

"Who?" Bill asked.

"Falco's partner."

"The one who's missing?"

"Yes. We also have a man who's trying to locate Saucier. Our man is a retired Orlando cop and has extensive experience in detective work. If

316

Saucier is still living somewhere, this man will find him."

"I'd wager a guess that Saucier's dead," Bill said.

"We have confidence in this man. He has many ties with OPD and has already enlisted their aid with a Missing Persons report on Saucier."

"What about Saucier's wife?" Miranda asked.

"We're looking for her as well. Believe me, we're bound to find something. It just might take a little longer than either of you are hoping for."

"You can say that again," Miranda said. "I'd love to see you nail that dirtbag right this minute."

Markum smiled. "If we could do that, we could. Unfortunately—"

"Yes," she said sourly. "I know. This takes time—all sorts of time. We just have to wait and be patient." She shook her head. "Two things I've never been very good at, by the way."

"What about Falco?" Bill asked. "Are you watching him as well?"

Markum consulted the binder on the blotter in front of him. "We've been watching him—as well as his place of business—for the last forty-eight hours."

"Anything look suspicious?"

"Not yet."

"I take it you've been able to establish a routine?"

"So far, we've found that the man puts in twelve-hour shifts at his business. He leaves his Aloma Avenue apartment at seven in the morning and gets home around eleven-thirty at night."

"That's a tad more than twelve hours," Bill commented.

"Both nights, we've observed him driving to one of the local steakhouses on Semoran for dinner, then leaving about half an hour later, driving to The Shamrock Bar north on Semoran, then returning to his apartment about an hour later."

"Alone?"

"Yes."

"And he lives alone?"

"We haven't seen anyone else in the place."

"No woman?"

"No man *or* woman."

Bill shook his head.

"What's up?" Markum asked.

"Something doesn't sound right."

"How so?"

"Falco's a dog. When he was living with Sam, he was constantly hitting on her. I don't think a man like him would change his ways much in twenty years—especially since he obviously knows how to get away with murder."

"You know this how?"

Bill didn't reply right off. Once again, strange feelings that had mysteriously settled in his brain were confusing him, and he knew full well that he couldn't possibly explain it. All he knew was that these feelings felt right, and he shouldn't argue.

"Trust me," he said. "Falco told me himself that he tried hitting on her several times when they were living together even though she kept turning him down."

"I get it," Markum said. "You're probably right. But how does this tie in with your idea that something isn't right?"

"I don't know. I just have a strong feeling that something about all this just isn't what it seems."

"And you say he goes to this Shamrock Bar regularly?" Miranda asked.

Markum studied her expression. Bill could tell the other man didn't like her question. Bill didn't like the sound of it, either. The dark look on the girl's face frightened him.

"What do you have in mind, Randy?" Markum asked.

"What makes you think I've got something on my—"

"How long have we known one another now? Two years?"

"Ever since I started with Peterson."

"Then tell me why you just asked me that question."

"Because we're your clients, and we need answers even though you're not progressing very quickly with this."

Markum frowned. "That was harsh…"

She ran a hand through her hair. "I'm sorry. I guess my impatience is wearing thin."

"I understand."

"Do you?"

"Yes. Of course I do."

She nodded. "Good. Now. You did say Falco goes to the Shamrock Bar on a regular basis, didn't you?"

***

That evening, as Bill and Laura were relaxing in the living room, watching an old Cary Grant movie classic, Bill's cell buzzed.

He picked it up from the end table and flicked on the display.

It said *Miranda*.

The instant he saw her name, he felt his pulse hasten.

"Who is it, baby?" Laura asked.

"It's Miranda."

"What's she want?"

He brought the cell up to his ear. "Hey, kid, what's up?"

"Hi, Dad...it's me...it's...Miranda."

The shaky tone of her voice made him uneasy. "What's wrong? Where are you? What's going on?"

"I'm sitting...in my car..."

"Okay..."

Silence.

"Miranda?"

More silence.

"Miranda, is someone there with you?"

He heard her groan. "No...I'm...all alone. By myself. All by myself..."

He cupped his hand over the cell and turned to Laura. "I think she's been drinking."

"Not good. You've got to do something, Bill. From what you said about how she was acting earlier—"

"I know." He took another breath to collect himself. "Miranda, where are you?"

Silence.

"Miranda?"

"Hi, Dad…I'm in my car, and—"

"Where's your car?"

A pause. "I think this is a parking lot. There's a store. A store. Over there. A big, *big* sucker—"

"Listen to me, now. Describe the parking lot."

"Did I tell you I was by myself?"

His nerves were jumping, but he had to find out what was going on. "Describe the anchor store, Miranda."

"Let's see…it's…I think it's…a Walmart, maybe?"

"Go on…"

"Did I tell you I'm…I'm in my car?"

"You did. Now…where's your car?"

"In the parking lot. Like I said." He heard her groan. "Weren'tcha payin' attention?"

"Which parking lot?"

"Outside. Where I live."

"You're sitting in your car in the parking lot where you live?"

She giggled. "Didn't I just say that?"

"Miranda, why don't you just get out of your car, go inside your place, lie down, and sleep it off?"

"S-Sleep *what* off?"

"Miranda, do you know where your place is?"

"Uh-huh…I think…I think I'm looking at it. Yep. There it is. Over there."

"Then why don't you just—"

"I'm not really…not really…in the parking lot there…"

He glanced at Laura and shook his head. "Where *are* you, then?"

"Across the street…from it."

"Can't you cross the street and then go inside and sleep it off?"

"Sleep *what* off?"

"Miranda, just get out of your car and cross the street."

"I'll get…get run over…"

His heart skipped a beat. "What are you talking about?"

"I'm across the street…from Semoran…"

His heart nearly exploded in his chest. "Miranda, *don't move!*"

"H-Huh?"

"*Stay in your car!*"

"Then how can I…I need to get out. Get out and—"

He ran into the kitchen to pick up his keys. "Miranda, stay in your car!" He tossed a wave at Laura. "I'll be there in ten minutes!"

"I'll still be here. You *want* me to, don'tcha? Be here, I mean?"

"*Stay* there. Stay *right* there. *Don't move!* I'll be *right there!*"

He heard her yawn. "Whaddya want me to do first? Don't move? Or stay here?"

"Both! Do not move! Stay there! I'm on my way!"

***

Miranda's Honda was sitting in the center of the half-empty Walmart parking lot, facing Semoran.

322

She was lying on her right side on the front seat, her cell on the seat not far from her chin. She seemed to be dozing.

The door was unlocked.

Bill opened it and shuddered at the long-forgotten memory that had quickly made its way to the center of his thoughts.

Sam lying on the couch in the same position, the bourbon bottle and a half-filled glass on the end table, her eyes wide open and glossy as she mumbled into the pillow mashed against her right cheek.

"Daddy...I'm so *sorry...I didn't mean...we didn't...you shouldn'ta been there, Daddy...Billy and me, we...I love him, Daddy...I love really* love *showing him how much I love him...you...just can't...you just* can't *be mad at me, Daddy...*please *don't stay mad at me! I mean...I mean you shouldn'ta—"*

"Sam?" It crept out of his throat before he realized it.

She stirred, turned her head, and slowly opened her eyes...

...and he cringed when reality came back, slapping him squarely on the cheek. Miranda. *Not* Sam.

She gave him a glossy-eyed look and smiled awkwardly. "D-Daddy?"

Daddy?

("please *don't stay mad at me...*")

Get a grip, man!

He shook himself, forcing the past back into the shadows.

323

"Miranda, I need to get you back to your place."

"I've been…drinking, Daddy…" She giggled.

"I know, baby. C'mon, now." He pulled her left arm and let it fall over his shoulder. Then slid his hand gently under her just below her upper arm and carefully pulled her upright. She moved loosely, like a rag doll, making herself much heavier when he tried pulling her out of the car.

"All by myself, Daddy," she muttered, smiling stupidly as he half-carried her over to his car. "I grew up…all by myself…"

You walked out on both of them, you idiot. And by doing so, you forced this sweet, beautiful young woman to fend for herself…

Bill forced his mind on the job at hand.

You need to get her back to her place safely.

He opened the back door of the BMW, helped her in, then laid her down gently on the seat. He closed the door and went back to the Honda. He removed her handbag and cellphone, pulled the keys from the ignition, and made sure the doors were locked. Then he got back into the BMW.

Except for the loud, erratic beating of his heart, the short drive to her place was spent in total silence.

Chapter 29

Miranda's one-bedroom garden apartment sat hidden behind a cluster of palmettos less than a mile west of Semoran Boulevard.

Using Miranda's key, Bill unlocked the front door, scooped her up, and carried her inside. Having her in his arms immediately caused a shiver trickling down his spine. He gazed at her sleeping young face and cursed himself once again for abandoning her and her mother at the most vulnerable stage in their lives.

Idiot. You should be shot for what you did—
Don't be so hard on yourself…

Once again, the strangely warm sensation that had been popping up more and more drifted into his psyche, calming him.

Focus, Nathan.

The living room lamp was already on. He carried her over to the couch and gently laid her down. She stirred and muttered something unintelligible. He positioned the pillow next to her head, making her more comfortable.

After closing the front door, he placed her handbag and cellphone on the end table. Then he returned to the sofa, removed her shoes, grabbed the Afghan that was draped over the back of the couch, and pulled it up to her waist.

The apartment seemed cold. The thermostat in the hall registered 65. He upped it to 70, then went back into the living room, fell into the chair facing the sofa, and lay back.

His cell buzzed.

It was Laura. "Everything okay?"

"In a manner of speaking."

"Is she…is she all right?"

"She's sleeping right now."

"You got her home safe, then?"

"I think I'd better stay here a little while. I don't want her freaking out when she wakes up hungover and can't remember anything. Besides, I've got to somehow get her car back. That'll have to wait till morning."

"That's a good idea."

"You don't mind?"

"Baby, I mind very much about almost all of this, but when it comes to your daughter, I think it's best that you take care of her any way you can."

He sighed. "I'm really glad you said that."

"I just know how badly you feel about all this."

"Do you?"

"I can only imagine."

"Think how badly you'd feel if you just found out that you had a daughter and that you had absolutely nothing to do with her growing up."

He heard her sighing.

"The least I can do is help her right now."

"Do what you gotta do, baby."

"I'll be back as soon as I can."

"Just make sure she knows we're here for her. From now on."

"Do you really mean that?"

"Of course I do."

"You really are fantastic, baby."

"Love you, too."

He pocketed the cell. For the next twenty minutes, he sat in the armchair and focused on Miranda. She looked so peaceful, yet he knew how troubled she was.

If only I'd just turned around and come right back.

As usual, the anger rushed right back, making the back of his neck hot.

I should have thought about what I'd done, gone back to the garage, grabbed the ladder, and climbed up to the roof to pick up that damned hammer. Sam would have come out to see what I was doing. We would have made up. She would have told me she was pregnant, and...

If only...

As he gazed at Miranda's sleeping form, he tried visualizing her as an infant...then a toddler...then a little girl...and then...

He'd missed it all. Everything.

He shook his head and thought once again about how stupid and selfish he'd been.

He'd also missed twenty years with Sam. Living with her, sharing daily memories of her and of Miranda. Sharing good times and bad while watching Miranda grow up to be the beautiful young woman he was staring at right now. Having a quarter of a lifetime of treasured moments to think about during the daily struggles and dilemmas of everyday life.

He realized that even though he and Sam had been missing from her life, Miranda had managed to become a beautiful, respectable young lady. In addition to her amazing resemblance to her mother, Miranda was like Sam in more ways than one. Quiet, soft-spoken, intelligent, perceptive...

How could we have been so lucky, Sam? he thought, closing his eyes.

It was in the cards, came the answer.

His eyes shot open.

"Sam?" he whispered, looking around uneasily. "Is that you?"

Silence.

"Sam?"

"Who's there?" came another voice.

He practically leaped out of his seat.

Miranda, stirring on the sofa, turned her head toward him and squinted. "Dad? Is that you?"

He took a couple of deep breaths and waited for his nerves to settle down before getting up from the chair.

"Dad?" She pushed some hair out of her eyes and tried sitting up. Groaning, she lay back down. "What happened?" She gawked at him. "Why are you...what's goin' on?"

"Relax, baby." He sat down on the edge of the couch and smoothed out her hair. Her makeup was a mess and her eyes were bloodshot. Her hair badly needed a few intense minutes with the comb and brush. He could smell the booze on her. He figured she might have spilled some of it on the front of her blouse. "Just lie there and let yourself—"

"I'm drunk, Dad..." She groaned and brought up both hands to rub her temples. "I'm really…really and truly fucked up—whoops, sorry…"

"It's okay."

She shook her head. "It's *not* okay, Dad. *Not* okay." He could feel her anger bubbling up quickly. "He killed Mom! That bastard killed my mother!" She grimaced and brought up both hands to her temples.

"I know, Miranda. I know."

She squinted up at him. She looked so helpless… "Aren't you pissed, too? I mean, you really loved her. You said you did. I know you meant it. Didn't you—"

"I loved her, Miranda. I really loved your mom."

She tried once again to sit up. She managed to bring herself up, then propped herself up on her right elbow. "Then you…you should be—"

"I know what I should be doing. I just don't know how to go about doing it."

"But he tried killing you, too!"

"He didn't succeed, did he?"

She just sighed.

"Let's wait and see what your friends at Brooks—"

"They're taking too damn *long*!" She straightened her right arm to help her sit up, then lowered her legs. When she was finally upright, she leaned forward and massaged her temples again. Her hair hung down.

He caught another flash of memory: Sam hunched over after a bender, her hair hanging down, moaning and promising herself she'd never touch another drink as long as she lived.

He put his arm across her shoulders. "You need rest. You should go right to bed. It's getting late anyway."

She stopped massaging her temples and groaned. She appeared to be nervous. "You wouldn't want to…I mean, would you mind staying with me? Would that be all right? Would Laura mind? It's okay if you can't. I'll manage. I'll just need to—"

"I'm staying."

She smiled. "I'm glad."

"It's all right."

"And you're *sure* it's okay with Laura?"

"It's okay with Laura."

"You talked to her, then?"

"I did."

"I musta been out cold when you did."

"I had to check your pulse to make sure you weren't dead."

She stared at him. When she realized he was joking, she laughed.

He laughed with her and squeezed her against him, and for the next few minutes, they sat close to one another in a tender silence.

He closed his eyes and once again felt the same warmth that had been caressing him during the last few days. It comforted him, made him feel like everything had somehow corrected itself. That everything that had gone wrong in his life had somehow vanished. And that for the first time in his life, he sensed that the self-anger lying deep inside

330

him had somehow detached itself from his psyche and began to drift away.

A few minutes later, Miranda straightened and stared at him. "How'd you know?"

"How'd I know what?"

"How'd you know I was drunk?"

"You called me."

"I did?"

"You don't remember?"

Confusion covered her face. She shook her head.

"You don't remember calling me *at all*?"

"I guess I was more shitfaced than I thought."

"I guess you were."

"How'd I call you, then?"

"Your cell—how else?"

"If I was that drunk, how'd I get all the numbers right?"

"Is my number in your address book?"

A nod.

"Okay, then."

"I don't know… I just don't think you can do complicated stuff like that when you're drunk."

"You were that drunk?"

"I *thought* I was…"

"How much did you have to drink?"

"Two shots."

His jaw dropped. "That's *all*?"

She shrugged. "I've never been able to drink that much. It only takes two beers to put me to sleep."

He wanted to laugh. Sam was the same way— very little tolerance to alcohol.

331

"What's funny about that?"

"Your mother couldn't drink much, either."

She shook her head. "I still can't remember doing any of that. I think my brain just switches off whenever a little booze gets in up there."

"I personally think you were more angry and upset than drunk."

"You really think so?"

"You're coherent now. If you were seriously drunk, you'd need much more time to recover. Maybe all night. You were obviously able to use your cell. It was on the seat of your car when I found you."

She thought that over. "I was pretty pissed off. That Falco jerk really has my panties in a twist. And Hal Markum's not working fast enough. Not as fast as I'd like."

"He's got to wait for everything to go through the process."

"It sucks."

"Most everything involving the legal process sucks."

She shook her head. "Weird…"

"Enough talk. You need to get to bed. How's your head?"

"It feels like a couple of little guys are running around up there with ballpeen hammers, trying to crack my head open."

"What do you usually do for a hangover?"

She sighed and shrugged. "I've only had two others before."

"What did you do?"

She reddened and smiled nervously. "I took off all my clothes, had sex with someone, then passed out."

He didn't reply.

She watched him closely before speaking again. "I was pretty wild for quite a while once I hit my teens."

"Define wild."

A shrug. "Long story short? Aunt Eileen threw me out."

"How old were you?"

"Sixteen."

The anger once again came back quickly. "She threw you out of the *house*? When you were *sixteen*? That bitch…"

"Relax, Dad. I stayed with Stepdad until I graduated. Then I went to Business School, and the rest, as they say—"

"How'd he treat you?"

"All right, I guess. Never saw much of him, though. He always seemed to be away on business. I didn't mind. It was like I had my own place. I had my friends in all the time. But they were pretty cool. We were always careful not to do anything really stupid, so the cops were never called in."

He shook his head. He felt even guiltier than ever before.

"It was all right," she said. "It forced me to grow up faster."

"Miranda, I'm so—"

"It's okay." She patted his hand. "I'm fine."

"You really are. I'm just glad that stupid aunt of yours didn't turn you into a man-hater."

Miranda laughed. "No need to worry. I love guys. Always got along pretty well with them. Sometimes I ended up picking the wrong one, but oh well…" She shrugged.

He just shook his head.

She suddenly looked worried. "Does this make you think less of me?"

He chuckled. "You're absolutely right. None of us has *ever* done stupid things or made dumb mistakes…"

Her eyes widened. "You, too?"

"I'm a guy, Miranda. Do the math."

She laughed, then cringed. Moaning softly, she reached up and gently massaged her forehead.

"Sorry…"

She forced herself to stand. For a few seconds, she looked like she was going to collapse, but regained her footing and looked down at him. "This place is really small. The couch is all I have. Sorry."

"It's all I need."

"I'm really glad you're here."

"Me, too. Now go to bed."

She took a few clumsy steps toward the archway. Then she stopped and awkwardly turned around. "Could you please do me a favor?"

"What is it?"

"Could you maybe…I don't know how to ask—"

"Just ask."

"Could you maybe…kiss me good night?"

His heart skipped a beat. He didn't know how to respond. He'd never imagined that a situation like this would ever happen. Now that it had, he found himself clueless.

"You *are* my *dad*, you know…"

"I know."

"You've earned the right."

"Have I?"

"Well, duh…"

"I don't know what to say…"

"You don't have to say anything. Just do it. Unless you don't want to…"

"I want to. Believe me."

"Look at it this way. You've got twenty years of good night kisses to make up for."

He felt a sudden tug at his heart.

"You're gonna do it, then?"

"Definitely."

"Good." She seemed to be waiting for him to make the first move.

"Something wrong?"

"Could I ask you another favor?"

"Okay…"

"Could you please come over here and make sure I make it to the bed without falling on my ass? I don't think I can do it on my own."

Smiling, he got up, went over to her, and wrapped an arm around her waist.

"I won't ask you to help me undress. That'd be *way* too weird. I'll sleep in my clothes. It seems like the easiest and best thing to do right now."

"Fine with me."

They went into the tiny bedroom. There was room for a single bed, a dresser, and an end table. He helped her into the bed, then pulled the covers up to her chin. Slightly nervous, he bent over her and kissed her lightly on the forehead. "'Night, Miranda."

"'Night, Dad."

He smiled, straightened, and went over to the doorway.

"Dad?"

"Uh-huh?"

"My friends call me Randy. I'd love it if you called me that, too."

"Actually, I like Baby Girl better."

"I do, too. But only when *you* say it…"

"Good night, Randy. My baby girl."

A smile. "'Night, Dad."

Chapter 30

The next morning, Miranda shuffled into the kitchenette in her pink housecoat and fuzzy white slippers while Bill was making breakfast.

Her eyes were glossy and her hair looked like it had been caught in a windstorm. But he could tell this wasn't a bad hangover. She wasn't shaking, unsteady, or exhibiting any of the other obvious signs.

"Coffee?"

"*Please...*"

He poured a cup from the pot and put it on the counter. She slipped by him and opened a drawer. Her hands seemed reasonably steady as she removed a small bottle of aspirin and dropped two onto her palm. She then left and lowered herself carefully onto the sofa. Sighing heavily, she rested the coffee cup in her lap and looked at it.

"Sugar? Cream?"

"Sugar, please..."

"No cream?"

She looked at him. "Once in a while. Don't feel like it now..."

Bill brought the sugar bowl out into the living room and placed it on the end table next to her.

"Did I do or say anything stupid last night?" She dumped a rounded teaspoon of sugar into her cup and stirred.

"Define stupid."

"Did I tell you about the time I got really drunk last year, then took my panties off and slipped them over my head?"

"No, but since we're talking about it now, I guess you can elaborate…"

"Oh God…" She lowered her face and covered her eyes with her left hand.

He laughed. "Don't beat yourself up. We've all done worse."

She lowered her hand and looked up at him. "Really?"

He nodded. "For instance, take the time I found your mother's panties and brassiere wadded up in the mailbox following a night of drunken bliss?"

She covered her mouth and nearly spilled her coffee. "How'd they get there?"

He scowled and shook his head. "She never would say. I accused her of cheating on me with the mailman, but it didn't go over too well."

Miranda laughed and spilled coffee on her housecoat. "Damn!"

"Need a paper towel?"

"I'm okay…" She wiped her wet hand on the housecoat and carefully brought the cup to her lips. Then she placed the cup on the end table and gazed at him again.

He noticed that even wet and bloodshot, her baby blues had the same power as Sam's when they'd centered on him.

"I'm really glad you're here this morning." She seemed content and happy.

"I figured you'd need someone to fix you breakfast."

338

"It's more than that and you know it."

He went back into the kitchenette and placed the bacon strips on a plate. Then he finished frying the eggs. He slid them onto two plates next to the bacon, took them out into the living room, and placed a plate on the cocktail table in front of her. "You can say anything you want because you know how guilty I feel about you." He put his plate on the seat of the armchair, went back to the kitchenette, grabbed some napkins and silverware, came back out, and handed her a napkin, knife, and fork. Then he picked up his plate and sat facing her.

She popped the aspirin into her mouth and washed them down. Then put the cup down and stared at it for a few moments. "You really shouldn't."

"But I do." He picked up a bacon strip. "There's no way I can justify what I did. And there's nothing you can say that'll make me feel any better about it."

"It happened twenty years ago, Dad. It's all in the past."

"I *thought* it was..."

"Lemme guess. You saw me and it came rushing right back?"

He nodded. It was amazing how perceptive this girl was. "In this case, I'm glad it came back. Otherwise, I would've never known about you."

She just smiled.

"Tell me something."

"Okay..."

"The truth, now..."

"Sure."

"I want you to tell me you don't hate me for walking out. Tell me right now. I know you won't because it wouldn't be true, would it?"

She sighed. "I'd be lying if I say I didn't."

"I wouldn't blame you one bit."

"My hatred for you didn't last very long, though."

"How so?"

"Certain things she did and didn't do made me suspicious—even when I was little."

"Like what?"

"Well, for one thing, there were never any pictures of you lying around. I always found that kind of odd."

"Did you ask her if there were any? There were several taken of us together, as I recall."

"I asked her a bunch of times. She said my mom was so angry at you when you walked out that she gathered up everything that reminded her of you and burned them."

"Sounds reasonable—for someone like her. I guess you couldn't help believing at least some of what she said."

"I did at first, when I was little and still trusted her. But after I developed some common sense, I realized that Aunt Eileen had made up a lot of lies about you."

"I'm sure some of them were true."

"Even if they were, I never had the feeling that you were the monster she claimed you were."

"How would you know?"

"I always had this feeling that you were a great guy. And you'd have to be. Otherwise, Mom wouldn't have been in love with you."

"How'd you get *that*?"

"I really don't know. All I can say about it is that the feeling has always been there."

"Very strange."

"Maybe…but I don't think so."

"Why not?"

"Did you ever have the feeling that something was gonna turn out all right even when you knew it couldn't possibly happen that way?"

"Once or twice…"

"That's how it was with you. Even when I was little, whenever I wondered about you, it always seemed as if there was some voice or feeling inside me saying you were a terrific guy, and I shouldn't hate you no matter what anyone said." She sighed. "I guess I was waiting to see if I could ever find you so I could find out if I was actually right."

He ate some scrambled egg and reflected on what she'd just said. And wondered if it had been Sam's voice in her head, guiding her.

"How do you explain that, Dad?"

"I don't think I can."

"Oh, I think you can."

He stiffened in the chair.

"When you were in that coma, you saw and heard things. Don't you remember?"

He nodded.

"And they all seemed to be about my mother, right?"

"Yes…"

341

"And some freaky things have happened ever since you came out of it, right?"

"Right..."

She smiled. "Need I say more?"

He didn't reply. He couldn't because he knew she was right.

***

After lunch, Dad told Miranda he had to leave.

"You seem to be doing a lot better," he said, finishing his iced tea, "so I think I'll be shoving off."

Miranda wanted him to stay longer. Although it had taken her most of the morning for the aspirin to dull the nagging head and neck pain brought about from her hangover, she discovered that sharing her tiny apartment with her father had been a most enjoyable experience. He was fun to be around, easy to talk to, and had proven that he was an excellent listener. She was so happy that she'd been right about him and was very glad that she hadn't believed anything Aunt Eileen had said.

She really wanted to spend more time with him but realized how selfish this would be. She had to accept the fact that he had his own life to live.

Even so, she considered the dangerous dilemma they presently faced and knew that they needed to discuss it.

"I really wish you'd stay longer."

"I wish I could, too, but—"

"We really need to talk."

He didn't respond right off. She could tell he was trying to guess what she was on her mind. "About anything in particular?"

342

His question disappointed her. It told her he wasn't as concerned about the Falco business as she was. "I think you know what I'm talking about."

He shook his head. "Randy, I honestly don't believe—"

"Markum's just not moving *fast enough*, dammit." The anger came out automatically. She hated that but she just couldn't help it. "It's really frustrating me. Tell me you're not frustrated."

"Listen…I don't think—"

"*Are* you frustrated?"

"It doesn't matter whether or not—"

"He tried to *kill* you, Dad!"

He didn't reply. He just sat there, watching her.

She could tell that her sudden burst had startled him. She hadn't wanted that to happen; it just came out. But they both knew that there was a man out there who had altered both their lives in a very bad way and should be in prison.

After a moment, Dad said, "I really think that if we give Markum a little more time, he'll find something that'll nail Falco."

"I'm having a real problem with that." She got up from the sofa and went into the kitchenette to pour more iced tea. "A really *big* problem."

"Tell me what it is."

She came out of the kitchenette and looked him right in the eye. "The same problem I've had ever since I told Hal about this. It's taking too damned long!"

"This sort of thing takes time, Randy. You know that."

"Yes, I know it." She plopped down on the sofa and shook her head. "I may be just twenty-one, but I've been around the block. I've seen things—lots of things. I've been working since I was seventeen. I know how the system operates."

"Then you must also know that you can't possibly change it. No one can."

"Of course I know that. I'm not stupid."

He was watching her. She could tell he was trying to sense what was going on in her head.

"There's something you're not telling me."

She sipped her tea and shrugged.

He sighed. "Baby girl, this isn't the time to be cute."

She tilted her head. "You don't think I'm cute?"

"You know what I mean."

"I just told you I know full well that you can't change the system."

"I know. I was right here when you said it..."

"And...?"

Dad scowled. "You got that look on your face."

"What look?"

"That same look your mother had when she was up to something."

"You think I'm up to something?"

"You know I do."

"What am I up to?"

"No good."

"Dad..."

"Tell me I'm wrong."

She shrugged. "You're wrong."

He went silent.

She hated lying to him but didn't want him talking her out of something that had been coming to her lately. Ever since Hal Markum demonstrated to them that this case would take more time than either of them would like, she began thinking of alternatives. And the one that kept coming back to her was the one that neither Markum—nor her father—would approve of.

"Why don't I believe you?" he finally asked.

She should have known he'd suspect that she was planning something. After all, he was a very perceptive guy. Besides, based on what he'd told her, he was very close to her mother and had stated several times how similar she was to her. This meant that he could read her very well.

Even so, she knew she couldn't possibly let him know what she was up to. It had to be this way. She didn't want him getting hurt if things went south.

"I don't know. Why don't you?"

"You're being cute again…"

"Can't help it. I'm like my mother. You even said so."

"Randy…"

"I just happen to think people should own up to their mistakes and face the consequences."

"What's *that* supposed to mean?"

"It means Falco hasn't been held accountable. For *anything*."

"Need I remind you that that's what Markum and his people are working on right now?"

"Need I remind *you* that Falco should be in prison by now?"

"And as *I* said, you can't change the system."

345

"No, but you can do a little tweaking."

His brows bumped together.

She knew right then that she'd gone too far.

"I don't...like the sound of that." He shook his head.

"Sorry. Can't help how I feel."

"No, but you can stop thinking that way."

"Why?"

"For my sake?"

"What about my mother's?"

He didn't reply.

"Dad, Falco needs to pay for what he's done."

"We can't go up against someone like him and you know it."

"Yes. I know."

"You really do?"

"I really do."

"You're not lying to me?"

"I'm not lying to you."

"Then tell me right now that we can't go up against that guy. If you say that, I'll be able to sleep peacefully tonight."

"We can't go up against that guy." She'd said it without hesitation.

He sighed in relief. Then he patted her shoulder and got up. "I guess I'll be going, then."

She got up and followed him to the door.

He turned. "You never told me why you called me last night."

Miranda shrugged. "I was lonely. And a little scared."

"Why didn't you call the keyboard guy?"

346

She laughed. "I wasn't that kind of lonely. Besides, anything wrong with a girl calling her father when she's scared and needs someone to come to her rescue?"

She could tell by his expression that she'd hit a nerve. The sudden sadness in his face was unmistakable.

"I'm sorry, Dad. I didn't mean it that way."

"I know."

"I'm really sorry."

"Well, at least everything turned out okay. I came to your rescue, didn't I?"

"Actually, I would've been surprised if you hadn't."

"Whaddya mean?"

"I kept getting this strange feeling that you'd come right over if I told you I needed you."

"Strange feeling, eh?"

She nodded. "Funny, isn't it?"

He glanced toward the ceiling, then smiled at her and shook his head. "Maybe not as funny as you might think."

He turned away. She wondered if he knew she'd been thinking of her mom just then.

Before reaching the door, he said, "I'm just five minutes away, you know."

"I know."

"You ever need me, you know what to do."

"Lemme guess. Call you?"

He smiled and patted her shoulder again.

She huffed. "Can't you do better than that?"

Smiling, he wrapped his arms around her and pulled her close. She felt safe in his arms and wanted to stay there forever. But before she knew it, he'd kissed her on the forehead and lowered his arms.

"You need anything—and I mean *anything*— just call. Or come right over. Laura loves you, too."

"She's really a great lady, Dad."

"I know."

"Sometimes I wish—"

"I know." He kissed her again, then opened the door and left.

She stood in the doorway, waving as he pulled out and drove slowly down the private one-lane road. Hoping with all her heart that he wouldn't hate her for what she was going to do.

You're right, Dad, she thought as the dark images drifted back. *We can't go up against that guy.*

But maybe one of us can.

Chapter 31

Donnie Falco hadn't been having a good week.

The sudden intrusion by that Nathan guy had messed up the entire week, and Donnie hadn't been able to concentrate on anything else since.

He hadn't expected anything like that to happen. Damn it all to hell. That mess with Samantha happened *twenty years ago*, for God's sake! He'd stopped worrying about its ramifications a long time ago. It had been one of the worst damn things he'd ever done, and he'd spent years trying to forget it. Trying to forget it with booze. And drugs. And sex. Lots and lots of sex. And keeping busy, working on engines, running the shop. Keeping his mind from going back there. And for the last few years, he'd been damn successful and hadn't thought of it much at all.

Hell, it shouldn't have happened in the first place. The bitch had been feeding him nothing but bullshit every damn time he tried getting her in the sack, and he'd been getting sick and tired of it.

No guy in his right mind would have passed on trying to get into those panties. A damn shame she'd been so stuck on Nathan. She cared only about that little brat and kept telling her bitch sister that Nathan was gonna come back. Said she could feel it in her bones. And she didn't care one damn bit about anyone else jumping her. Wouldn't even give him the time of day and was interested only in his rent money.

He'd had it with the bitch, plain and simple. Watching her traipse around the place in shorts and those tight-fitting tee shirts was enough to make any guy turn batshit crazy.

He couldn't help it if he lost his cool that afternoon when she came out of the garage in her shorts and loose-fitting gray sweatshirt, carrying that hammer she'd been using on that stupid rocking horse she'd had sitting on the workbench even before he'd moved in. Said her daddy had given her that silly thing when she was a little brat. She'd also said Nathan had been working on it for her but hadn't finished because he'd just walked out the door one day and never came back.

Donnie figured she'd probably pulled the same sort of bullshit on Nathan too many damn times, and he decided he didn't wanna take it anymore.

It was a damn shame the hottest babes were always the ones that gave a guy the most trouble.

Donnie had finally had it with her and told her she needed to find some other sucker, but she didn't care one damn bit and told him he'd signed a rent agreement. Told him the agreement was legal and binding. Told him she'd sue him if he walked out. Then, before he could say another word, she turned her back on him.

Turned her back…

No guy can tolerate a broad turning her back on him. He couldn't help it that he saw red. Couldn't help it that he snapped. Everything in his head seemed to turn upside down. Even now he couldn't remember the exact moment when the rage took over, turning everything hot and blood-red. Making

350

everything in his head blurry and muddled as he reached out, grabbed her, then spun her around to face him.

That same business had happened a few times before, in high school. They told him it had something to do with his old man leaving when Donnie was just ten, then his mother hooking up with a guy who didn't like Donnie much. Then Momma, who'd always been close to her son, picking her new guy over Donnie and discarding him like yesterday's trash.

Made him angry, the way she'd turned away from him like that. Made him feel like he shouldn't have been born in the first place.

The rage had always been bad. It had happened a few times since, usually when a simple argument got way out of control, but aside from putting a few guys in the hospital, he'd been lucky no one died or tried to sue him.

Not so with Samantha.

You don't turn your back on me, bitch!

Couldn't help it if she lost her footing when he'd grabbed her by the arm and spun her around to face him. He had no idea she'd trip, then fall backward. He still couldn't believe how the back of her head slapped the concrete, cracking her skull wide open and forming a pool of dark red under her.

Couldn't help it. Not at all.

If only she hadn't turned her fucking back on me!

Good thing he'd had the sense to call 911 and report it as an accident.

The fiasco turned even deadlier when he saw Samantha's bitch sister Eileen pulling up the drive while he was cleaning up the blood. He still remembered how he'd nearly crapped his pants when that happened. He'd managed to give the bitch a story about how he'd found Samantha lying there like that. The sister hadn't cared much for Nathan and asked if Donnie had seen him. Donnie had never seen the dude at all but got the feeling he should tell her yeah, he had. He figured it might get the sister to stop asking questions. And when he'd told her he thought he'd seen the dude sometime earlier, on Colonial Drive, he guessed he was home free.

He needed a good, stiff belt or two before making his weekly trip to Bernie's Babes, where those half-naked broads really knew how to turn a guy on. He needed to forget that nasty business. The sooner, the better.

And he really had to forget about Nathan coming into his place last week and bringing it all back.

A few strong belts would really hit the spot. Some whiskey, a stripper, and an hour or so of some juicy groping in the back seat of his Ford 350SL.

That would be all it took to get things back to normal.

He knew better than drive back to Gordon's Watering Hole. That was where he'd bumped into Nathan and was forced to do him in. He hadn't planned it that way—hell, he had no idea he would ever see Nathan again. He still didn't know why Nathan had popped up in his office that day last week. Donnie had been tense during their talk but had handled it as best he could. Nathan hadn't seemed suspicious. Donnie figured the dude had been out of touch and maybe decided to find out what had happened and didn't want to deal with that Eileen bitch, if she was still around and kicking.

But last week, when he'd parked the truck outside Gordon's and saw Nathan coming out of the bar, he wanted to freak and knew he'd have to do something about it. He had no idea what Nathan was doing in one of his haunts; he wasn't even sure if Nathan had spotted him getting out of the truck. But panic had set in, and his head went all kinds of funny again. The rage had come back—this time with a shitload of fear that told him Nathan knew damn well what was going on.

Donny knew right then that he'd have to put down the bastard or the thing with Samantha would open up wide.

He'd put him down, all right, but before he could check to make sure Nathan was dead, two other vehicles had pulled into the place, and he knew he was better off if he just snuck back to his truck and waited until the coast was clear.

Had he killed Nathan?

He had no idea. He certainly didn't want to call ORMC and ask. Even if Nathan hadn't croaked, he'd probably be in a bad way. The jerk had gotten belted full in the face, sucker punched just as he was getting out his keys. And to top it all off, the dude had hit his head on the bumper of the BMW on his way down.

It had been the perfect one-two punch.

His nerves were giving him a slight case of the shakes as he left the garage, went outside, and walked over to his truck. Steady, he told himself. Things would turn out. They had before, hadn't they? No reason why they shouldn't do it again.

***

Miranda recognized Falco right off.

She remembered the photos Hal Markum had shown her from what his investigators had collected during the last two days. Looking at the man's face had made her tremble with uncontrollable rage. But she managed to keep her emotions in check, promising her mother that she would do everything she could to make sure Falco paid for his crime.

As Falco climbed into his truck, Miranda eased out of her parking space and took the Honda down to the other end of the lot, which led straight to Semoran.

Her adrenaline was pumping madly, making her tremble even worse.

She realized she was angrier than she had ever been in her entire life.

The trembling in her limbs had grown hot, making it difficult for her to keep her grip on the wheel. *Control yourself,* she told herself. It wouldn't take much at all to mess this up. And if she did, all would be lost. Falco would guess what was going on. He'd either skip town or try and turn the tables by finding a lawyer to slap a stalking charge on her and quite possibly her father as well.

The drive to the Shamrock Bar took just ten minutes. Her plan was to find a parking place far enough away to hide, then wait until Falco showed up.

Then she would do something she knew her father would never approve of. Or Hal Markum. Or anyone at Peterson & Sloane who knew her. She didn't want to do it in the first place but was convinced this might be the only way they could nail Falco.

She pulled into the gravel lot fronting the bar, found a spot in a long row of parked vehicles extending about fifty feet from the building, and parked between a large black SUV and a Dodge Ram. She decided to wait here for half an hour. If Falco showed, she'd wait a few minutes, then go inside and watch to see what he did. If he didn't show, she'd call it a night and drive back home.

Just as she parked the Honda and switched off the engine and the lights, her cell hummed, startling her.

She picked it up and flicked it on.

And groaned when she saw the display.

**

As they were finishing up the supper dishes, Laura said, "Are you gonna tell me what's bothering you?"

Bill didn't want to get into it with her. He'd been in a strange mood since he'd gotten out of bed that morning. He guessed that it involved another dream about Sam, and he didn't want to give Laura something else to worry about.

He and Laura had spent the day quietly, making a trip to the grocery after breakfast and spending the afternoon out by the complex pool, watching the activities while catching some sun.

While watching the others, Bill found that he just couldn't stop wondering what had been bothering him all day.

Was it the simple fact that he was just tired?

Or was it something else?

He hadn't slept well at all the night before, waking up several times when he thought he'd heard a voice trying to communicate with him. He couldn't tell if the voice belonged to a man or woman but realized that its source hadn't concerned him nearly as much as the message. At first he'd had a problem interpreting it, but the moment he fixated on it, the voice stopped and was instantly replaced by Sam's image.

The image flared for just a moment before blipping into nothingness. Once this happened, Bill tried to interpret what it meant. All he could glean from it was that Sam looked worried.

The image had troubled him all day, yet he saw no reason to tell Laura about it. For one thing, he had no idea what it meant. For another, he didn't want to get her all worked up as well.

But later that day, as they cleaned up after supper, he realized that he didn't have much choice.

Laura sensed something was wrong. He couldn't in good conscience lie to her about it; they'd been through too much together. Keeping something like this from her would do serious harm to their relationship.

However, he saw no reason to burden Laura with any of the details of his dreams.

356

He just shrugged. "I'm just a little tired, is all."

"Stop lying. It isn't you. And I won't buy it for a second."

So much for trying to keep from burdening her...

"I've got this horrible feeling."

"About what?"

He hesitated.

"Is this about Miranda?"

He sighed heavily. He should have known she'd be able to figure things out.

"I'm worried that she could be in danger."

"What makes you think that?"

"A dream I had last night."

Laura glared. "Don't tell me this is about Samantha..."

He just nodded.

"Was it something she said in your dream?"

"Nothing that I could understand."

"Then what makes you think—"

"I saw only a brief image of her. She looked very upset."

"What do you think is going on?"

"I'm afraid Miranda might be up to something."

"What sort of something?"

"I'm afraid she's gonna try and speed up the process."

"What process?"

"She's going crazy over this and doesn't like sitting around, waiting for Markum to come up with something the courts can use."

"She *said* that?"

357

He nodded. "Not in those exact words, but close."

"What can she possibly do?"

"A lot of things."

"She's a smart girl, baby. I'm sure she wouldn't do anything that could jeopardize the investigation."

"I'm worried about her doing something that'll jeopardize her own safety."

"You think she might get personally involved?"

He nodded.

She stopped scrubbing the plate in her hands. "Bill, if she tries to confront Falco…"

"I know. And if that bastard even gets a *glimpse* of her—"

"Who knows *what* he'll do?"

"I know what *I'd* do if I was a psycho who killed a woman years ago, then twenty years later saw the very same woman I thought I killed."

"Bill…I'm getting a very bad feeling about this…"

He didn't reply. Something had been working into his brain during their discussion. He needed to talk to Miranda as soon as possible.

"I think we need to find out for sure. Can you call her and see if she's—"

"Already on it." He went over to the counter, where they kept their cellphones.

***

Falco's Ford pickup turned into the entrance, crawled over to the front row of parked vehicles facing the bar, and stopped at the far end, next to a beat-up red Challenger.

Miranda's pulse accelerated. For a moment she considered flicking on the ignition and driving back to the apartment. But she knew she couldn't. Not yet, anyway. She'd come this far—it would be stupid to call it quits.

The cell in her hand hummed again, yanking her back to cold reality.

Her body shook as she glanced once again at the display.

Dad.

She couldn't bring him into this. He couldn't know what she was about to do. He was calling to ask all sorts of questions and she knew how difficult it would be to lie to him. She'd done it before but hadn't liked it at all. After all, he was her dad. Despite the odd circumstances that had brought them together, she'd grown extremely fond of him in just days.

But she *couldn't* let him know what she was doing!

Preparing herself, she pressed the prompt. "Hi, Dad..."

"Randy, where are you?"

"Whaddya mean?"

"I mean, where are you right now?"

Out of the corner of her eye, she saw Falco walking up to the front entrance of the building.

Once again her nerves began twitching.

"I'm home, why?"

Silence.

"Are you really?" he asked a moment later.

"Why would I lie?"

"That's right. Why would you?"

359

Falco disappeared inside the building.

She told herself to give him half an hour. For a heavy drinker like him, half an hour would probably translate into at least two drinks. Two drinks wouldn't do much, but they might make him slightly more relaxed. Then he just might be susceptible to—

"Randy? You still there?"

"Still here, Dad…"

"I want you to tell me what you're doing, and I want the truth."

"Just here in my apartment, watching the old widescreen…"

"I don't hear anything."

"I…I muted it…when I saw your name."

Another pause.

"Dad, I'm kinda tired. I think I'm gonna head off to bed early tonight."

Silence.

"Dad?"

"Randy, I sincerely hope you're telling me the truth."

"Dad, I really am tired."

"I hope you know how much I care about you."

She felt herself softening but forced herself to keep her mind focused. "I really care about you, too."

"I don't want anything to happen to you."

"I'll be all right. I'm right here in my living room, and I really am going to bed, so I wish you wouldn't—"

"Okay, okay. Call me if you need anything, all right?"

"Love you, Dad."

"Love you, too—"

She hung up and forced herself to focus.

Falco, remember? Forget about Dad for right now. He's better off not knowing about this.

Consulting her pocket mirror, she made sure her black wig was positioned just the way she wanted it. It looked perfect, some of it falling over her right eye and cheek the way it was supposed to.

Couldn't look *too* much like Mom when she went in there, could she? It would freak out the bastard.

The last thing she wanted was for Falco to suffer a heart attack and die before anything could be done to bring him to justice.

She checked her watch. Twenty-five minutes until she went inside.

Chapter 32

"She's lying to me, Laurie. I know she is."

Bill paced the living room, trying very hard not to panic.

"Maybe not." Laura watched him anxiously from the doorway.

He couldn't help feeling this way. Miranda did not sound like herself—not at all. He knew he shouldn't be so agitated so soon after his recovery, but he couldn't control himself. His growing fear was that she was about to do something dangerous. It was driving him crazy, and he didn't know what to do about it. He sincerely hoped he was wrong, but his gut told him otherwise. If he was right, the outcome would be disastrous, and he knew full well that he'd never forgive himself if something happened to her.

He stopped pacing. "She's up to something. I can feel it in my bones."

"But what can you do about it? You have no idea what she's doing or where she is."

"I'm pretty sure she's not home. She told me she was, but she isn't."

"Where else could she be?"

She's going after him, and that means she knows where he is.

Remember your last talk with Hal Markum.

The image came to him quickly. Once again he wondered if it was his own mind talking to him or something coming from some other source.

362

"When we were talking to Markum, he told us some of the things his team had found. One of them was Falco's routine, which sounded simple at the time."

"Go on..."

"Markum has a guy staking out Falco at his home and his business. They know how long he spends at the garage, what he does when he leaves the shop—"

"He goes straight home?"

"No, he—"

The Shamrock Bar. He drives to the Shamrock Bar right after work.

"Bill? What is it?"

"The Shamrock Bar. It's in the Fern Park area."

"You think Miranda could be there?"

"She's there, Laurie. I know she is."

"Why would you think—"

"I think she's gonna take him on, and I believe it'll be tonight."

"How do you know?"

"I don't. Not for sure. But for the last few hours, I've had this strong feeling that I should be with her."

"Bill, you can't go there by yourself!"

"I have to."

She approached him. Her eyes were enormous. He could feel the fear emanating from her. "That man is dangerous!"

"Baby, she's my little girl!"

"I know, but—"

"I walked away from her once before."

"You walked away because you and Samantha were having major problems. You had no idea Samantha was even pregnant, and—"

"It doesn't matter. I *can't* desert her now. I have to be with her. She's all that's left of Sam and me, and I can't let *anything* happen to her."

"But—"

"Laurie, I deserted her for the first twenty years of her life. I'll never do that ever again. I can't. I won't ever be able to live with myself."

Laura sighed tiredly.

He went to her, wrapped his arms around her, and kissed her.

"I'll be back, baby."

"You'd better be. I'll never forgive you if anything happens to you!"

Without another word, he pulled away, moved past her, grabbed his wallet and car keys from the kitchen counter, and ran out the door.

***

Sitting on a barstool, Donnie Falco eyed the cute little redhead.

While gazing at her reflection in the mirror, he visualized her struggling in the back seat of the pickup while he held her down and ripped those damned buttons off that lacy blouse. She seemed the type who'd probably put up a fight. He'd always liked that. Liked them to fight, to struggle, to cause a fuss. It really turned him on. Covering their mouth with one hand while feeling them up with the other also got his engine running in high gear.

A lot of babes went for the rough stuff nowadays.

The redhead was sitting with two guys, but anyone could tell she wasn't really into them. One looked like a bookkeeper—skinny, thick glasses, well-dressed—while the other was more like some guy you'd expect to see working in the mailroom—jeans, tennis shoes, dress shirt buttoned at the top.

He decided to watch them for a little while and see what happened. He didn't think they'd try anything—neither dude was sitting close enough for any groping. They were chatting up a storm, all three talking at the same time. Not one of them was laughing or acting drunk or silly. They all looked serious.

They'd probably come from the office for a drink and some gossip. He couldn't see this ending in a messy threesome session in the back seat of a car.

Larry the barman brought him another shot of rye. "Another Bud?"

Donnie checked the bottle. Just a little less than half left. If he had a refill, it would be number three. Three beers and three shots of rye. A little much since he'd only been sitting here for half an hour, but why the hell should he care? He'd just gone through a rough week—why not let loose? He still had to check out the strip club on his way home. He knew he'd better stop after he'd finished this last one and scope out the redhead. He didn't want to be shitfaced if she pulled off something weird and left the bar alone.

A quick peek at the bar mirror told him he ought to forget about her and start focusing on the strip club. Right now, she and her buds were getting ready to leave. Shit. He really liked how she filled out that blouse. Now his best bet was to drive over to Bernie's, scope out a pole dancer, and start all over again.

Sighing heavily, he chugged down the rye and grabbed the half-empty Bud. He had just raised it to his face when he spotted something really interesting out of the corner of his eye.

A smoking hot black-haired babe had come in.

Donnie's gaze followed her as she surveyed the room, then walked right over to a vacant table behind half a dozen other tables about twenty feet away.

Something about the babe tickled his fancy, but not the way he expected.

This one looked familiar. Was it someone he'd been involved with recently? Or had he seen her somewhere else?

Since she was sitting behind three crowded tables, with customers and waitresses wandering around, he couldn't see her very well. Every so often, he caught an image of the face and hair...but even so, he couldn't get over how familiar she looked.

If he didn't know any better, he'd swear she looked just like some other chick he'd known a while ago...

His vision had blurred—probably from the smoke and all the different perfumes, B.O., and everything else. He put down the bottle and vigorously rubbed his eyes. When he could see clearly, he began looking for her again.

Customers wandered around, squeezing between tables—which hid her from view. He caught an occasional glimpse, but only for a second. If just one of those damn tables cleared out, he could see her better. But they wouldn't comply. Figured. Even so, he couldn't get over how familiar this chick looked.

Just then, a couple at the next table got up, giving him a clear shot.

She'd just turned away from looking at him.

And then he knew he wasn't imagining it.

Damn if she didn't look like some babe he'd once nailed!

But who the hell *was* she?

***

Bill was getting frustrated fighting the heavy traffic.

He should have known it would be this way. After all, it was Friday night, and everyone knew how hectic Friday nights were in Central Florida.

But it didn't matter. Semoran Boulevard was crazy nearly all the time. He would probably have to put up with this all the way to the Shamrock, so he should do his best to be patient. Miranda's life could be in extreme danger. Fighting heavy traffic was a small price to pay for keeping her safe.

"We'll get there, baby," Laura said, sitting close beside him. She reached over and rested her hand on his upper thigh.

Her touch, though reassuring, was somewhat distracting. But at least it convinced him he was not alone in this.

367

Even so, he cursed himself for letting her come with him. He hadn't wanted to get her involved in this messy business. But she hadn't given him much of a choice. Her unsettling expression as she came running out of the condo told him that she was coming with him. He hadn't even had time to start arguing before she'd circled the car, pulled open the door, and jumped in. And immediately told him to stop gawking at her and get the BMW moving.

"Just be patient," she added. "We'll be there before you know it."

"I just hope we have time. If she Falco sees her, it'll definitely set him off. He's liable to—"

"Don't even think of that."

He sighed. "I still wish you would have stayed back—"

"You *want* me here with you. Admit it."

"But you might get—"

"Admit it."

Once again, he realized how useless any argument with her would be. "You're right."

"Now stop thinking about that and start concentrating on what we'll do when we get there."

He had no idea what their plan would be. For one thing, Falco had already seen him. Hell, the bastard tried killing him and would not tolerate Bill coming after him—especially in a crowded bar. But he had to keep Miranda from getting hurt, and this could mean using himself as a shield if push came to shove.

Strangely, that last thought didn't bother him as much as he thought. Each time he visualized what

Falco had done to Sam, he knew that if he had been there, Sam would still be alive.

"He can't do much damage in a crowded bar, can he?" Laura asked.

"It depends on how much he's had to drink. Don't forget—the man's got serious anger issues."

She didn't reply.

"Face it, Laurie. This is up to me. I'm gonna get her out of there. If he doesn't like it, he'll have to kill me—"

"Don't talk like that."

"But if he does—"

"He won't."

"Please let me finish."

She sighed.

"If he kills me, I want you to make sure Miranda will be all right. I know she's a grown woman and all, but she's been without her mother all her life and has had to look out for herself—"

"Don't worry about that."

He told himself that when this was all over, if he managed to survive, he would never put Laura through anything like this ever again.

I've got to do this, he told himself. *I* think *I can, but—*

You can, came the strangely familiar voice.

Sam?

Silence.

Another image swept boldly into his consciousness.

Yes. Why hadn't he thought of that before?

When they were just two intersections away from the Shamrock, he pulled out his cell, flipped it

369

open, and went into his Directory. His nerves made
him jumpy as he pressed the appropriate number.

Chapter 33

Miranda quickly discovered that coming to this place hadn't been very smart.

Donnie Falco was a scary-looking dude. She'd been trying to avoid his seeing her, but it just wasn't turning out the way she'd planned. The crowd wasn't cooperating. People kept moving away when she wanted to keep out of sight. She'd come here to observe him. This way, she'd have something she hoped Hal could use. She didn't come here to meet up with him. But each time she tried sneaking a glance, she caught him watching her from his barstool.

It made her blood run cold.

You can do this, baby...

The voice had come out of the blue, and she immediately relaxed.

Despite her fears, she caught herself smiling. It was her mother's voice—she was sure of it. She also firmly believed Momma visited Dad while he was in the hospital, although she had no way of proving it and would never admit it to anyone. She didn't want people to think she was crazy.

However, she was convinced Momma's spirit remained at her side, and nothing would ever change her opinion.

She just hoped she was right and hadn't been imagining things. The way things were beginning to look, she knew she was going to be in very serious trouble if there had been just one chance in a million that she'd been wrong.

Falco had gotten down from his barstool and was walking over to her table.

***

As Donnie approached the brunette's table, he found that he was still wondering why she looked so damn familiar.

He'd known a shitload of babes over the years and found that as he grew older, his memory tended to blur their faces and make them all look the same. He didn't think it was his memory going bad on him. Hell, he still had a handful of years to go before he hit the big five-o.

This babe was a little young—which made him think she favored someone he'd known a while ago. Maybe a younger sister of someone he'd nailed a few years ago. That babe who'd come in to have her brake fluid checked a year or two ago had a younger sister. She'd been around eighteen or so, and he clearly remembered seeing her checking him out from the reflection of the store window when he'd lifted the hood to peek at the engine.

This wasn't exactly something to lose any sleep over nowadays, not with cosmetic implants and surgeries they'd been coming out with over the years. Females looked just like one another these days—it was a common fact. He was always getting them mixed up—especially while watching something on the widescreen. They looked like they'd popped out of a mold.

With this brunette babe, it didn't really matter. A babe was a babe—why should he care *who* the

372

hell she looked like? The only thing that mattered to him was that she was here. That meant that she was looking for action.

Well, she certainly came to the right place.

"Hey."

She didn't reply. It made him wonder if she'd heard him. This place was kind of noisy, folks laughing it up and clinking glasses and all.

"Been here before?"

She still didn't reply. She looked nervous, for whatever reason.

He wanted to smile. This might turn out just great. He liked them nervous. When they were tense, it was easier getting their clothes off.

Okay, baby. We'll do it your way...

"Haven't seen ya here before."

She shrugged. "My first time."

He nodded.

Just then, she said, "You're staring at me," and sounded pissed when she'd said it.

"You're a *babe*, dammit. What did ya expect?"

She didn't reply. She definitely looked pissed. He wondered what was going on. Babes didn't come to a place like this if they didn't want to be gawked at. That didn't make any damn sense.

"Want me to buy ya a drink?"

She shrugged and snuck a quick glance past him, toward the front door.

Yeah, this hot little number's tense, all right...

"Whaddya want?"

She glanced at the door again. "A beer would be great."

"On tap?"

373

"Sure. Why not?" She was playing with her hands.

We'll find something you can use later on to keep those hands busy, baby…

"Right. Okay, then. Two beers comin' right up."

He turned and squeezed through the wandering drunks to get to the bar.

While he waited for the barman to come over, her glanced to his right for another glimpse of the chick. And growled.

She was rushing over to the front door.

***

"Who are you calling, Bill?"

He discovered that he was so anxious, he could barely keep his hand on the wheel as the light turned green. "Hopefully, someone who can help."

"Are you okay?"

He took a couple of deep breaths. "Not really."

"Baby, talk to me."

"I don't know if I can handle this one, Laurie. This is way the hell beyond—"

Just then, he heard the familiar voice in his ear.

"Mr. Nathan, what's going on?"

Bill sighed in relief. "How soon can you get one of your men to the Shamrock Bar on Semoran in Fern Park?"

"I had someone there until about half an hour ago."

"Why isn't he there now?"

"Falco wasn't there, so my man waited the usual thirty minutes and left."

"Something tells me he's there now."

"Want to give me a clue what you're talking about?"

"Take a wild guess."

A short pause. "Does this involve your very impatient daughter?"

"It surely does."

"Go on…"

"No time for it."

"Just give me the details, then."

"Unless I'm wrong, I think she's at the Shamrock, and she's probably gone there to confront Falco."

"I'll have my man back there ASAP."

***

Falco caught her outside, just as she turned toward the side lot.

"I thought you wanted a beer."

She spun around and gawked at him. In the haze of the front lights, she looked scared. And surprised. And confused.

Falco gasped. This was not right—not at all. That face. Those eyes. The way this chick just spun around.

It was like…like a long time ago.

Twenty years, maybe?

Why the hell did this feel so wrong?

How could it be? That was twenty years ago! This chick is twenty? Maybe twenty-two?

Weird. Seriously weird…

Concentrate on what's really going on, will ya? This bitch tells you to go get her a beer, and as soon as you turn your back, she's out the door. And now you're thinking things that could get you committed and stuck in a padded room?

"You heard me, didn't ya? You told me you wanted a damn beer!"

"Changed my mind..." Her voice sounded funny. Weak. Shrilly. She was acting scared.

"I was gettin' your beer for ya. You knew I was. Hell, you watched me walk right over to the damn bar. Why didn't ya tell me you were gonna leave?"

She was shaking a little, avoiding his eyes. Yep, the bitch was scared, all right. He could always tell.

"I just remembered," she said in a soft voice, "I gotta get to bed...early tonight. I've got a...a meeting. In the morning."

He was definitely going to nail this babe. She was acting like she really wanted to go at it. That was probably why she was acting so damn weird and flaky. Some babes acted that way because they liked playing games. They wanted to make you think you needed to force them into doing things.

He felt his blood heating up. This babe was really getting his engine revved. The way she was standing there, shaking, trying to turn away but unable to. He could tell she was getting turned on just as much as he was.

"How 'bout we find a nice, quiet place somewhere else?"

"I just said I've got to—"

"I know what ya said. What's that gotta do with what *I* just said?"

376

She was looking down at her feet. "I really need…to get back…to my place."

"I'll take ya."

"I've got…my own ride, thanks."

"We can come back later and you can pick it up."

She didn't respond, just continued shaking and staring at the ground at her feet.

"Okay with you?"

She sighed and raised her face to look at him. Her face was still kinda pale, but she seemed to be holding it together. "Listen—"

"*You* listen, dammit." He was getting tired of this shit. Arguing was okay for some things, but not when a guy wanted to get laid. "My truck's right over there." He jabbed his left thumb in the direction behind him. "You're goin' over there with me and we're gonna get in, and—"

"I really need to get home!" Then she spun around and started walking away.

Spun around.

Turning her back.

Walking away.

The rage had come back in a giant hot wave. He couldn't let her do this—not this time. She was going in his pickup and that would be that. If he had to carry her over there and toss her inside, so be it. Once he had her in the back seat and got those clothes off, she'd warm up just fine.

He took off after her, reached out, and grabbed her arm. Then he spun her around to face him. And immediately felt a coldness running down his spine.

This time, it registered like a hot coal sizzling deep inside his gut.

The short hairs on the back of his thick neck bristled.

Her body shook as she gawked at him. There was something in her eyes that told him something was very wrong. It was a darkness that made his blood chill, and suddenly her face told him something he did not think was possible.

He realized right then that he was looking at a dead woman.

Just then, she'd stopped trembling and became very still.

Her arm suddenly felt like ice, making him pull away sharply.

Her lips parted, and a chill in his limbs he'd never experienced before nearly made him lose his balance.

"Do yourself a large favor," she said, in a voice sounding very different.

He opened his mouth to say something, but nothing came out. A giant lump had filled his throat. He found it difficult to breathe.

"Don't you *dare* hurt my little girl," the voice said in a hoarse whisper. "If you do *anything* to her, I'll haunt you for the rest of your natural life!"

***

Bill pulled into the front lot of the Shamrock and parked three rows down, between a late-model Mustang and a beat-up VW Bug.

It only took him a few moments to spot Miranda's Honda, which was parked in a short row of vehicles about fifty feet or so from the west end of the building.

"There's her ride," he told Laura.

"I see it. Now…what do you want us to do?"

His first instinct was to get out of the car, rush inside, find her, then drag her back outside. But after thinking about it, he decided that it would be unwise. He had no idea if Falco was even in the place. And if he was, what would he be doing?

More important, what would Miranda be doing?

She'd obviously come here to find him, so what would she do if she saw him? Walk up to him and tell him who she was? Or would she just sit in a dark corner, watching him? Would she call Markum? What would she tell him? She couldn't very well ask him to send someone to arrest Falco. For all they knew, the man was merely getting drunk in a crowded bar.

Legally, they had nothing on him. They were still building a case. If Miranda did manage to bait him, Falco might have grounds to turn the tables and sue her.

"Bill?"

"Yeah."

"What'll we do?"

"I'm not sure. I want to go inside and yank her out of there, but I know how stupid that would be. She'd hate me, and she'd never forgive me if I messed this up. She's a grown woman—not a little girl."

"Any idea what Falco drives?"

379

"None. I'd assume that since he's a mechanic, he'd drive a truck, but that would only be a wild guess. For all we know, he could own a Porsche, or Maserati."

"I don't see a Porsche or a Maserati anywhere," she said, scanning the lot.

"I just hate sitting here, waiting, when he could have her trapped in a stall in the bathroom."

"Wouldn't that be risky? This place is obviously crowded. People will be coming and going to the restrooms every couple of minutes."

"You're right. But if Falco *is* in there, we don't know how long he's been here. This also means we don't know how much he's had to drink. For all we know—"

"He could be much too drunk to care about much of anything."

"Hopefully, we're just assuming the worst."

Laura glanced at her watch. "How long did Hal Markum say it would be before one of his men gets here?"

"He said as soon as possible, but in this traffic—"

"I just hope he gets here soon."

"So do I."

"One thing, though…"

Laura continued talking, but suddenly Bill couldn't hear her.

A strange voice was calling him.

It sounded like Samantha, and her voice sounded urgent.

"Bill? Are you paying attention to me?"

"I'm picking up something."

380

"Whaddya mean?"

"There's a voice in my head."

"Help her, Bill!"

"Bill?"

"Please!"

"Is it Samantha?"

"I don't know…not for sure…"

"Is it coming from the bar?"

"No."

"Follow my voice!"

"What's going on?"

He flung open the door. Before he got out, he turned back to her and said, "Stay here. And *please* don't get out of the car. For *any* reason."

"Wh-Where are you going?"

Without another word, he pushed the door closed and began jogging toward the far end of the large block building.

Chapter 34

Miranda opened her eyes and discovered that she was lying on the ground.

Falco was straddling her. Her arms were pinned beneath his weight. Her black wig sat on the ground at least ten feet from her head.

Confusion set in.

How did this happen? Out of the corner of her eye, she caught the blurry image of a building about fifty feet away. A scrub area and two small storage buildings extended from the rear of the building. Two cars were parked next to the storage buildings. Judging by the thumping coming from inside, she could tell it was a bar.

The Shamrock.

Had Falco just dragged her back here?

Had she blacked out?

Last she recalled, she and Falco were arguing outside the bar. Falco was angry with her for leaving.

Now he was going to kill her.

She knew that what she'd done was not only stupid, but also very dangerous. So dangerous, in fact, that she was going to die. And no one would even know until it was much too late.

He followed me out of the bar, and then—

A strange feeling had suddenly taken over. Everything grew blurry and dark. It was as if someone had just shoved a thick plastic bag over her head. After that, she could barely feel the ground beneath her feet.

Then she heard Momma's voice.

It seemed to be coming from her own throat.

"Don't you dare *hurt my little girl. If you do* anything *to her, I'll haunt you for the rest of your natural life!"*

Just when the confusion set in, Momma's image blipped in her head.

In that same instant, Falco had turned around. His face resembled a death mask, and for a moment she wondered if she were looking at someone who had just escaped from Hell. Falco's mouth opened. A searing rush of foulness spewed out, smothering her face. The words coming from him were incomprehensible and sounded like the growl of a wolf. His hand came up and ripped off her wig. When he saw her natural hair, his eyes bulged.

Then the blackness consumed her.

And what seemed like just moments later, the blackness vanished, bringing her back to harsh, painful reality.

He was sitting on her chest, drool from his snarling mouth scorching her cheeks and forehead. His huge hand came plunging down, encircling her throat. Her air was immediately blocked off. She opened her mouth to scream. His free hand shot right down, covering it.

My God...I'm about to die!

The pressure had become unbearable. She could feel her consciousness rapidly drifting away. But just then, the pressure on her throat immediately vanished, and a strange noise escaped his lips. Falco straightened, raised his head, and gawked at something just behind her.

"Y-*You*?" Falco gasped loudly. "What the *fuck*?"

She could move her head just enough to see what Falco was looking at.

Momma?

She gasped when she saw her mother's image.

Am I hallucinating? Or have I just gone insane?

A surge of inner strength bubbled up, and she suddenly knew she was not going to die tonight.

Gritting her teeth, she pulled her arms free. Then reached up and struggled to rip the hand away from her mouth. She finally succeeded, and a scream exploded hotly from her throat. The moment she felt his weight shift, she twisted around to look at the phenomenon once again.

Momma's image had vanished.

Then, in the next moment, a dark figure had rushed over from the direction of the parking lot and slammed into Falco, forcing him to the ground several feet from where Miranda lay.

***

When Bill saw Falco sitting on Miranda and choking her, his mind went into predator mode.

Wasting no time, he accelerated into high gear, bringing muscles into play that hadn't been stressed in years. He knew he was about to attack a much stronger man, but all that mattered was that his daughter was being choked to death.

His thoughts turned chaotic the moment he flung himself at the other man. He hurtled through the air, grunting loudly when Falco's large head slammed into his gut. The rage taking hold, he wrapped his arms around Falco's neck and brought the bigger man down. The ground came right up, twisting sideways, and before he knew it, he was rolling on the ground with Falco's head cradled in his arms as the other man's huge fists pummeled into his sides.

What seemed an eternity later, Bill lay on his back. Falco knelt over him, face contorted, eyes bulging, his fists furiously slamming into him. Bill made one feeble attempt to block the onslaught, but Falco had gone totally berserk, totally oblivious of Bill's efforts.

The excruciating pain eventually ebbed, and Bill's body went numb.

Blackness came quickly.

Everything turned soft and warm.

The soothing voice in his ear brought an easy smile to his face.

***

An emergency unit was parked just a few yards away from where two paramedics were placing Miranda onto a gurney.

Lights flashing, two police cars were parked in the grass just off the main road. Two cops had Falco pinned on the ground and were cuffing him while a third stood off to the side, talking to his radio.

Once Miranda was safely positioned on the gurney, the paramedics wheeled her over to the emergency unit. The doors of the unit were wide open. Someone else was lying on another gurney, which sat outside the open doors. The victim was being tended to by another paramedic. Laura was standing next to the gurney, holding his hand. Bill shuddered when he saw the victim's face.

"You saved her life, you know."

Sam was hovering a few feet from one of the parked cars behind the Shamrock Bar. Her spiritual form was much brighter than the dim lighting of the hazy twin floodlights spreading a slim golden sheen onto the lawn.

"Am I dead?" Bill asked in a soft voice.

She shook her head. "Just unconscious."

"Damn." He groaned. "Another coma."

She smiled. "Not this time. You should be awake in a few minutes."

He sighed in relief. Then he turned to watch the paramedics positioning Miranda next to the other gurney.

Out of the corner of his eye, he saw another emergency unit backing up in the grass next to the first unit.

"I'm very proud of you, Bill."

He shrugged. "It was no biggie. I just followed your voice. You did the grunty work."

She turned serious. "You *heard* me. You *listened* to me. You could have just ignored me."

"You honestly think I could've done that?"

Her smile returned. "Not really."

The cops had shoved Falco into the back seat of the squad car and slammed the door shut. Two men in suits were talking to the third cop. One of them was Hal Markum. Bill guessed that the other guy was the one working for Markum.

386

"Why am I here?" he asked Sam. "If I'm not dead or in a coma—"

"We're having one last talk."

"One *last* talk?"

She suddenly looked sad.

"You mean—"

"We won't be talking again, Bill. Not in *this* life…"

"Really?" He felt his heart sinking fast.

"It's no longer necessary."

"That doesn't tell me—"

"It should tell you everything you need to know."

She was right. Things had obviously happened the way they were supposed to.

"I really miss you, Sam."

"I know."

"I wish—"

"Don't go there, now. Laura's a great lady. We both know that. Don't mess it up."

"Like I did with you?"

She shook her head. "I'd say we both had a hand in that, wouldn't you?"

He realized right then that their petty problems no longer mattered. Everything had turned out as well as could be expected. He couldn't have asked for a better outcome. "We had some great times together, didn't we?"

"We did. And we've got proof now."

"Proof?"

"Miranda, silly. Together, we brought a beautiful, intelligent young lady into the world."

"She's that, all right."

387

"I'm *so* glad you saved her from that animal."

"*I'm* glad we were able to make him accountable for your death."

"Well, at least that chapter can finally be closed."

He gazed into her beautiful blue eyes with a sadness he had never known before. This was it. In just a few moments, he would never see her again. At least, not in this life...

"Take care of her, Bill. She's all grown up now, but you can still take care of her."

"How can I do *that*?"

"Be there for her. You're all she'll ever need."

"I wasn't there for you, Sam. If I had just—"

"No more regrets, okay? It's over. Time has washed it all away. You'll always have those memories. Now you've got the chance to make new ones. Make sure they're good ones."

Her glow began to dim.

"But Sam—"

"I'll be around to look in on you from time to time."

"I'm really sorry, Sam. For everything."

"You more than made up for it tonight."

"But—"

"Make good memories, Bill. It's all I ask."

"I love you, Sam."

"I love you, too. Make sure you keep loving Laura."

"I will."

"And tell Miranda I'll always love her, too."

"I will."

"Now you can go back."

"Back?"

"To the world of the living."

"You mean now?"

"Yes, Bill. I mean right now."

Then she was gone.

He gawked at the semi-dark emptiness that had just replaced her beautiful, glowing form.

Was she really there?

He closed his eyes.

And suddenly felt intense pain in his throat, arms, shoulders, sides, and stomach.

When he opened his eyes, he was lying on a gurney, staring up at the worried face of Laura, who was gently stroking his shoulder.

Someone else was holding his left hand.

It was Miranda. She was smiling at him from her gurney.

"Hi, Dad." Her voice sounded weak.

"Hi, Baby Girl."

She frowned. "You've got a really bad habit, Dad…"

"Howzat?"

"You've got to quit getting unconscious all the time. It's getting old—if you know what I mean."

He laughed in spite of the pain in his gut.

Chapter 35

A week later, Miranda dropped by the Brown Brokerage to have lunch with Bill and Laura.

She'd recovered from Falco's assault. Despite some cuts, bruising, and sporadic neck and back pain, she showed no ill effects.

Bill was proud of her. So was Laura. Both Bill and Laura were relieved and amazed that the girl didn't appear to suffer mentally or emotionally, as others would have from such a violent trauma.

Although Bill's memory remained somewhat cloudy from the event, some things that he could not begin to explain continued to plague him. The fact that he had been having recurring dreams about Sam convinced him that her spirit might have somehow returned during the assault and could have been instrumental in preventing Falco from doing them even greater harm.

Certain phrases

("Take care of her...")

entered his mind at odd moments during the workday as well as in the evenings, as he and Laura were having dinner together.

He could hardly explain any of them

("Be there for her...")

but was convinced that the messages were from Sam,

("Make good memories...")

and that she had been watching over them.

390

This brought back other memories that had come during his recovery from his coma. He couldn't help thinking Sam might have been watching over both him and Miranda much longer than he'd originally thought.

Sam could have been waiting for them to meet. To connect. And to become the family they should have been.

If someone had told him something like that just a few weeks ago, he would have thought them crazy.

Now he knew better.

Sam's essence had never completely left. But now, since he and Miranda had finally reunited, he had the sinking feeling that there would be no further need for Sam's spirit to return.

He sensed a sudden ache in his heart when he realized he could be right.

***

Bill, Laura, and Miranda rode the elevator down to the ground floor, where the Paradise Bar & Grill was having their lunch buffet.

The bins were filled with sauteed shrimp, scallops, oysters on the half shell, fried clams, and a large assortment of salad combos.

They chose a window seat facing Robinson and ordered vodka tonics from the skinny brunette who had picked up their trays.

Miranda seemed in high spirits. She picked up a scallop with her fork and said, "Hal just gave me another progress report. This one's even better than the one he gave me yesterday. Isn't that great?"

As Bill drank some ice water, he was thinking how great it was to be having lunch with Laura and Miranda. Aside from two cracked ribs, a few minor aches and pains, as well as a nagging headache from the black eye Falco had given him, he felt reasonably well, and very fortunate that the three of them had survived the nightmare.

He knew he should be interested in what Miranda wanted to tell them. However, he found that he just didn't care. He also knew the reason for his attitude. Miranda was to blame. She hadn't stopped impressing him since the day he first saw her, and he just couldn't get over how his luck had changed. He no longer cared about Falco or what the man had done. After twenty years, karma had finally caught up with him. And now, Falco's fate would be dictated by the courts.

All that concerned him now were the two women sitting at his table. They were his life. He knew he should feel differently, but he just couldn't shake the strong feeling that nothing else mattered.

"Dad?" Miranda looked confused. "Did you hear me?"

"Huh?"

"You're not paying attention at all, are you?"

He couldn't help smiling. "Me? Not paying attention?"

"He's been doing that quite a bit lately." Laura picked up a wedge of buttered toast.

"I do not. I'm paying attention. I really am."

"All right, then." Miranda looked like she was about to laugh. "Tell me what I just said."

"You told me I wasn't paying attention."

"Before that."

"You asked if I heard you."

"Keep going…"

He drank more ice water. "Let me see…"

Laura and Miranda laughed.

"Give me a second, now…"

"Give it up, baby." Laura elbowed him in the side. "You've just been exposed."

"I can't help it if I happen to be thinking about other stuff."

"What *other stuff* are you thinking about, Dad?"

He picked up a sauteed shrimp. "*Much* more important stuff than that idiot Falco."

"Like what?" Laura sounded skeptical.

"Well, you." He turned to Miranda. "And you."

The women looked at each other, stared at one another for about five seconds, then broke out in laughter again.

"Let me get this straight." Laura sat back in her seat and was about to say something when the waitress came with their drinks.

Bill took his glass and sampled it.

"Can I get you anything else?" she asked.

"If you've got a psychiatrist handy," Laura said, "you could bring him right over. My guy, here, seems to be ready for the rubber room."

Miranda laughed. So did the waitress.

Once they were alone again, Laura said, "In other words, you don't care about Hal Markum's progress with the Falco case because of *us*? Miranda and me?"

He nodded solemnly. "That more or less covers it."

"Care to explain that so we don't think you actually *are* going insane?"

He had more of his drink. "Not really." He put down his glass and picked up another shrimp.

Miranda had turned serious. "You wouldn't mind too much if I told you a couple of things, then?"

He shrugged. "Go ahead. I'm listening."

"Hal said they found dirt on Falco, stuff that could get him for embezzlement, tax fraud, and more than a dozen other offenses."

He nodded but said nothing.

"He also said Falco was involved in a couple of lawsuits two years ago. Several customers sued him for unnecessary expenses as well as overcharging. One angry guy really got into it with him and Falco broke his nose and several ribs."

Bill speared a scallop on his fork and slipped it into his mouth.

Miranda sighed impatiently. "Dad…"

"Yes?"

"*Please* tell us what's going on…"

"Going on?"

"Why you're acting this way. Why you don't seem to care. Why you're acting so…so *spacey* right now."

"Spacey?"

"Spacey." Laura nodded. "You know. Dazed. Confused. You're not on any meds I know nothing about, are you?"

"I'm definitely not doing any meds, nor am I dazed or confused."

"What *are* you, then?" Miranda asked.

"Well, for the first time in my life, I'm in a very comfortable state of bliss. In the last few weeks, I've managed to escape death on three separate occasions. I've been absolved of the worst mistake I ever made. In the process, I have been reunited with a beautiful daughter I never knew existed, and I've managed to handle all of this without losing you." He smiled at Laura, grabbed his glass, and held it up. "Anyone still wanna know why I no longer care about Donny Falco?"

Laura and Miranda raised their glasses and they all clinked together.

There were tears in Miranda's eyes as she put down her glass. "Right back atcha, Dad."

Laura's eyes were also wet. "I've always wanted a daughter, but I never knew I'd get one under these circumstances. I'm very happy to say that I'm quite pleased with how things turned out."

"You may not be my mother," Miranda said to Laura, "but I kinda think my mom wouldn't mind if I treated you just as I'd treat her."

***

That evening, after Miranda had finished dinner with Bill and Laura in their condo, Miranda asked Bill to walk with her around the grounds.

It was a warm night. As they walked, they passed a couple of the other tenants out for their evening stroll among the palmettos and freshly mowed grass. Distant splashing from the community pool echoed in the night air. Other sounds consisted of cricket chirpings and sporadic traffic moving up and down Semoran Boulevard nearly a mile away.

As they passed the tennis court, where a middle-aged couple exchanged serves, Bill sensed that Miranda had something on her mind. He could tell by her silence that she was hesitant to bring it up.

"Just say it," he said, watching her as she stayed close beside him, staring at the pavement straight ahead.

"I feel really bad," she said.

"Why?"

She stopped walking and looked up at him. She looked sad and confused. "I never really thanked you."

"For what?"

She gave him the strangest look. "For saving my life."

"Oh…" He just shrugged.

Her jaw dropped. "Just an *oh*? Is that *all* you thought it was?"

He smiled sheepishly.

"You really did, you know. You risked your own life to save me. Falco's a psycho. He's also big and strong and…well, you didn't seem to care. You just rushed on over and slammed into him. He almost killed you, and it was because of me."

He didn't feel particularly heroic. All he cared about was that Miranda was in trouble. And that he had to eliminate the threat. "It really was no biggie."

"Are you serious?"

He sighed. "You're my daughter, and you were in mortal danger. I didn't care anything about how big or tough Falco was. I just did what any father would do to save his kid. I didn't much care if Falco ended up killing me. You had to be safe, and it didn't really matter much what I had to do to—"

She wrapped her arms around him and held him tightly against her. He closed his eyes. He could sense a genuine warmth hovering close to them again and realized once again how lucky he was to have been given this second chance.

Long before he wanted the moment to end, Miranda pulled away. There were tears in her eyes, but she was smiling.

"You're welcome," he said, and they both laughed and resumed their walk.

More than a minute passed, and he began wondering why she'd become quiet again. However, this time he sensed a strange darkness settling over her.

"What's wrong now?"

"Huh?" His voice had startled her. She looked up at him and smiled, but he could see something in her eyes that suggested fear, or doubt.

"Something's wrong, and you're afraid to tell me."

"Nothing's wrong."

"Really?"

"It's just that…well, actually—"

"Actually what?"

"There's been something I've been wanting to ask you from the beginning, but since a lot of this other crap started up, it kinda got lost in the chaos."

"There's no chaos now. We're all alone. Just you, me, a bunch of annoying crickets, and a shitload of hungry mosquitoes." He swatted one that had landed on his forearm. "Laura's not even here—if she's one of the reasons why you don't want to tell me—"

"No. Laura's great. I love her. This is...this is something I need to know. It's something I've wanted you to tell me without anyone else around."

"Well, let 'er rip."

She stopped walking and looked up at him, and he suddenly saw a nervous little girl looking up at her father to ask him something very important.

"I'm your dad," he said softly. "I know I just recently came into your life, but I'm here now, and I'll *never* walk away from you ever again. You can tell me anything, and you can ask me anything. I won't bite, and you're entirely too old to be sent to your room."

She laughed and wiped her eyes.

"Go ahead, baby girl, ask away."

"This is something I've been wondering ever since I first met you."

"Okay..."

"And something I thought about a long time ago, when I was living with Aunt Eileen."

"Gotcha..."

"I've got to know, and I need you to tell me the truth."

He put his hands on her shoulders and looked deeply into her eyes. "Take this one to the bank. I'll never lie to you. *Never*."

398

She nodded. A moment later, she took a deep breath. "Just tell me this. If you had known about me back then, would you have walked out of my mother's life?"

"Are you serious?"

"Very."

"Randy, if your mother had told me she was pregnant, I would never have left her in a million years."

"Never?"

"*Never.*"

Despite the tears gathering in her eyes, she smiled and put her arms around his neck.

Bill wrapped his arms around her waist and hugged her tightly.

***

A few minutes later, a tall, slender, white-haired woman stopped walking and stared oddly at them as they were about to pass.

The woman wore white shorts and a sleeveless turquoise tee shirt, which showed off her tan and long, toned legs. She had taken off her glasses and was carefully cleaning the lenses with a small white rag while watching them intently.

"Hello," Bill said. "Is something wrong?"

She laughed nervously and put the glasses back on. "Just my double vision flaring up again," she said. "It hasn't done that for a while, but..." She shrugged and looked embarrassed.

"Double vision?"

She nodded. "When I first saw you coming around the bend, I thought I saw three people."

"*Three* people?" Bill turned around. So did Miranda.

"This young lady." The woman looked at Miranda and laughed again. "I could've sworn I saw double."

Miranda and Bill exchanged confused looks.

"There really aren't *two* of you, are there, dear?"

"I don't *think* so, ma'am..."

The lady sighed deeply and nodded. "I thought so. I guess I really do need new glasses, then." She glanced at the streetlamp. "Musta been the glare of the streetlamp blurring these lenses."

"Must've been," Bill said uncomfortably.

"Anyway, have a lovely evening." She waved as she passed.

"You, too," Bill replied, waving back.

Miranda was still staring at him. "Dad? Are you thinking what I'm thinking?"

He didn't reply. He was still thinking about what the woman had said.

"Dad?"

"Could've been," he said with a shrug.

"Could've been what?"

"Glare."

"Maybe..."

They resumed walking.

About a minute later, Miranda said, "You really think it was?"

"Do I really think it was what?"

"Glare. From the streetlight."

"I honestly don't know."

"Is it...I mean, is it possible?"

Sam? Are you still there?

No response.

But the sudden warmth at the back of his neck brought a smile to his lips.

"Dad? What's wrong?"

"Nothing, baby girl. Nothing at all." Suddenly invigorated, he put an arm around her shoulders and they went down the street that led to the condo.

As they went up the front steps, he knew for a fact that, from now on, life would be great.

ALSO BY DAVID BERARDELLI

THE APPRENTICE
THE WAGON DRIVER
STEPPING OUT OF MY GRAVE
COLORS
AND DARKNESS FELL
AFTER DARKNESS FELL
IN ANOTHER REALM
BEYOND RECOGNITION
THE NIGHTMARE COLLECTOR
BEYOND GUILT
REDEMPTION
ENLIGHTENMENT
HIDDEN
AWAKENED
WINTER SCENE
THE PLANNING COMMITTEE
LEGACY

Titles available through:
Gravestone Press
Fiction4All